MW01616038

HOLD FAST

a novel

Spencer K.M. Brown

Wiseblood Books

Copyright © 2022 Wiseblood Books

All rights reserved, including the right to reproduce this book or any portions thereof in any form whatsoever except for brief quotations in book reviews. For information, address the publisher.

Printed in the United States of America

Set in Baskerville Typesetting

Cover Design: Amanda Brown

Paperback ISBN-13: 978-1-951319-32-8

For my son, Leo Vincent

"Ablaze, I trust myself to this lone paddle,
this calm on and on, no return in sight."

—Wang Wei
"Adrift on the Lake"

THOM

1

From inside the snow plow, Thom Algonquin looks at the forest and feels fear in a way he has not felt it in many years. He stopped the truck because he thought he heard something, a voice. He thought he heard a voice say his name, say, *Thom, Thom, Thom*. He stopped the truck to listen. The snow dampens everything and the sound of the wind and the trees rises and dies, rises and dies.

There is nothing more to listen for. *Never was*, Joe whispers into his mind. *You need to sleep*. I can't, Thom thinks. He is tired, a strange sort of tired, bone deep and numbing. Yet he is wide awake, his mind set loose and running off like wild horses.

Thom drives on a little farther, turns down the long road that cuts through the woods, and drops the plow again. A random mailbox here and there stands to mark driveways leading to houses that don't wish to be found or seen. Thom likes the idea of that. Still he prefers to be around people: not talking or interacting or *with* people, just *among* them, nearby, silent in the corner as everything spins along on some days, burns down on others.

There is one set of tire tracks on this road, half-filled with snow from earlier this morning. Thom can hear nothing but the slow crystallization of the settled flakes. All other sound hibernates in the cold hush of the forest. On either side of the road myriad genus of bushy conifers stand under thick coats of snow and ice, bowing close to the earth under the weight of the sky. The green is dark in places, the path to the forest darker still just behind it. On either side the trees stare at Thom as he drives past.

It comes to him: the feeling of the forest, the smell of the woods. Piney and sweet as molasses in the slow warmth of summer.

Forests are strange things. Living, breathing things. In them there is life, death, communication, community, preservation. We may like to think of the world, of human life and its all-consuming day-to-dayness, as separate from nature. We tend to forget: we are nature.

We hang paintings of forests on walls, take pictures of autumn-leafed paths covered in sunlight, or an early snow. We take walks through them, go to them in mind's eye for solace, release. Yet, some of us ignore a forest's capacity for terror—its whispers and rustles, its shadows where dark things lurk. Its isolations. Some forests are dense enough that you could stand in them and shout and nothing would be heard even a few dozen yards away. Other woods will carry sound for miles and miles as if the trees were tossing the sounds from branch to branch. People might shout, and go unheard, HELLO or IS ANYONE HERE or HELP ME—or they might, by beauty or by terror, be stunned into silence. It depends on the forest.

We're talking now of late August evenings in Minnesota. That world consists of the din of lawn mower blades turning in raucous slicing circles like buzzards over prey, the throb of a racing boat's outboard motor on the Lake. Garden hoses run with cool water and wash over the last flowers of the year before the autumn turns all the green to brown. In the afternoons, children run through sprinklers on the lawn and men burn piles of last autumn's leaves. Mothers prepare suppers and read novels under the shade of summer hats, carefully watching over their children from afar. All is safe and good in the summer. But Thom Algonquin can no longer hear the lawn mowers humming, boat motors churning, the hoses splashing or the children playing. He doesn't smell the leaves burning or help his mother prepare supper. Thom Algonquin is seven years old and he has walked too far into the woods near his home on Lake Superior. He hears nothing save the sound of sunlight and trees, birds, and his own feet pattering along atop the underbrush. He is not so sure he can hear these things exactly though. It has now become clear to him that he has gone too far, too deep into the old woods. He is accustomed to going a little farther than his mother allowed, but he has walked miles past that line now. Though his heart races he does not scream or run or cry. He looks around for home but each direction is identical to the others. He remembers his Cub Scout manual saying that moss grows on the northern side of tree trunks because there is less sunlight. But the aspen trees have no moss on them at all, and the big white oaks have moss on every side of their trunks. He holds his breath and listens. He hears his heart beat, and somewhere behind that, he hears water, waves and lapping tides. The Lake. He can always find home from the Lake. His father told him to simply keep the water on his left hand and walk until he is home, should he ever get lost. Thom moves toward the sound of water. He walks quickly but doesn't run, doesn't panic. If he runs he will know that something is wrong and that he is scared. He does not want to know these things, does not want them to become real, so he walks quickly but calmly.

He hears it before he sees it: the deep fathomless growl. The moaning and grunting. The smell of it rides on the hot heavy air like a bad dream. He slows only a moment but keeps moving toward the Lake. From his hip he takes his little Bowie knife from its scabbard: a birthday present from his father. He holds the knife tight in his hand. He comes to a full stop, smells it distinctly and sickeningly now. Blood and raw fish and decaying dirt and wet fur. Through the pale scatter of aspens and birches and high grass the boy sees the bear among the underbrush. The emerald canopy of trees has thinned out here and sunlight pours down like rushing water. The bear's mouth is wet with carmine blood. It eats and eats from something that a flourish of buckthorn hides from the boy's line of sight. The bear growls and the boy can smell its hot breath on the breeze. Flesh and blood and blackberry brambles. The boy doesn't know why he won't run faster toward the Lake and then faster for home. He doesn't know why, but his feet inch closer toward the creature. He has never seen a bear up close. Perhaps it is to have a story to tell his friends. Perhaps because his heart has been bursting to get out of his chest—though now it is only a sonorous vibration. Perhaps it is this new feeling of powerlessness, helpless-ness, losing all control, entirely human and fragile, melting back down to mud and a little breath. Primal, ancient. He doesn't wish to lose this mysterious desire. So he moves like a fawn through the forest, quiet, patient, fated. His eyes widen as he gets closer and he stares at the bear and feels as if he were about to meet God. The bear looks at him as it smells his boyish sweat on the wind. At the creature's feet and caught between its claws are pieces of a person. Thom sees the parts scattered around the bear the way his father once scattered pieces of a disassembled boat engine across a table to fix it. As he is closer, the smell on the air is unlike anything Thom has ever smelled before. Again, he is out-side himself, looking down from the high branches, and yet he is entirely within his bones, every fiber and sinew twitching with fire and fury.

The bear sees the boy and grunts irritably as it stares him down. It moves, ursine and lumbering, mammoth, shaking the earth to stand between its meal and the boy. It growls again. The sound is near deafening. Thom feels it pushing over his skin and entering his soul. His heart is going like mad once again, but he doesn't move now. The bear paces side to side, baring its teeth, and climbs the air to stand on his hind legs. It roars louder and Thom stands there, petrified and awed. He wishes to be brave, to show no fear. He doesn't know if he can be brave or not, so he stands there. He wants to know who the person is, dead at the bear's feet; he feels a human sorrow because the body once belonged to a human, flesh of his flesh.

Thom breathes deep and howls back at the bear, showing his own crooked teeth. He screams and holds his knife out in front of him. The bear roars again and falls back to its feet. It moves back over the body, staring at the boy as it lowers its head to take another bite.

Thom moves away, backwards, and then he runs as he hears the Lake. He reaches the shore and runs along the rocky edge of the slick shale until he is home. He tells no one about the bear, about the body. Often he will dream of the forest. He will feel the bear's weight pressing down on him and its teeth digging into his own flesh. He will look up at the bear from under its paws. He feels himself being disassembled and torn apart, one bone, one muscle at a time. Even then he tries to growl back, from under the beast's bulk; he tries to gasp for breath and howl until he has no breath left, until his bones are scattered across the silent forest. And as he feels himself slipping into such fathomless darkness, and then into the dark after that, he wakes, he comes up for breath again.

2

Thom Algonquin sits in the unmoving plow somewhere near the national forest on Highway 53. He recalls a few things, but the images pass him by like roadside billboards. Outside the sky is like a television turned to a dead channel. He wishes to think about things, to truly feel his mind at work on something else. But lately it doesn't move. He sits, feeling the cold winter winds assail the cab of the plow, worm their way into the cracks, and wrap around his body, bone deep.

Sometimes, he wishes he didn't exist. Not to disappear completely. But not to exist, like how animals or forests don't exist. To detach his soul for a moment, to drift along unmoored from his body. He'd come back at some point.

He shifts the truck into gear and hums a song his father used to sing. *"Would you like to swing on a star, carry moonbeams home in a jar, and be better off than you are, or would you rather be a fish?"* He can't ever recall any other line of the song but this one. And always, he answers the question: Yes, he would like to do those things. Yes, perhaps, to be a fish.

He'd come back at some point. When he was ready.

He drives on and enters the forest. Ahead in the distance, he sees something in the road. The sight terrifies him. He stops the truck in the middle of the road. No. No, it can't be.

JUDE

1

Midway through our hibernation I awake to Dad out in the driveway melting snow with a makeshift flamethrower he built. He told me part of the thrill is knowing he could blow up at any second. It's rare to see him smile the way he did when he first told me that.

I'm surprised the flames haven't burned his beard off. I have this passing image of it catching, of Dad going up in flames and letting himself burn up. It goes away and I'm lying in bed, still half asleep.

The flames wake me up again. They roar up in manic bursts through the window like a yawn from some great beast. The bright flares of golden-orange flames disrupt the predawn blackness covering everything on our street. What little morning light there will soon be struggles to break through the thick December sky. The river of warm meltwater from Dad's fire runs down the driveway in a quick trough, disappearing into the snowdrifts the plow left at the end of the driveway. It really pisses Dad off and gets him going when the other guys do that. Our house isn't on his route, but sometimes he plows our street anyway. Our house is at the end of a cul-de-sac, right on the Lake, and by the time the plow gets to us they're kind of like, fuck it.

It sounds like a river or rain from my bedroom but the sky and earth are quiet. Dark and quiet, waiting to blow up at any second.

2

Everything is dark in the house. This is what ghosts must feel like, navigating in the blackness, hoping the light will come through a little more, but not too much. Seeing only the shape of things, never the things themselves. One thing Dad and I agree on is our hatred for artificial light. We'd rather wander in the dark than have to walk through blaring fluorescent or LED lights. It's just not natural.

My eyes widen owl-like as I trip on the first step coming down the stairs. I catch my balance and feel uneasy on my feet, like my body isn't quite my own. I sit a moment, let my heartbeat slow down. That's how Mom died, falling down these stairs. I feel more like the old man every day. He probably thinks I'm still asleep because I'm rarely up before noon these days. He left a sixer of Milwaukee's Best sweating on the kitchen counter. Two cans already missing. Dad doesn't sleep much anymore.

I still feel bad for yelling at him how I did. Five years ago now, before I had left for school, but it feels like I just said it, like I'm still saying it. Eighteen and a God-damned idiot, he told me—Dad said the two always go hand-in-hand. He smelled like beer one morning when I was leaving for school, the way he always smelled when he got off work on the plow in winter, and I got all high and mighty about it. Said if he ever took another sip in front of me I'd never speak to him again. Not sure if I really would've followed through with it, but something in my voice rattled him. Five years later, he's yet to have taken a drink in front of me, no matter the occasion. Now, we both just sit and drink coffee or water—anything besides—each of us smelling the alcohol on the other's breath. Both of us too chickenshit to drink in front of the other, just in case one of us never speaks again. Not sure either of us could take something like that. I know I couldn't.

3

Dad pulls the trigger on the flamethrower in quick bursts, hiding a can of beer in his gloved hands. It's only just now five-thirty in the morning. Better than five o'clock, I guess. He's silent out there in the dull gray light. He hasn't shaved since Mom died. It's been nearly a year now and his beard has become Whitmanesque. Mom would have hated him looking like this. Would've made him shave it, wouldn't kiss him 'til he did. He probably would have done it himself before that point, though, if she were still here.

Dad looks like Charlton Heston in *The Ten Commandments* after talking to God on the mountain, only a little more gray and a little less immaculate. Dad looks like a grizzly bear. Wild and tired of the fight. There's still something fierce behind his eyes though. Something is alive in them and won't die, even if he has given up on his body.

The front door is open and the house is cold. The door must have been left open for a while—probably since he came home sometime in the middle of the night. We do things like that now, he and I. Doors stay open a while, a few days at a time, then they close. Laundry and trash pile up, then Dad just burns it all in the backyard. We go shopping together after the fire. We do things on our own time, in our own way, in these ghost days we're stuck in. Best we can anyway. But not because we want to. Only since Mom fell, since I hurt my arm and came crawling back home to hide out and hibernate from everything. I think some part of Dad thinks that if he leaves the doors open maybe she'll come back. Like wind or light or a wild animal. He'd even take a brief haunting, footsteps in the night, papers flying around, a message drawn on a foggy mirror—he'd take anything he could get by this point. Just some sign that he's not alone.

4

I take my coffee to the front porch and watch Dad melt the bottom layer of ice on the driveway. The flames are more powerful than either of us thought they'd be when he first built it in the garage. He was sick of shoveling.

He pauses and looks back at me, gives a tired wave. It's early. He doesn't want to wave at me. I don't want to be waved at. We do these things because it's normal. It's what people do. I suppose we want to be normal, too.

His face looks sunburned and pink-blazed as if he's just been slapped twice. It's just the fire. Standing in shorts and a thick winter coat wrapped around my bare shoulders like a chrysalis, I watch him and sip my coffee. The cold wakes me up more than the caffeine. Dad makes the coffee thick as motor oil. He looks like a feral animal or homeless man I've just found and brought home, ready to turn on me at any moment. Ready to go up in flames.

Maybe he's already burning.

The first time I saw Dad light himself on fire I clapped. Mostly because everyone else was clapping. I clapped, despite the tears. I cried because my father was on fire two feet away from me, burning, and everyone was just sitting in lawn chairs watching and clapping. And I clapped right along because it's what I thought I had to do.

He performed magic tricks at birthday parties when I was little. It quickly escalated from card tricks to juggling to bending spoons to setting himself on fire. Somehow, Dad puts in effort more for his own satisfaction than anyone else's. To see what he can do, how much he can take.

Seeing your father on fire is unlike anything. Of things

I can speak, seeing your father burning is most like watching him talk to God, only he can't tell you anything that was said.

5

Dad unhooks the straps of the kerosene tank from his shoulders, and for a moment I brace myself for an explosion.

"Read that book you gave me," he says. He cuts off the fuel line and stabs the flaming end in the snow. The quick sizzle is muted by the sound of running meltwater.

"What'd you think?"

"Goddamn depressing," he says. "Why would you ever want to read something so depressing? All that work for nothing in the end."

"I don't know. I haven't read it. Just saw it and thought you'd like it. Reminded me of you."

He looks like he wants to punch me. I think part of me wishes he would. He certainly has reason to.

As he walks closer I smell the beer and fire on his skin. I love that smell. My father's smell. "You little shit," he says—flashing a grin, I think, but his beard hides it.

"Bigger than you, old man."

He walks past me and on into the house. I close the door behind me. Things get a little darker until our eyes adjust. In the kitchen, Dad stands there staring out the back door for a long time.

"What is it?" I ask.

"What do you think about a sunroom?" he says.

"It's December. We don't need a sunroom."

"I wouldn't mind having a sunroom," he says.

I sit at the table, pulling a blanket around my legs, and he remains standing, measuring things in his head. He holds the weight of this world in his hands, in his mind. He puts the six-pack in the fridge, as if I weren't here and it was just root beer, and pours himself some coffee. We sit and smoke cigarettes and drink coffee, not speaking for a long time.

When I was training, when I was still rowing, I swore I would never smoke or do anything to harm my health. I'd read this quote from Socrates that put a hook in my heart. "It is a disgrace to grow old through sheer carelessness before seeing what manner of man you may become by developing your bodily strength and beauty to their highest limit." Rowing was the one thing I knew, the one thing I was good at, the one thing, I'd convinced myself, that made life worth living. I avoided any need for vice by becoming addicted to competition. Dad, doing what he does, living how he lives, disgusted me. That changed, though. The glory faded. The hubris ached within me. And after the accident, I guess I just didn't give a shit.

Dad's looking at the back door, at the walls, cutting boards in his head.

"I need to do something with my hands," he says suddenly.

"Like build a sunroom?"

"Doesn't have to be that. I just need to do something with my hands. They itch."

"Think we can turn the heat on? It's December and it's fucking cold, Dad."

"No. Waste of money. Wait for the real cold. Put more clothes on if you're cold." He looks to the back door again, fitting panes of glass in his head.

I choose my next words carefully and breathe them out like eggshells. "We should maybe look into what Mrs. Clemens was saying about selling the house. Might be a good idea. She said it's a seller's market right now."

Dad is quiet for a moment. Then he says, "We'd get

more for it if it had a new sunroom."

"I'm serious, Dad. It's too much house for just us anymore."

"No, you're not. You only want to be serious," he says, and he might be right. "It's not too much, it's the same house it's always been." He stays quiet, looking out the windows at the snow and the cypress tree out by the Lake as the dawn lightens the world. Then he says, "Besides, where would we go?"

6

Dad has done most everything in his life like his hands were on fire. Fished, built, cooked, laid brick, hung drywall, drove trucks, cut trees, washed windows, laid pipe, dug earth, carried water—most any task you can think of, he has carried out. Everything no one sees or wants to do but is glad someone else did. For four years Dad was a part-time janitor and groundskeeper at my high school because he said he wanted to keep an eye on me. But in all that time he never said one word to me at school. I think he knew what other kids might have said if he did. He cleaned bathrooms and smoked cigarettes on the soccer field with the burnouts and another janitor. I'd see him through the classroom windows. I think he really liked being close by, just not too close. Every night at dinner he'd ask me how school was that day, even though he knew exactly how it was.

He never went to college himself, but he helped build additions to four different universities across the state. He always says he's seen the insides of enough classrooms and auditoriums to have five degrees.

For a while he got a job digging graves for the county cemetery. He said it was better than just about anything because no one else wanted to do it. Said he had the best job security a guy could have. People never quit dying, no matter who is president.

Dad used to take apart every mechanical thing in the house just to see how it worked. Mom would get pretty pissed off when she wanted to do her hair and found the blow dryer on the kitchen table in a thousand little pieces.

Dad could take apart the toaster and have it back together again like a Marine fresh out of boot camp and ready for deployment.

Now he's sitting here, staring at the back door and wall, wondering whether, if he changes it, builds something new out of the rubble, something will change within himself. Maybe it'd be different then. Maybe.

7

The sun comes up after breakfast, but you wouldn't know it. Clouds hold the sun back in its scabbard, only the faintest murmur of light. Dad is full of bacon and big ideas. He looks like a grizzly bear and I wonder for a moment if I'll ever have to wrestle him.

After a hot shower the house feels even colder on my skin as I come back downstairs. Dad's boots crunch over a million pieces of shattered glass, remnants of the windows he's smashed. He stands in the snow-filled flowerbed outside the door, smashing the back wall down with a sledgehammer. Pieces of brick and wood fly off in a thousand directions. Behind him a pile of dirty laundry is on fire and burns slowly in the yard. He's still afraid to touch the washing machine because it was the last thing Mom touched before she fell. He tried to wash his blankets a few times and I found him crying on the laundry room floor. I think he feels that if he touches it she'll vanish just that much more. I do the laundry when I can, if he hasn't burned it already.

I stand and watch the old man work. The hammer moves smooth in his hands. The downswing lands perfectly where his eye has told it to go. The whole house shakes with each strike. The rhythm of his body is calm and even. Black smoke rises from the pile of burning clothes like some SOS. It drifts toward the house and is carried into the winter sky by the cold breeze coming in off the Lake.

On the table he has laid out dozens of articles on building sunrooms, all of them printed off the internet. A dozen more hand-drawn sketches lie scattered among them. I should have known. The paradox is, nothing about him is sudden or spontaneous. Even this. He's researched and researched countless hours of the day. Whole nights have gone unslept with his mind wriggling like a sardine in a net as he compares one DIY builder's plans to another's. Dad must have been walking through the kitchen for months just eyeing things up, measuring and cutting boards in his head. He knows every last spec of that wall. He knows where the windows will go, how thick they'll be, and precisely where a three-fifteen ray of sunlight will hit on a clear afternoon in May. He knows it. He's already built it in his head.

The only sudden or spontaneous thing about the man is that first swing of the hammer. That first spark sets his hands ablaze—the one he's been thinking about and rolling over in his mind for weeks and months, knowing every possible outcome. Only that first hit, that first match strike, takes your breath away. You didn't know it was coming, didn't know such a thing would ever come, until you're suddenly on fire.

I smoke a cigarette at the table, only a few feet from the chips and feathers of debris flying through the room like sparrows. The cigarette smoke drifts and entwines with the brick dust and laundry smoke. Like some endless and thundering dynamo, Dad makes such travail seem no more burdensome than an exhale. His thick arms bend effortlessly; the muscles work like snakes beneath his yellow and gray flannel coat, as if they were doing that very thing they had been created to do.

"Why'd you hate that book?" I ask him through the dust and smoke.

He holds the hammer still against his shoulder, looks

up silently. He didn't hear me.

"The book," I say again. "Why'd you hate it?"

"Yeah, it was terrible. All about that old man trying to catch the fish and when he does the sharks come." He gnaws on his tongue a moment, chewing over something he doesn't want to say. "Never hated sharks so much in my life. He loses everything. Terribly sad, waste of a story."

"But the point is that he *did* it. He caught it and fought for it. It wasn't about anyone else, only that he could still do it. One last good fight."

"Thought you said you never read it?" he says.

"Of course I have. I only said that so you wouldn't yell at me. Didn't want to put any opinions in your head."

"There's no point to it. Just sad and depressing. Trying too hard to be meaningful."

"Well, sometimes things are like that. We don't always win the way we thought we would."

"No, Jude. Life is just how life is. That book was someone making a joke of it, sensationalizing it. Writing something sad just to be sad. Just to get a rise out of people. Trying to seem genuine and profound or some shit. That's just bullshit's what it is."

"It's a classic, Dad. *The Old Man and the Sea* is a classic. I don't think you can say all that."

"I can say whatever I like. And it's a bunch of bullshit."

The hammer comes down evenly on a few corner bricks that were giving him trouble. They shoot out easily now like rotted teeth. Pieces go flying through the kitchen, disappearing under the fridge.

"Heads up," he hollers.

He comes back inside, where he searches through drawers and old boxes in the mudroom. Dad is murmuring, the sound's insistence like the throb of an open wound: pulling out words by their guttural roots, holding them by the tails like wriggling mice. His tongue dances upon vowels like a hungry bear mouthing the bones.

He's looking for something but doesn't know what. He does this at least twice a day now.

The dust settles, the smoke, and Dad sits with me. He looks through me for a moment and then into the fridge; he's looking into it and opening one of the beers.

My right arm still twitches every time I look at a fridge. My heart skips whole beats. A Goddamn fridge. An appliance. How is it that an appliance can ruin a whole life? Or stairs, for that matter.

"No work today?" he asks.

"Not 'til tonight," I say, rubbing my shoulder where the scar cuts crossways from armpit to collarbone.

He and I both wish we were working all the time. We know how necessary it is to stay busy, especially now that it's winter. The house gets too cold and quiet when we don't work, then we start knocking out entire walls to build sunrooms just to break the silences. I can almost feel my hands burning too, itching for something, but I don't know what.

8

Winter comes in through the emptiness Dad's punched into the wall. A breeze comes in off the Lake through the spot where the back door used to be. Winter skulks like a guest you didn't invite and yet can't ever seem to be rid of.

"I think that book messed me up," Dad says. "I feel like that old man sometimes. I feel like I know him."

"Sorry. Maybe I shouldn't have given it to you."

Outside the sky has banned all flying things, killed off all growing things. Outside the sky smiles. A light snow drools from its lips like sugar.

"It's cold," Dad says.

"Yeah, it is."

"A sunroom will be nice."

I just look at him, watch him sitting there.

We both turn at a sudden sound of cracking twigs. A thin, gaunt wolf comes up to sniff around the backyard. It's too skinny to frighten us. It moves around the bonfire of Dad's dirty clothes and comes up to the open wall. We sit there watching it. The wolf stops and looks at us, then carries on through the backyard, down toward the Lake shore and to other backyards. I wonder if it isn't warmer outside than in here.

Gray light settles on the shattered glass and splintered wood. I watch the pieces shimmer just slightly, suggesting the faintest glimmer of warmth.

"It'll be a nice sunroom, Dad."

He nods and sips his coffee, wishing it was a beer and wishing I wasn't here just now.

We're silent, and in the silence we somehow hear it; I

am somehow thinking it. Dad hums to himself as he builds a sunroom in his head. Dad hums a tune we both know well. He's murmuring like a wound, pulling the world apart and putting it back together again.

Dad looks like a grizzly bear, too restless to hibernate, too tired to hunt. I hope I never have to wrestle him.

9

I've sometimes thought about what our life would be like if Mom were still here. I wonder about what I'd be doing, where I'd be if I never had my accident, if Dad had taken the job in Ann Arbor. Dad used to say that each decision had a million possible outcomes in a million separate directions, like a flock of frightened birds, all shooting off at once into the sky. In one of those worlds I might stay home and sit here with Dad and we'd talk for a while. We'd eat together, watch a movie, and maybe work through some things we've always needed to. Maybe we'd become friends again. We'd tear things apart and build them back up again, this time a little stronger at the broken places.

But we don't. Not in this version.

In this version I eat a can of sardines and get into the car and go to work early, leaving Dad there in the house alone. It'll be a normal night for me, boring and quiet like all the nights are now. But for Dad, something happens.

10

This man I didn't know once told me that the quietest place on earth is Antarctica. I couldn't hear what he said at first with all of the screaming kids learning to dive in the deep end of the YMCA pool, so I asked him to repeat it. He said it can get so quiet in Antarctica that you can even hear the muscles of your heart twitching and pulsing and your organs squirming around doing what they do. Not just feel them, but hear them working. "You can hear yourself living and being alive," he hollered over the screaming kids and thrashing water. "Closest I can come to that silence anymore is underwater. Deep, deep. But it still ain't even close," he said, in his drawling Southern cadence. He then rolled foam ear plugs in his fingers like little lime-green joints and stuck them in his ears. He jumped into the water, sinking down sixteen feet to the bottom.

At that time I really didn't care what he had to say—what anyone had to say. I'd seen him once or twice before, but I was pretty much only concerned with myself at that time. Or rather, there was myself, and there were only two things I cared about: the pain in my right shoulder, and the five rings tattooed on my forearm.

Two months before that chubby man in the Speedo said that thing about silence, I held the Minnesota state record and the U.S. National record for rowing in the single scull and the coxed eight team record, both for the University of Minnesota. We qualified and got the news that we were going to Rio de Janeiro for the Olympics that year. We trained harder than ever—but first we went out and cel-ebrated, right after we got the news. Half-drunk, eyes marbled over like Grecian statues, high on our hubris, me and the other guys on the team went out and got our tattoos together, because nothing except some catastrophe or act of God stood in our way of going to the Olympics. As it turned out, nothing else did stand in the way of the team—only me.

You could call it a catastrophe or an act of God or a fluke—call it whatever the hell you want. I've called it everything I possibly could, but giving it a name or trying to find some greater reason for it happening doesn't change a thing.

I'd gone to the refrigerator in my apartment in the middle of the night for something, and the door didn't shut all the way. It was heavy and never closed without some extra effort. When I turned to close it I tripped over my own feet somehow, and in my half-dazed state, I tried to catch my fall on a shelf in the fridge. My weight and the inertia sent my right arm through the cold glass shelf and subsequently through the cold panes of glass in the other four shelves. A shard of glass no bigger than an index finger shot up through my armpit at just the right angle (or the wrong angle, rather), severing muscle and tendon and sinew in my shoulder. It only nicked my brachial artery, but the glass stayed in place long enough to keep me from bleeding out. The same shard of glass that ruined my future also saved my life, and all in the amount of time it took me to fall over.

When I stood on the pool deck waiting for my physical therapist to start rehab for the day, I didn't have anything to say to that chubby guy who floated down to the bottom. Now, a year and a half later, I want to know why he went to Antarctica in the first place, why he always came to the pool to sink instead of to swim. Was it because something was ringing in his ears that he needed to go to the end of the world to silence? I believe that it was. Some sounds and noises seem to never die but only to swell. There are two in my head, always. The sound of the glass shattering in the fridge, and the sound of my mother falling down the stairs. Those sounds were enough to send me back home, to hide out and hibernate from everything and everyone with Dad. But I always get to wondering how many noises drove that man to the end of the world. Will they ever go away? I like to think maybe they will. One day, maybe.

11

I stop and get a coffee on my way in to work. From sunrise to sunset, the day doesn't change much. All is heavy and low and cold as steel.

Work is washing dishes at Belle Mer Bistro, one of those jobs like Dad's always kept, one that no one wants to do but are glad someone else does. Someone has to, after all. It's the most expensive restaurant in the county, and it sits right on the shore of Lake Superior. People pay thirty or forty dollars for some herbs and a fish they could've caught themselves not a few hundred yards away in the Lake. It is delicious, though, I'll give them that. I sometimes eat whatever's left on the plates, if it hasn't been mangled up too badly. You'd be shocked how many people order a fifty-dollar prime rib and hardly touch it.

When I first got the full ride to the university, I always thought I'd leave town, go off to college, see the world by rowing, and make this great life for myself somewhere else. I'd come home on holidays and everyone would be so excited to see me. There'd be signs, like the one the mayor put up when I won Nationals and was heading to Rio. It read: WELCOME TO WOLF FALLS, MN, HOME OF 2016 OLYMPIAN JUDE ALGONQUIN.

They took the sign down last autumn. Dad put it in the garage somewhere. I could have had a great life, but now I'm a dishwasher who can barely lift his right arm above his head, with a tattoo of five rings, massive and permanent, on that same arm: a grand stigmata of hubris.

Tonight, Dad is driving the plow for the county until dawn, and I'm washing the wealthy citizens' dishes. There's

something zen about that, if you look deep enough. Plow
the snow, clean the plates: someone has to do it.

12

When I get out of the car I nearly slip on the rock salt they've spread heavy-handedly all across the parking lot. If the ice doesn't kill you . . . .

"What's going on, Jude?" Derek says as I walk up. Everyone in town calls him Dynamite Derek because he blew his right leg off at the knee on Fourth of July when we were kids. He has a wooden leg now, and the metal hinges freeze over if he stands outside too long in the wintertime.

Derek and another line cook smoke cigarettes as they empty oil from the deep fryer into the tank outside the door. The smoke rises in a great cloud as they maneuver the giant pot.

"Hear what happened to your buddy Nick?" Derek says.

I've known Nick since I was seven. We learned to swim in the Lake together. He's a First Call driver for the county morgue. He picks up bodies and takes them to wherever they go.

"No, what happened?"

"Get this, right, so he picks up a guy from Methodist Hospital, and he's driving along when he hears this noise, weird strange kinda noise, like some moaning or growling type shit." Derek smokes and paces back and forth in the alleyway behind the restaurant to keep his wooden leg from freezing. "So he slows down, right, and looks in the back and hears the noise again—some like moaning or wailing or something he said—and, get this, it's coming from the damn body bag, man, from the damn bag. So he's freaking out and gets out of the van and walks around to the back. He's ready to lose his shit, right? So he sees the bag moving—something in the bag is moving…" Derek stares at me with a stunned can-you-believe-this-shit face.

"From inside the bag?" I say.

"So Nick's about to renounce his atheism and become a Bible-banging fool because he's near fucking certain the dead guy he's carrying has come back to life. And, well, you just have to see something like that. Lazarus, Lazarus…" Derek shouts out to no one. "So he starts to unzip the bag and his hands are all shaking, right? Bam! He sees these two kids, weird fucking kids, just going at it in the body bag. Can you believe that? Can you believe that shit, Jude? So they hop out all buck naked and are scared shitless. Meanwhile, Nick's having a heart attack or stroke, thinking he's just had the beatific vision, and falls on the ground. The kids just run off through the woods, naked. Yeah, so these two freaks were like goths or some shit, all obsessed with death, blah, blah. Weirdos. They were going at it and didn't even know they were being hauled to the damn funeral home." Derek hits me in the shoulder, hard. He pauses a moment. "Oh, shit, sorry, man. Is that the bad one?" He flicks his cigarette off into the snow. "Anyway, must have been pretty good if they didn't even know they were being hauled to the coffin, eh?" Derek laughs and kicks his wooden leg out suddenly, making sure it doesn't freeze over.

13

You can think or not think when washing dishes. You have plenty of time. The trick is getting the water to the right temperature. If you can get it right, the world is running water.

I've never broken a dish in the year I've been working at Belle Mer. I was hired on that promise: that I wouldn't break shit.

"It's just a white bread plate to you, just a wine glass," the owner said to me. "But to me, it's $4.50, $13.75, and that adds up. Don't break shit. The last guy broke shit constantly. Just don't do it."

The world is running water to me. You want the water to sting, like a sweat bee, not a hornet. A balance of hot and cold. The sink and dish pit are in the far corner of the kitchen, near the freezer and opposite the dining room. To my right a stainless steel trough, where waiters drop their dirty dishes, closes in around me and blocks off all view of the cooks. The clean racks of dishes are stacked to the left. Right in front of me is a three-foot-deep sink and dirty white wall with outdated government-sourced information about sanitizing dishes and employees needing to wash hands with diluted bleach. The sound of the industrial dishwasher beside the sink drones out the language of the line cooks and clanking pans in an infrasonic and hypnotic lullaby. The faucet drips and babbles, drowning the hot pans plunged below the water. I used to listen to music when I first started, but it got to be too loud. It got my head spinning and got me thinking too much. There was something in the sound of the water, of the scrubbing, that seemed urgent and present only just then, and I somehow felt I needed to listen to it.

The night started off slow, and by seven-thirty it hasn't picked up much. I work on a pan that a new sauté cook left in the Salamander too long. Half a duck charred and burned right into the metal. The scrubbing and running water muffle the chef's screaming as he calls the new guy every horrible thing he can think of. His voice is only vowels. Everything—Dad, the restaurant, rowing—pushes away in rings through time as I press my weight into the pan. The Brillo pad cuts through the charred blackness, carving clean lines through the emulsified grease and bone marrow. I rinse the pad every few minutes and watch the water run black and then clean again. It all spirals down the drain in a kaleidoscope of little specks of burned duck and grease.

There's nothing to think about except what my hand does. Soap-soft and water-logged, the patterns of my fingers push the steel wool pad. The water runs over everything, makes it clean again. There's nothing to think about and I imagine I'm sinking to the bottom of an ocean. There's a silence there. One that can only come when you're not thinking and filling your head with ghosts.

14

I roll the big garbage cans down the alleyway and out across the parking lot to the dumpsters. The plastic wheels twist and crunch over the rock salt, echoing off the building's outer walls like ribbons of thunder unfolding. I toss the heavy bags of uneaten food and trash into the dumpster. The smell is fetid but not quite rotten, as the cold slows the process of deliquescence. I smoke a cigarette and lean on the wooden fence that overlooks the Lake. The surface is frozen miles out. Snow blankets the Lake in a silent and endless desert. Nothing moves out there, nothing speaks, and the clouds lower and grow heavier with each lulling moment. And the moments lull in winter, in silence. Growing fat and heavy, ready to break open, ready to stand up and set themselves on fire.

In the alleyway Emily and Cherry smoke and bounce from heel to heel to keep warm. Everyone smokes in restaurants. It's something of a prerequisite: that and hating people, all people, and being pissed off all the time. Emily and I dated in high school and for a while after. I was going to marry her. But things sort of fell apart when I went off to school and she stuck around here. I got this stick up my ass about how I would be this great athlete and do something with my life and couldn't waste precious training time with my old burn-out friends anymore. But somehow she still talks to me, still invites me out. If she hates me, if she ever did, I'd never know it. I get more upset that she doesn't hate me, and then I hate myself a little more because I can't say I'm sorry and tell her that I still love her, that I always have.

They're talking, and Cherry swallows a Plan-B pill with a long gulp of Mountain Dew. She has a little girl at home with her mother and says she'll be damned if she'll ever have another one.

"And Derek was like, 'Well, what if I want kids?'" Cherry tells Emily. "And I told him, 'Well, grow a Goddamn uterus and fuck yourself then.'"

She laughs. A rasping smoker's laugh that turns to a coughing fit. I hear it and my eyes start to water. I try to slip past them without talking but Emily stops me.

"What are you doing after work, Jude?" she says.

Her mouth is like sapphires from stealing sips of red wine all night behind the bar. When she speaks, a spark cuts across the air that comes to me alone. I always wish I could tell her that I love her, but her voice is precious as gems, strong enough to fracture jaws. I only ever speak in running water.

"I don't know, probably just going home," I say.

I love you I love you I love you.

"We're all going out to Golden Hours if you want to come."

"It's been a shit night. We gotta get shitty to balance it out," Cherry says, coughing and laughing.

"Maybe. I'll see how late I am here."

Cherry used to be pretty. She still is, only she wears a life of sorrow and heavy drinking and pills on her soul like a demon she can't exorcise. I always get homesick when I'm around her for too long. Somehow customers love her; they revel in her shocking forthrightness. It turns out honesty and being an asshole are two different things.

I've taken my time tonight, so that by closing time, the dish pit is loaded high with dirty dishes. I don't mind it. It's my excuse not to go out with them and not to go home right away. Work for as long as you can, Dad always says. I feel more like him every day.

"I wish all these losers were like you, Jude." Adam, the head chef and co-owner of Belle Mer, reaches up past the sink to the stainless steel ledge behind it, where he sets down a pint glass of gin and bitters on ice for me. He holds up his own glass and drinks. He drinks two pint glasses of gin and bitters and ice after every shift, and then he moves on to pints of porter or stout after that. He'll have half a dozen before he locks up and drives home. He brings me a gin because it's usually only the two of us left and he doesn't like drinking alone.

"Why's that?" I say, loading a rack of plates into the dishwasher.

"These assholes don't know how to work. They just whine and bellyache. Everything is always someone else's fault. Bunch of entitled pricks. You're one of the good ones, though, man."

I just nod and start the dishwasher. I drink and nod again. He walks off toward the empty dining room, shooting the lights off as he goes through the kitchen.

"Just let me know when you're done mopping the floors," he says.

A little while later I go up to the bar where Adam's sitting, watching the television. I sit next to him and finish my gin.

"All done," I tell him. "You're not going out with everyone else?"

"Hell no," Adam says. "I won't ever go out with those idiots."

He stands, dons his coat, and goes out front for a smoke. I follow him. As soon as the night air hits me, I see my leather apron is still on. It's frozen stiff in a matter of seconds; I knock the teardrop icicles from the bottom.

Adam sits on a bench overlooking the water and sighs. "You can work Christmas Eve, right?" he says.

"Yeah, that should be fine."

"We got a hundred and fifty on the books already," he says.

"Damn, not bad." I never know how to talk to Adam. I try not to say much. "So you fire that new guy?"

"Nah, he'll get up to speed. Just takes time."

"You laid into him pretty good."

"That's just to scare him and make sure he doesn't burn another duck. That's thirty bucks he burned. Shit adds up."

I take my coat off, untie my apron, lift it over my head, and get back in my coat as quickly as I can. The cold lingers on my skin and I can't help but shiver.

"So you were in the Olympics or something, right?" Adam says.

I look at him a moment. "How did you know that?"

"Saw your tattoo," he says. "And Emily mentioned it the other day."

"Oh, right. No, I never went. I qualified and everything, but didn't go. The rest of the team went."

"What happened?"

"Messed up my shoulder pretty bad. Eight months of physical therapy. Missed the window."

"Damn. That sucks. Can't you qualify again?"

"Nah, it's done. You have to be training at such a level it's insane. I sort of gave it up after that."

"What sport?"

"Rowing. I did the single and team, the eight-man coxes."

"No shit. I used to row some in high school. My dad

taught me to row."

"Mine too," I say. "God, I've spent most of my life on the water with an oar in my hands. Kind of crazy when I think about all those hours. What a waste of time."

"Nah, at least you were trying for something. If you didn't spend time doing that, you'd have found another way. We always find ways to distract ourselves."

"Yeah, I guess so."

"Who knows though, maybe you'll get back in a boat again. Just not on the twenty-fourth. I need you working."

"Deal," I tell him.

15

The road is empty and the sky is lilac-blue, blending with the white metal-gray clouds like watercolors. It's cold. Sixteen degrees at four-thirty p.m. Seven degrees now at two a.m. Cold and colder still as the sun is gone. As if God's hand were pulling a wool blanket across the sky and light. The clouds gather again, conspiring, like doomsday loose on God's fingertips.

I read somewhere: "Winter is a thoroughly honest fellow, with no nonsense about him, and tolerating none in you, which is a great comfort in the long run."

Sometimes you pray for a little bit of nonsense, a little bit of light when winter comes. But mostly, winter and I get along.

I wonder how Dad is holding up. The draughty cab of the snowplow rolling along the empty white roads. Alone, and bitterly, heartbreakingly so. Cold. I hope he remembered to wear his gloves.

There's one final glimpse of the Lake, the white flat sea, before it dissolves into sky and that black hemlock distance, shadow-backed and limb-laced in the assembly of snow and shades, lilac to blue to gray to black. The sunrise no more than a hope we don't dare tempt or question. It'll snow again tonight. But this land, the trees and frozen Lake and emptiness, don't seem to care, keeping close and anchored to the earth.

I hope Dad's holding up all right.

16

You don't have to talk to anyone when you're driving the dead. Nick told me that once, after he took Mom away in his van. The metaphor and story remain silent, hidden somewhere backstage, and all you have is the present moment, he said. Cold. Dark. Silent. Tires flex over cold pavement, no one out on the road. Silence in the car, only thoughts and the heater murmuring, simmering on all that's left unsaid.

"It's the only way to do this job," Nick said. "Not to think about who's behind you."

The finality of life and death is what gets me. You can't undo dying, same as you can't send back life except with death. A life of million-threaded ends and paths is bookended by such permanence. In between is a beautiful torrent of webbing branches, one moment into the next. Cherry would call it "a shitshow." I call it tangled: a mess we tell ourselves we're making sense of. Following our reason one moment, free will and appetites running like wild horses the next. Sometimes we're pushed forward because we need a hand; we'd just remain stagnant otherwise. As if the gods were watching and getting bored and wished to move the plot along, fast-forwarding to the good parts.

I should be ready to sleep, but my mind is off to the races. My foot is heavy driving through snow. I should slow down. That's what I tell myself. Out loud I say, "Slow down, now."

I wonder what Dad is thinking about.

I picked up a First Call driver's shift for Nick one time and felt something like Kharon or Vasudeva. Carrying souls across the river. In this modern world there is so much travel to do before you're laid to rest. To the hospital, to the morgue, to the funeral home, all the while they're poking and prodding at you. Only then, finally, does the rest come.

When I think of my mother I always think of the freckles on her skin and back. She was covered in freckles and little raised moles. When I was so little that she still sometimes brought me into the shower or bath with her I would watch the water slide and roll down her speckled skin and move in little rivers over the moles and freckles. She was beautiful. It's hard to think of her gone. But it's almost worse to imagine all of those strangers poking and prodding her at the end. Of the people driving her from place to place. It upset Dad enough that he drove down to the hospital, after Nick took her away, and picked her up himself to take her to the funeral home. He was the one who drove her in the hearse to the cemetery. He dug the grave himself. He has a hard time trusting anyone.

I pull up to the house and just sit there in the street out front. Everything is dark, and yet it glows against the pale fires of the snow, *misericordia* on the night wind, snow gathering and gathering overhead, ready to let loose over the landscape, but not yet, not just yet. Five degrees outside now, at three forty-five a.m. The house is dark and silent. It must be just as cold in there.

I drive around the block once more and listen to this radio show talking about UFOs and ghosts and angels, anything bizarre or paranormal. The host has this deep bellowing voice. There's something so genuine and sincere in his tone. The callers are so absurd and weird, as if it were free telephone hour at the Greylocke Mental Hospital. But the host listens to them, *actually* listens to them. He asks questions, like he believes every word they utter as gospel. Maybe he does.

Dad said he saw a UFO once, while he was out plowing years back. Said he saw all these bright lights on the road suddenly, right there in front of him. He stopped and got out, thinking a car had stalled or something. He heard all these voices talking, something like Chinese, but not Chinese—that's what he said. Mom said he must have fallen asleep and dreamed up the whole thing. Who knows. He believes it though, to this day he swears by it.

It's almost four in the morning, and I'm parked in the driveway. The radio plays low and becomes static every time the wind picks up off the Lake. It sounds like wolves coming on the radio, howling with the wind, as if they're transmitting from some cave on a forgotten island on the Lake.

When I get up to the porch, the door is cracked open already. Dad didn't bother with closing it all the way. I walk inside and close it behind me. I can see my breath in the darkness. Everything's blue and black and white as if I were lying at the bottom of a vast and endless ocean, as if I were hiding out in a cave in Antarctica. Nothing moves in the house, nothing makes a noise. Sometimes I wonder if everything didn't just pause when Mom died. When she left, life slipped into hibernation, waiting for her to come back. I empty all the air from my lungs and pretend I'm sinking down to the bottom. I pretend that great cloud of my breath is Mom for a second. Then it's gone.

I sit at the table and have one of Dad's beers. The back of the house is open and blends with the elements. Snow has blown in and covers the brick-dusted kitchen floor. I can't help wondering if that wolf came back into the house while we were gone. Maybe he's still in here somewhere.

A cold draught fills the house like the Holy Ghost. The snow starts. There's something about the cold that seems good for the soul. I've always wished I could move like wind does and cover the earth. I've wished I could burn my way to the center of all beauty, that I could live like my hands were on fire. But it's a slow walk to the top of the mountain.

This month feels abandoned. Frozen and hibernating. Soon it will be cold enough that Dad and I will fall asleep and dream of spring and the icebreakers on the Lake. I can't help but feel like something has happened to Dad, something sparking around him and he's about to go up in flames. Like a rocket, not a martyr. We're just waiting for something to come; we want to do everything, so we do nothing. We want to say it all to each other, but we bite our tongues till they bleed. I can almost feel Dad growling like a bear, restless and hungry. Somehow I can't shake this feeling like I'll have to wrestle him soon, that I'll have to drag him from the bottom of the Lake by his hair.

I hope he remembered to wear his gloves tonight. He forgets sometimes.

THOM

1

Thom Algonquin peeks in the door to check on his son, as if he were still a child. He is, in a way. They never stop being your child. Never. Jude is asleep in the warm darkness. Shades pulled and daylight slipping and wriggling past the heavy curtains. You never get used to nightshift, Thom thinks.

Thom pours a beer into a coffee mug, adds a little coffee, only enough to change the color and give it a bit of a kick. Just in case Jude wakes up and comes down. The sun is a few minutes away and sleep is farther off still. Thom's bones still rattle and quake from driving the plow all night, like he is still being tossed around by the sea hours after swimming. He pulls at his beard and moves a hand over his thick gray-yellow hair, smoothed down from his wool knit hat. Thom thinks about absolutely nothing for as long as he can. When thoughts come, and they do, he looks back into his head and sees the snow. He looks at it, deep into it. Blackness. Nothingness. Cold and colder still. At times he feels like those satellite images of planets. A glowing mass surrounded by blackness, moving through the dark. Pushing away in ten thousand directions at once, or maybe being sucked into it. Cold and colder still. He tries not to think about her but he can't fight it off today. Some days he can, but this morning he allows one memory to slip through. Just one, he tells himself.

His wife sleeping. He watches her, watches for as long as he can until everything becomes smoke and echo.

There's not a moment goes by that I don't think about you, he thinks. I wish I didn't. I want to feel you against me. Feel your skin, your hand in mine. But we both know that will never be again. There's no going back to that. I move like I imagine a ghost moves, Helen, and feel like the damned must feel: broken, fey, cursed. Sometimes I wish I didn't think about you, that I could forget you. And that makes me sadder than anything. Jude says it'll get better soon. Everyone does. But we both know "better" is a far shore. I feel like climbing in a boat and rowing across the Lake to wherever you are. Maybe I'll find you, if I only row far enough.

Grief flutters southward in the heart. All guilt and dull ache, sitting alone in rooms. All resources for living have gone; the light grows fainter with each moment. The heart is too tired to beat on anymore. What can be done? Hold onto hope, perhaps. In something unseen. For who hopes in what they have seen? But Thom does not wish to hope any longer. He has hoped long enough. He wishes only to see, to stick his fingers into the wounds and feel flesh and blood. To exist in that truth that is truth, to live in that joy that relies on nothing. Nothing. Maybe to not exist for a moment. Just a moment. That would be something.

The breeze coming from where the kitchen wall used to be hits him and Thom closes his eyes. It'll be better soon, someone told him yesterday.

2

Thom walks into the backyard, out into the snow and gray-dark morning light. He prefers dawn. The darkness at dawn is a different kind of darkness, one that promises light on its edges, that shows signs of an end in its folds and structure. He prefers to be awake before dawn because of this, to see the night come to an end.

A winter wind from the north harasses the skeletons of red pine and black spruce. The back of his house looks like a bear's cave. Just a dark opening where the back door and wall stood for sixty-five years. They're gone, knocked out like teeth. He can see the sunroom and knows the work it'll take. But the work is all right. He never minded the work and was always willing to work when others wouldn't.

Above, the sky sits in stillness and silhouette. The last lisp of cloud lingers. The ash pile of clothes and the charred waistband of a pair of Wranglers lie covered in frost and dusted with snow like forgotten things in a basement. Among the little drifts of snow a smoothed-over lump of leaves sits off in the shadows, long and corpse-like.

Thom remembers something from the road last night.

How the soul starts to talk to itself in the deep slumber of winter. How the heart no longer beats but only whimpers and folds. Thom spoke to some part of himself while he drove the plow. For the sake of his own sanity and for convenience he refers to this part as "Joe." He'd begun talking to himself in high school when he apprenticed to a carpenter in town, Bill Mors. "All carpenters talk to themselves," Bill said. "All carpenters worth their salt, that is." Thom liked this. He found that almost all skilled and tedious jobs required talking through things. He preferred to talk aloud to someone other than himself, rather than directing empty questions to machine parts or pieces of wood. Joe always answered.

Thom heard a noise coming from the motor of the truck. Carburetor, he said.

"No, it's not that," Joe said. They listened.

Sure as shit, it's the carburetor, I'd know that whine anywhere, Thom said.

"We'll see," Joe said. "We can't know for certain till we take a look."

This is the moment Thom saw the wolf in the road. Nearly ran over it as his eyes closed on a straight stretch through Minnesota wilderness on Highway 53, listening to the motor a little closer.

A gray-white timber wolf lifted its head from whatever mangled carcass it was eating. Bright red blood stained its fur and mouth in a strange half-smile. It didn't move at the sound of the horn, didn't move when Thom flashed the high beams on and off. It stood staring at Thom, took a bite of the meat, keeping its eyes on the man. Thom found himself amid the absurd scene. Not a carcass, he realized, not an animal.

"You know what it is," Joe whispered.

An orange hunter's vest around a thick coat, brown boots, black winter pants. Then, a hand, cold blue. Then, the back of a head, gnawed half-open like a melon.

Thom climbed out of the truck. Pumped a shell into the twelve-gauge he kept in the truck and fired into a snowdrift on the roadside. The wolf ran off to the night-black tree line, stood there watching, pissed off and ready to fight for his dinner.

Thom kept his eyes on the wolf and went to look at

what it ate. A man. What was left of a man.

"My God," he could hear Joe say somewhere deep within.

The wolf took a few skulking steps in a half-circle around the truck, coming up on Thom's left-hand side. Thom aimed the barrel and growled like a grizzly bear. He'd read somewhere that predators only respond to bigger predators. They don't know what the hell a shot-gun is.

Thom growled like a bear as the wolf made a hostile step toward him. He pumped another shell and fired. This one sent the wolf off for good.

The body didn't smell and was near stone-frozen. He'd been dead awhile. Thawed enough for a smell to catch the wolf's nose, freezing again now. Thom got on the radio and called the Rangers and waited for them to arrive. He could hear the wolf moving around in the tree line, waiting for Thom to leave or turn his back, building up bravery to go after the man. Thom sat in the plow with the high beams entombing the dead hunter in the road, staring at the spattered ring of blue-red blood around the body in the snow.

"He's been dead awhile," Joe said from somewhere behind his ribs. This somehow made Thom feel better. Better to die first, then get eaten and torn apart. He'd heard stories. Seen men missing whole arms up to the shoulder, faces clawed open and scarred over. Better to die first. Who cares after that.

3

Sometimes Thom Algonquin wishes he could not exist for a few minutes. Not die, not disappear completely. Just pause his existence for a minute or two. To float adrift in that quiet on and on. To move like the wind moves and cover the earth. He'd come back when he was ready.

4

Thom has another beer in the yard, no coffee this time, because the first one never counts. "There's not a moment goes by I don't think about you, Helen." More and more it feels like being dragged through the day. Toe-tied, a dull ache works on his bones, sips at the marrow. These are things he keeps to himself, that he'll never share with his son.

Instead, he works. He knows how important it is to keep busy in the winter. He'd just sit around drinking beer, smoking cigarettes, and reading books his whole life otherwise. He would feel sorry for himself. His wife always said he would do these things if she weren't there to keep him level. So he keeps busy. Keeps moving. Move, move, move, to the other side of dawn. Dismantle the broken scaffolds of his life. Always easier to tear down than to build up again.

There must be some symbolism in the wolf and the hunter, Thom thinks. Jude would see it. He loves that, loves to see things that aren't there on first glance. Never in his own life, only for others and in stories. Jude is a reader and lover of stories, and for this Thom is most proud. He never cared about college or degrees or jobs; he didn't care about rowing records or the Olympics. He was proud, of course, like any father would be. His heart brimmed and pulsed with pride and love and joy for his son. But what Thom wants most is for his son to be a good human being. Rowing a boat teaches that. It teaches patience and humility and how to be powerless. This was why he taught Jude to row at such a young age. Books, even bad books, teach how to be moral and mortal. Thom has always been a reader, a researcher and learner, and he couldn't be more proud to see that his son took to words and stories and language like he did, even if Jude never fell in love with tools like he did. Thom wishes he could tell him that, tell him it doesn't matter what he does with his life as long as he is a good man, a kind man, a loving man, as long as he never stops searching for what the world has numbed and forgotten. A word would be good enough, a single verse to contribute. Thom used to think that language was divine and sacred; words are what caused the wound and would make him well again, if only he still believed it. He believed that language whispered and moved and showed you the way. He used to believe in words, as he believed in things he could not see or understand.

He wants to be someone who believes again.

And yet he knows there is something more waiting for him, even now, at the end.

What could be waiting? Thom thinks. "You know what it is," Joe says. It is there within him, as ever. He seeks it in the work, in the detail and infinitesimals of morning's break and day's dark end. Only he forgets about it, numbs it and drowns it out in the day-to-day-ness of life. But he always finds his way back here, back at this morning view: the view of something just there, just beyond the reach of the dawn within him. All at once, the view is not the view, but what is just beyond it. A line of tiny moments align; the heart rends, and something within it splits like dried wood falling away from the axe. Then, for a moment, it is there: the path, the way, the search. Then it begins, and the thought of "too late" no longer exists: with a breath, a heartbeat, a golden apple, a magic thread. Other times Thom refuses the search:

drops the clue, flings away the apple, freezes solid, turns to dust. Thom knows what winter can do, what the day-to-dayness can do. He knows the face of despair, its exact nature—and that is being unaware of being in despair. There comes a passage to his mind. He has recalled it so often that the author is lost, and it has become his own: "Turn over a stone and there I am, split open a tree and there you will find me." But what, what could I ever find? One can never arrive too late for redemption, to the search and the morning view, but is that what is to be found within the trunk, under the stone? "Isn't it?" Joe says. I don't know what it is. "Surely you do, your tongue salivates with the word," Joe says. Thom stares at the tree standing at the edge of the water. He looks at it, and then he looks out at the Lake. Frozen, cold.

Is it God, is it some enlightenment or transcendence? he thinks. "You know you can't answer that," Joe whispers. Thom knows he can't. But there it is, nonetheless. Like some light just over the hills, like a beacon on the far shore of the Lake. He knows he has to move toward it. Move, move, move. But not numb, not listless, not languid: rather, to move as the lilies move, to roll on as the tide rolls on.

Consider the birds of the air, Thom thinks.

Please, don't start with all that, Joe says.

The lilies of the field, he thinks.

Thom, Thom, Thom.

"I want my heart to move again," Thom says aloud. "To move. Not merely to beat, not only to pump, but to live. What do you say to that?"

What do you *say to that?* Joe says. *What do you seek?*

Thom looks at the Lake. He looks and breathes, and in the moment, nothing hurts. Not looking at the Lake, not seeing the tree, not thinking of all that such a sight brings rushing into his heart these last months. Thom walks to the Lake's edge. He crouches low and brushes the powdery snow away and lays his hand on the black obsidian ice. Just below it, there is a darkness and a darkness after that. There is life there in that frozen depth. Life and living things and an abundance of it. But he can't see any of it. Everything is still and solid, frozen cold as tombstones. He feels the cold slide up his bare hand and he lets the cold enter him. He rises and lets the winter brush against his cheeks.

What do you seek?

It is the search to find that joy which depends on nothing, he thinks. He stands there looking at the frozen Lake and wants to believe such a thing is possible.

5

Days end in dark confusion and begin like a match strike. Full of promise and hope, soul-shaped and peregrine, fresh off the highway out of Eden. Thom watches the sky open through the cloudbreak. Curtain call for dawn's rosy blush; things to do but not to be said. Jude's been quiet lately, Thom thinks. Quiet and pushing off like rings on a pond.

"So have you," Joe says.

It's winter, Thom thinks. And winter's the only thing that can tear a soul down. There's never a reason to be unpleasant in the spring or summer or even autumn—but winter is something else entirely.

"Working late nights can weigh you down, sit on your chest and keep you there. It's probably just the nights," Thom says aloud, and decides not to think about it anymore. He doesn't want to look for what isn't there at first glance.

He picks up the hammer from the toolbox and pries out the nails that were holding down the baseboards. One gives him trouble. He wiggles it with a cold grip, hands almost numb, and tugs harder. His hand is cold and it slips and the nail slices the skin open. He sets the hammer down and looks at the cut across his palm, holding his wrist tight to slow the blood. The blood comes anyway. He stares at the cut. It is deep and in the severed flesh, there in the pink-red muscle, he thinks he can see her face for a moment. Her eyes, the round glow of her freckled face. But his wife is not in his hand, she is not there.

"She is and she isn't," Joe whispers.

He washes the cut at the sink and wraps a handkerchief around it, ties it tight to stop the blood. "You should sleep," Joe says. Thom sits at the table and looks out of the massive hole in the back of the house like a bear from his cave. The sky opens a little more. Light and dawn come and make a tear in the pewter-dark wall above, just big enough for a soul to slip through. He imagines walking out onto the Lake, breaking through the ice, sinking down. "Don't," Joe says. Thom stares at the wall and imagines sitting in a sunroom. It'll be a good room, he thinks.

"You should sleep," Joe says. Thom can feel his heartbeat in his hand, moving out in sonorous rings to his fingertips, and then farther out to nothing.

There isn't a moment goes by I don't think about you, Helen. I feel like I imagine the damned must feel, broken, fey, and cursed. Not a day goes by I'm not falling through the dark, not a day I don't think about you and feel damned and cut off from what is pure, what is sacred.

Out in the garage Thom starts up his truck and moves his hand to the remote on the visor to open the door. He stops and pulls his hand back as he smells the exhaust creeping through the windows. He wonders if he shouldn't just close his eyes and sleep and dream of afternoons adrift on the Lake. Close his eyes. Let everything pull apart. Sleep. Jude, though. Jude. Jude . . .

Thom breathes deep and coughs a little.

"Open it," Joe says, impatiently. "Open the damn door, Thom."

Daylight fills the garage and Thom backs down the driveway half-dazed and coughing. The tires crunch over the rock salt and snow like a plow over bones. He can feel his heart beat and break in his hands, he holds it there.

He can feel the wolf tearing him apart, one piece at a time.

Not a day goes by I don't think about you . . . .

6

Thom loads the truck with pine boards, brackets, boxes of nails, a new saw blade. Expensive, but the end justifies the means, he knows. What's the point of saving if it's not for something? Thom takes his time doing things. He feels the weight of each two-by-four and six-by-eight, feels the weight of the nail boxes and brackets. Flurries dance through the air in a riot of wind. It's not new snow, just the wind blowing the dust off things. Fog and cold. Thom has another cigarette, counts what's left in the pack, and tosses it into the passenger seat, telling himself no more until he's back home.

He stares at the snowdrifts in the Lowe's Hardware parking lot, blackened with oil and dirt. He sees the neon orange vest of the hunter sticking out of the snow, sees the blood; he can almost feel the phantom kick of the shotgun against his shoulder. The wolf is somewhere in the tree line. He feels it coming up behind him.

Thom slides his cell phone out of his pocket and calls Ricky at the ranger's office.

"Doing all right," Thom says. "Say, Ricky, I was wondering if you found an I.D. on that hunter. Wallet or anything?"

"Yeah, hang on," Ricky says. Thom can hear the rustling papers. He's known Ricky for almost fifteen years now. He calls him when there's a tree down on the highway, or a stalled car, or when a wolf is eating a hunter in the middle of the road.

"Name's Fred Sørensen. Fifty-seven. Lives up near Orr. Well, lived."

"Orr?"

"That's what it says." Ricky is quiet a moment before going on. "You holding up all right, Thom?" he asks again. "Hell of a thing to see out there."

"I'm holding fast," Thom says. He has learned to say this when people ask that question. *Holding fast.* Thom's father used to say this, and so Thom does now, too. It's different enough, so no one ever asks much more most of the time; different enough so they know he's still with it. "Was it the wolf that got him?"

"No. He'd been dead a week or so by then. Heart attack. Wasn't any fresh blood. Only living things bleed. His wife put out a missing-persons report when he didn't come home. Must've lost his way and gotten too tired or something. It gets rough out there. Pretty common, sadly."

"Jesus."

"Yeah, you said it." Ricky sighs. "Damnedest thing. You holding up, Thom?"

They talk a few minutes more about how they should get together for a beer at the Black Caribou there in town. It's been too long since they just sat and had a cold beer. Thom's on autopilot while talking. His voice carries on with Ricky but he's far away, already driving out toward the wilderness.

When he hangs up he looks at the time, just now eight a.m. Jude won't be up for a while still. Orr is a bit of a haul, but it's a straight, quiet drive. "None of that matters, though, does it," Joe says suddenly. Thom knows that it doesn't. There's something there within him. He has to go. He doesn't know why, only that he has to, *has* to, go see the man's wife.

Thom pulls out of the parking lot and turns right

toward the highway, away from home. He merges onto 53 Northbound. The highway is mostly empty and silent as he drives through the fruit of his nightly work in the plow. He doesn't know why he's going. Only that he must. He has to find something. Maybe to find again what he once was before he became what he now is: this bear, perpetually trapped in this year of hibernation.

7

Later, Thom will wonder why he went at all. What purpose did it serve? How useless it was. How sudden and spontaneous and bizarre for a man like Thom Algonquin to turn and drive north without a word or thought for his son. Later, he will wonder if he wasn't dreaming, if it wasn't some dark force hovering over his shoulder compelling him against his will to forget his grief and despair and move toward the dark, and on into the darkness after that. He'll wonder these things. He'll wonder what it was he went out in search of. Then he'll let all those thoughts go. In some other version, one of those million-threaded paths, Thom went home and cut boards and hammered nails and tried not to think of his dead wife. He had lunch with Jude and they talked like father and son. But not in this version.

In this version he pulled into the driveway of Louise Sørensen at a quarter past ten on a Monday morning in December. Sometime later, Thom will wish he had just gone home instead.

8

The house is made of long brown timbers, chinked together with thick stripes of white mortar. It's at least seventy or eighty years old, Thom guesses, but it has been well cared for. They don't build them like this anymore. It sits at the edge of the forest on the shore of Pelican Lake in northern Minnesota. Thom wonders if such a cabin doesn't look perfectly picturesque and peaceful in the spring or summer. But in winter it is lonesome and still.

He parks the truck near the porch and is slow to climb the stone steps to the door. What will I say? he thinks.

"This isn't about words, though, is it?" Joe says.

Thom knows it isn't. He is vacant of words and their meanings, has been for a long time. All that is left are the details, the infinitesimal parts and pieces that hold it all together, the little things he can control and then get lost in. Words move and oscillate. They've always stung his tongue like match heads and set loose a fire before he ever could control them. As an old man, Thom has learned it's better to bite your tongue and taste the blood. Now, his language is mute and languorous. All is petrichor and only a memory of the storm.

"You've come too far not to knock," Joe says.

The woman who answers the door is prettier than Thom had drawn her in his mind. Her eyes are tired and dry, as if waiting for more tears at any moment. Thom knows the feeling well.

"Mrs. Sørensen?" Thom says.

"Yes—?"

"I am Thomas Algonquin, ma'am. You don't know

me… I drive a plow for Saint Louis county." He pulls his wool hat off and kneads it in his cold hands. "I was the one who found your husband, ma'am."

She swallows a lump in her throat that seems it won't ever go away and looks out at the snow behind Thom. She stands in the doorway, waiting.

"I know you've probably had enough people coming to your door lately, but I just… I had to come and… well, I lost my wife a year ago now. It's, well… I know how…"

She watches Thom stammer and twist his tongue over words that say nothing of what he wishes. She opens the door wider.

"Come in, please," she says.

A tired old husky looks up from the cold hearth but remains supine. The house is cold and the woman sits on the sofa, wrapping herself in blankets. Thom knows she's been sleeping in that spot on the sofa. He knows the feeling of trying to return to an empty bed.

"Is there something new they've found, Mr. Algonquin?"

"No, ma'am, not that I know of." They sit there, rapt in the silence. "I guess I just couldn't get it out of my head. When I heard he had a wife, I just felt this… something in me that I had to come and talk to you. I don't know why, I just…."

Mrs. Sørensen is silent, staring off at the fireplace that has no fire burning. Thom kneads his woolen hat in his hands, leaning forward on his knees, hunched and uncomfortable. "Why did you come?" Joe whispers.

The words come now.

"I thought it might be easier if you had someone to blame," Thom says. "Instead of just . . . random, reasonless things."

"Someone to blame?" She looks at Thom, moving her

eyes slowly across the room to him. "Did you kill my husband, Mr. Algonquin?"

"No ma'am."

"There simply isn't someone to blame sometimes," she says. "There is no fault, other than being human, being alive. And that is never a fault. Freddy had health problems. I told him he shouldn't go. But did he deserve to die like this? Was it fair? Was it his proper time? Would he still be here if he didn't go on that hunting trip? I don't know. But all these are useless questions, Mr. Algonquin. Useless, because the soul and the heart deserve a chance to grieve. Not to be distracted with all our excuses or blaming or empty reasons. Sometimes it just isn't for us to know things. But even then, the heart deserves that time to be left alone."

Thom stands after a moment and pulls on his hat. His beard is bristly, feral.

"I'm sorry for your loss, ma'am. And I apologize for coming out here. I just… thought it might be easier for you, to blame someone. I wish I had that. I guess I wanted to feel something different, that by talking to you I'd find an answer or an end to my own grief." Thom looks around a moment. "Pretty selfish, I guess. I'm sorry. I shouldn't have come here."

"Like what?" she says. "Find what?"

Thom looks at her. "I needed to see that I wasn't so alone for a moment. That I wasn't the only one. People can give you their thoughts and prayers all day, but they don't know. I thought maybe there was some connection with you and me." Thom looks at the woman. "My wife died because she missed the top step of the stairs by half an inch. Stairs she'd gone up and down for thirty years. And half an inch changed everything. It makes no sense. None at all. And I have to have things make sense, ma'am. I have to. The pieces, the details simply have to fit together. They have to, they just have to…"

"Why do they have to? Because you say they do?"

"Because without the little bits we can hold in our hand, that we can control, we're helpless. There's just nothing real if we don't have that little bit to hold."

"I've often wondered if we're ever in control of anything, even those little bits. Would it be so bad if we weren't?"

Thom pulls at his beard and looks at the dog lying inert on the cold black stone of the hearth.

"Often I feel like the damned must feel," he says. "I feel cursed, like a ghost trapped between having her here and letting her go. And yet, either way, I feel adrift. Cursed and damned. And those little things I can control are all I have."

"I've heard it gets better with time," she says, and smiles as if they share an inside joke.

"What comes after grief?" he asks.

"Something beautiful? Maybe? If you can be willing to go so far to find it. Something that pushes you off alone and rolls onward. But you have to go so far to find it. You have to go meet it."

"It's a long walk for something like that."

"Always has been, I think," she says.

Thom nods and moves to say more, but doesn't. He wishes to say something, to say everything pent up inside. So he says nothing at all.

She adjusts the blankets around her and he can see she is crying now, as if the act were out of her control. Thom knows the feeling. He walks to the fireplace and the old husky moves aside, brushing up against his legs. Thom stacks a few dry oak logs on the iron grate and twists a piece of newspaper. He pushes it under the wood and strikes a match, lighting the paper at both ends. The flames struggle, so he blows gently on them, and they crawl up the dry wood. In a moment, the fire is steady and hot.

He moves to the door and waves a solemn good-bye.

"It is something beautiful," she says, staring at the fire dancing. "If you can go the distance, it is beautiful."

Thom closes the door behind him. It's snowing again, soft and dreamlike. He gets in the truck and pulls out of the long driveway. He wonders if Jude is up yet. Thom wishes he could hug his son now. He feels more alone than ever. He should never have come. What is he without that which he can hold in his hands and control? Who would he be without the details and the pieces? He wishes he could tell his son these things, all he fears. But he knows that he won't. There's work to be done. Boards to cut, nails to hammer. The details, the controllables. He knows that if he pulls a saw, the wood will give in and be cut to size; he knows that if he hits a nail, it will dive down and hold things in place. He can control these things, and he knows that if he holds fast in doing so he'll find the words, the way.

Now, though, Thom feels worse than before. He wishes he had never come here to see this woman. It was better to be alone, to leave things in their familiar places. He was just beginning to be comfortable in the despair; it was becoming the new normal. Thom found it harder to hope that despair could end, harder to know life might call to be built up again. It's easier to tear things apart than to rebuild them.

JUDE

1

I have often wondered if we aren't marked indelibly on the soul or heart with who we are to become in this life: with this one *thing* we were meant to do. We spend a great long time finding it, trying to understand it, and if we do, we grab hold of it with both hands and try to hold on to it, often forgetting our lives in the process.

Dad told me a story once about this baseball player from back in the late 1800s or so. He was the best pitcher anyone had ever seen and he changed the game forever when he threw the first sinker-pitch. But the owners were paying him shit money, despite how many fans he brought out to the games. So one day this local businessman offers the pitcher a bit of cash to not play so well in this one pretty meaningless game. So the pitcher took it. He needed the money to feed his wife and two daughters. All he knew was baseball, as if he'd been born for the sole purpose of playing and making people happy. He'd never done a single dishonorable thing in all his life, and one can argue he never did at all. He had a choice, Dad always said: to feed his family or not. But it took no time at all for everyone in town to find out what happened, how he took the money. The story made it to the newspapers. The pitcher was banned from baseball for life—they had to make an example out of him, they said. He tried to get back into the game, even changed his name, moved to a new city, but no one would take him. He was tainted, and he had tainted the purest thing in America up to that point. He died only two years afterward from an unknown sickness. But Dad always said it was because his soul died. It died because it could no longer do that one thing it was born to do. It seems entirely illogical and rather silly to think playing a game could be someone's sole purpose in life, but Dad believed it. Still does.

2

My earliest memory is of being on the Lake in a boat by myself. The water calm as glass, no one around, and me just sitting there, looking out at the endless water. Nothing makes you feel as perpetual and yet temporary all at once as water you can't see across. I don't know why I was alone on the water, or where Mom and Dad were. But it didn't matter. I felt I was at home. Mom told me later that I went down to the dock and got in the boat by myself and just drifted out onto the water. Dad had to swim out there and pull me back in.

By the time I was old enough to hold an oar I was rowing with Dad. I became obsessed, because even then, there was this great and mysterious truth deep within me. I was good at it. Sometimes that's reason enough to dedicate yourself to something. Mom said it was because I was born under the sign of the Water Bearer, but no matter what, I felt that I was meant to be on the water. I felt as if I belonged on the Lake, with the oars in my hand.

The beautiful thing about rowing is that there is never a destination if you don't want there to be. Even if there is, you can't think about it. The boat and the water won't let you think about it. Even in competition each individual stroke is the most important thing, not the destination. The way the wrist moves, how the shoulder pulls, how the fingers are placed, even the balance of strength in both arms, must be perfect. If you're not conscious and present, an inch too far to the left can put you miles off course in no time at all. You must be completely and entirely focused on what you're doing. But those are just the things you can control.

The water is something else entirely.

Water is a strange element, the softest substance. In your hand it is nothing at all, and yet it is everything. Water has the strength and force to wash away entire cities and divide continents. Its force is quiet and subdued, but it is constant. Water never yields. One way or another, it will find a path to wherever it must go next. Nothing in this world stands in its way for long.

When you're rowing on open water there is no telling what you will have to fight against. A lazy tide can start unnoticed early in the morning on a far shore, but by the time it reaches you it has become this mythic, living thing. One thing I have always loved was that when the waters turn, there isn't a thing you can do about it. Nothing. All you can do is keep rowing and smile as you test your mettle. Even then, the water can force you to stop rowing altogether while it tosses you around on its belly. Then all you're left to do is sit and wait.

I found that I was never once concerned with the finish line during competitions. This pissed a lot of people off. When I rowed crew (usually an eight-man team) I was always placed in "stroke" position. All the other rowers follow the stroke's rhythm and timing. We rowed with a coxswain sometimes, and it never failed to end very poorly for whoever was in that position. They were always looking to the boats beside us and at the finish line ahead, but never at the water. They constantly tried to quicken our strokes per minute, but that was only because they couldn't let the end point go. They couldn't feel the water beneath them and in their hands. My goal was to row fast, to glide, but to do so in the rhythm of, in respect for, the water. Not to fight it. When you fight the water, you will always lose. Always. I let the water do part of the work for us, let her carry us over her surface. It was rare to find a coach or another rower who held this same perspective. That in turn led me back to rowing single scull. I sometimes prayed that I'd never reach the finish line and could row on forever. Subsequently, I won almost every single scull race I was in.

Up until the accident, rowing had been all I thought about, all I did. I would wake up at four in the morning and go out on the Lake for a few hours before school each day. I hate training in facilities and the infinity pools. When the Lake froze over in winter, I would find rivers or ponds small enough that I could break them up with my boat, and I would row until I was numb. As a kid I slept with an oar beside my bed, always within arm's reach, and I'd lie awake dreaming of rowing across the Lake, rowing as far as I possibly could. Maybe I'd come back. Most of the time, I knew I wouldn't. Sometimes in the summer or autumn I'd go down to the boathouse and sleep in Dad's old rowboat, long since gone now, and listen to the sound of the water. If I was feeling particularly brave and adventurous, I'd even row out a little way onto the Lake and lie down, looking up at the Northern Lights as the boat rocked and drifted freely in that calm on and on.

In less than a year all of it has changed. I can barely stand the sight of a fucking rowboat now. I can hardly walk with Dad down to the dock to look at the Lake without feeling completely angry and hopeless. It feels at times like my own soul has died. It feels like I've been evicted from that one *thing* I was meant to do in this life. Other times, I have come to feel suspicion of that very sentiment, suspicion of myself for entertaining it. Maybe it is only a cop-out, a shortcut to thinking. Truth of the matter is I messed up my arm so badly that I can barely raise it over my head. Dad says that's all psychological, but it doesn't matter. The facts are the same. And all because of a little misstep, because of a God-damned appliance: a one in a million chance that I should fall in such a perfect way as that. But more than sorrow, the accident has opened my eyes to the fact that I have wasted my life on a Lake, wasted my life by sitting in a boat. A life spent there just…sitting. I'm more pissed off about that than anything else. How God or the Universe or whatever could lead me down such a path only to pull it out from under me and send me into the dark. Fuck that. And now I'm in this place of perpetual *stuckness*, waiting for someone or something to come along and show me the way, to push me off the rocks. Emily told me that that was one irony of working in a restaurant: everyone is waiting. Waiting tables, waiting for the next customer to come in, waiting for the next order to be plated. No one is a professional waiter by choice, usually. They're all waiting for their real lives to begin, waiting to go back to college or to get a better job. All of them, myself included, caught in this restless *stuckness*. Stuck in between living and being alive. I'm sure Dad would have something to say about whining like this. He's full of useful tricks for how to get things back on track, or at least to keep moving forward somehow. His tolerance for whining and bullshit is dangerously low. He and Mom once went to some friend's house for a party and their friend's toilet was running. Dad could hear it as soon as he walked in. He remembered it had been running the last time they were there too, months before. So he brought it up to the couple. "I took a look at it, but nothing really helped it," the guy said. "I guess it just runs like that, ever since I installed it."

"Bullshit," Dad told him. "Toilets aren't made to run constantly. Did you look at the manual that came with it? Did you research it?"

"No, I think I tossed that out with the box."

"Of course you did. That was a damn stupid thing to do," Dad said.

The story, the way Mom told it anyway, goes that Dad spent the rest of the night tearing apart the couple's toilet and rebuilding it. He worked on it until almost two in the morning. It worked how it was supposed to after that. He went as far as resealing the base and cleaning it for them. I think he even went into the basement and adjusted the water pressure valve. Dad always said people like that are just poor stewards of what they have been given; they don't learn because they don't care about knowing or understanding or caring for what they have. It makes him more sad than angry at the state of the world, at people. Sometimes Dad talks and it sounds like he's reading from a motorcycle repair manual. He'd probably tell me I'm so clever for this idea of *stuckness* but how useless it is all the same, how it's all been said and done before. But maybe not anymore. These last few days he's been different. I guess I have too.

But truly, I'm starting not to mind being stuck. It's comfortable and unwavering if you can let it be. Mostly I think I am afraid now of being unstuck, afraid of having to continue life somehow. Doing some other thing. Just that thought ties my guts in knots. But I've found that all of that goes away when I'm washing dishes. Everything drifts away when I'm standing at the sink and thinking or not thinking. It just depends on the night.

3

There's nowhere to sit in the house that isn't freezing cold, now that Dad's knocked out an entire wall of the house. Bed is the only warm place, but staying in bed after I'm awake makes me feel homesick and slightly depressed. A pit forms in my gut. I have to get up when I'm awake, have to do something. Dad's the same way.

Emily called to say she's coming by on her way into work to just say hi. I wish it was time for work already, but work is still hours away.

I have this urge to read something, but Dad's gotten rid of most of our books. He said there's no point in hoarding books, specifically novels, as people rarely re-read a novel, so they just sit there being useless. I completely disagree with this; I've read my favorite books dozens of times. But I lack the energy to argue about it, to argue about anything really. I got a new library card in place of the yelling.

It wasn't only the books though. Dishes, furniture, clothes, VHS tapes, old records; he got rid of most of it one day, rid of anything that reminded him of Mom that wasn't hers. All of her own things remain. They stay exactly where she left them.

The bookshelves are filled with instructional manuals. Dad will never get rid of these. Everything from computers to small engine repair to welding, Dad has a book or manual on it. He even has one on building boats that I'm pretty sure he has never looked at. But it's here, just in case he gets the itch to build a boat one day.

For today's reading I've chosen a 1982 RCA television owner's repair manual. I read at the kitchen table by the open wall and drink coffee. It's freezing, but with the wall gone the light is perfect. These manuals always begin so mind-numbingly boring that the light is important to keep you focused. However, somewhere along the way they really take a turn and become quite interesting. They become like a prayer or a meditation. The act doesn't change the world around you; it only aligns you to the moment you're in.

I have never had much difficulty with the quality and expression of wonder. This is where Dad and I part ways in our thinking; at least, our perception of the world takes different paths here. Donald M. Sumner, the author of this manual, has examined and explained every tiny detail of the RCA XL-100 "Colortrak" TV. Every nut, bolt, wire, tube, and dipole coaxial cable input—he knows it intimately. It's probably safe to say that nine out of ten people sitting in front of a television have absolutely no idea what makes any of it work. Other than the power cord sticking into the wall, they have no understanding of why they see images on that piece of glass. And that's perfectly fine. They don't need to know why any of it works, as long as they can appreciate the wondrous fact that those images do appear and can appreciate that someone's imagination and invention put them there. This is the juncture where my road and Dad's diverge further. I constantly marvel at such feats, both in technology and in the natural world. But where I am satisfied with my wonder and minute appreciation, happy just to be in the presence or use of such a thing, Dad can't sit still. If he did he would burst into flames. He is one who *must* know why those images appear. Not only why, but how they do, and why in such order. Why does this wire attach here and not here? Dad can't marvel. He has to understand things to the farthest possible degree. I'm not entirely convinced that this is solely because he can't stand not being in control of something, but I do think that is a major factor. Dad has never called a repairman to the house, has never asked for help of any kind. He does it himself. If he doesn't know how, he learns it on his own. Not only learns it, but becomes an expert in whatever it is. He protects himself from criticism, from needing someone. I do believe Dad's biggest fear is needing someone else in order to get by. He is afraid of having to rely on people because, in his experience, people are most often unreliable and you are usually alone in life. I don't disagree with this outlook, but I'm not quite so pessimistic in my drift.

Roads are one thing Dad takes very seriously. He read this statistic once of how many car accidents occur in bad weather, especially snow and ice, and so the next day, after Mom and I spun out and ran off the road into a ditch, he got a job plowing roads for the county. All because he didn't trust whoever had been doing it. It's the same with the sunroom, I think, but that has more to do with *doing* something.

Dad converted to Catholicism when he married Mom. I'm not really sure why he did—other than to make her happy and to get married in the Church—but he's always seemed to be disgruntled and at odds with religion and God and church-going. He rarely went to Mass with Mom, except when she made him go on major feast days and Holy Days of Obligation. He hasn't gone now since her funeral. At first he liked the history and tradition of it all. Then he dove pretty deep into the catechism and philosophy and Canon Law. He loved how all the bits and pieces made sense, fit together. But he could never see the point in just sitting there in a pew, praying silently, meditating on things and just being still. Because when he is still, he's not *doing* anything. Dad is as far as possible from the pop-culture "fear of missing out" or fear of not being "connected enough," but his fear of idleness is there all the same. We are a society of *doers*. We have this false simulacrum of a value that we must always be doing something. If we're not doing, we've come to believe that we're rotting, dying, and wasting life. We've said: Life's short so we must do it all, no time to waste on sitting still, on *non-doing*. There's this strange unspoken pressure that you must have something to show for your day, for your time on this earth. You must make something of yourself, be successful. The first question we generally ask each other is, "What do you *do*?" And this is always a loaded question. I've found that we often ask this to see if we are doing better than that person, to compare our life to theirs. We feel great if we're better. And if we find out our life pales in comparison, we either become sick with envy or become inspired to do more, both of which usually send us off immediately to go and *do* something. But I think it is in the non-doing that we are most alive. At least, I'm beginning to think this.

A few weeks ago I read this one instructional manual on growing herbs that Dad had bought for Mom at some point. I decided to read it as if it were a novel (I was craving a fictional world to escape into), and that helped make the whole experience much better. I came to this part where the narrator was warning the gardener about too much sunlight on the leafy main characters. That, yes, they needed plenty of sunlight, but they also needed plenty of darkness too. In the light, photosynthesis starts and converts carbon dioxide into oxygen. But after a full day of light, everything needs to rest and to purify, to return to its base level, to balance out. In the darkness the plants reverse and convert oxygen to carbon dioxide, cleaning and healing themselves in the process. We need that balance too, of doing and non-doing. When you sit there for long enough, all the shit you've been thinking and doing will begin to disassemble and tear down. We need this. We need time to heal and to purify.

When I tell people I've given up rowing and that I'm washing dishes at a restaurant, there's this look that comes over them, a look of pity and sorrow, but also one of them feeling better because they won out in the comparison game. "How could he have fallen on such bad times? Why isn't he *doing* something with his life?" it seems they want to say. The reality is I wish I had always been washing dishes. Things would perhaps be much better if I had.

In college, before the accident, I used to walk a few blocks off campus to Saint Sebastian Catholic Church some nights and sit in front of the Blessed Sacrament. I hadn't been a practicing Catholic since the end of high school, since I went off to college and stopped going to church with Mom each week. I wasn't having a return to the faith necessarily, but the chapel was the only quiet place I could find. Truly, those nights sitting in that empty chapel were the quietest moments I can recall. I would sit there in a pew toward the back, silent, just sitting in the warm orange glow of the candles, with the faint perfume of incense still balancing in the air. I would just sit, staring at the monstrance holding the consecrated Host, and I'd sit for hours, not doing anything, letting everything wash away and disassemble. At the time I did it in order to organize my head for rowing and school, especially before big races or exams. But looking back, I think it was the beginning of something else. Not that I know what that something else is; it just feels now like there's something there, something I didn't see at first. The one thing I know about it is I can't *do* anything to find out more about it. It only comes in non-doing, in being still—useless, Dad would say. In just sitting there. And just sitting there is often harder than doing something. People, like Dad, they can't sit still. Always restless, even when they're resting.

4

I've learned all about the audio reception on this old model of television, and Dad still isn't home. It comes to mind that maybe he got into an accident last night. Then again, that fear is nothing new. Every morning that I wake up and Dad isn't downstairs doing something, that thought always comes up. My head goes to the worst things. I'm terrified of the day I'll wake up and they'll be true. But I never call him, not because of that, at least. I always think up another reason and convince myself that it was why I called. If I let myself call out of fear, what I fear might become real.

It's raining outside, a freezing rain that will be snow before long. Blue skies are a memory in winter, daylight too. Only a weak grayness leaks through the windows, pours through the hole Dad has knocked into the wall. But it's not full light, only the sun's short breath before going back into hibernation, only a flash of sunblade before it's in its sheath of clouds again.

Dad's words from the other day hit me differently, or maybe just for the first time, as I reshelve the TV manual. How he said I'm only pretending to be serious. He might be right. He must believe I am only serious how most people are serious: in an attention-seeking, control-feigning sort of way. Which is not seriousness at all, only despair wearing a presentable mask.

5

I stand in the back yard a moment, look out at the blankness of everything. Winter now, Spring only a breath away, but a long breath, and, lately it feels we've lost our lungs, Dad and I. There's all this life around, all sorts of moving parts and pieces, and yet we're here on the shore. We just watch the water run past, waiting for the bravery to stick a toe in.

It strikes me just now how people like to say two things: how everything is temporary and how all this matter matters very little in the grand shape of it all; while at the same time they say how much things and people mean to them. They care so greatly about all those things that they'd never let them go, so much sometimes that they'd die for them or start little apocalypses because of them. But why care that intensely about something you are so damn certain is only temporary and, in the end, meaningless? It depends on the thing or person, I suppose, but it shouldn't. If you believe one thing to be only temporary (in the great timestream of it all), then you should equally believe all things are just as temporary. If one life is of the greatest value, then all life must be of equally important value. But most people don't go this far. Monks maybe, people in contemplative life—but rarely any of us below the mountain. This is one of mine and Dad's opposing perspectives.

The truth is I don't know what I believe about most things.

Somehow, in this modern age, we're suddenly expected to have made up our minds about everything; lines are being drawn and we're supposed to live life hopping back and forth, instantaneously. I don't know how anyone does it.

Dad says it comes down to what he calls *Qualitas*, Cicero's translation of the Ancient Greek—*poiótēs*, quality, a peculiar and essential nature of a thing. He always says that caring for a thing has only a little to do with the thing itself, but everything to do with the person caring for it. For Dad, there is no dichotomy. I think he sees himself as much a thing of nature, as much a piece of technology and of non-being, as everything else in this world. Dad takes his time doing things, learning all he can, as a means of elevating the quality of his belongings, and in turn the quality of himself. But all this is, in my opinion, his way of trying to establish and maintain control amid chaos. Much like the rest of us.

I guess I am holding out hope for something to come along and cut me down. To rock the boat and either push me to the far shore or else capsize me and let me sink to the bottom of everything. Either way...

Mom always said God never gives us any more struggle or sorrow than we can handle. I used to believe that; at least, I always wanted to. God might allow some sorrows that we can handle, but we sure as shit pile on our own little hells. And that's enough to break anyone's spirit. Still, I'm holding out for something.

6

Emily is standing in the open doorway. She says "Knock, knock" aloud in lieu of a door to knock on. It's only now I realize Dad has taken the front door off its hinges. It was working fine yesterday, but I guess not well enough for him.

The fur lining of her coat is crystallized with frost and ice. Her nose is a blushed rosy pink, the only bit of color against her otherwise Nordic pale skin. Just seeing her standing there, I begin to think of memories she'll never have, whole fictions I built and then tore apart back in another life. We're both here now in that life I wished to build, only a simulacrum of what our life could have been.

Emily sits and starts talking. She shivers a little, bouncing her knees under the table. I can see her breath, it smells sweet like Pepsi. I see the plastic bottle in her coat pocket. I don't know how she can drink soda this early. I used to try and form her into these romantic images that I'd dream up. Never real: always mercurial and despairingly antic. I wanted her to carry herself like something out of a sonnet, wanted us to be tortured lovers in a Hemingway or Fitzgerald novel: brimming with love and no idea what to do with the overflow. I wanted her to smell like a certain blend of cool spring air and mountain flowers. I wished I were more of a man. But she and I were always stuck with the little realities. Lovers, sure; tortured, most assuredly.

She smells sweet like Pepsi, and her hair traps smoke from her mom's house. It comes out in little puffs whenever she turns her head or brushes her hair behind her ears. I've come to love how she smells: more perfect than anything I could dream up.

"So Cherry was already drinking before we got there and was going on and on about how she was done with Derek," Emily says. "And the next thing we know, they're off in the corner making out and feeling each other up."

"Could've told you that was going to happen," I say.

"It was crazy, they're both crazy. Why didn't you come out?"

"Just didn't feel much like drinking."

Emily is quiet and stares at the missing wall of the house as if she is only noticing it now. Maybe she is.

"Yeah, Dad knocked out the wall yesterday," I tell her.

"In December?"

"He wants to build a sunroom."

"…in December?"

"I don't know. He just wants to build it. He cares enough about it, doesn't matter the weather."

"So when you and your dad *care* about something, you just tear it down to rubble?"

I look at her, then move my glance quickly to the weather blowing in.

I can't talk about what I know she wants to talk about. I don't have the heart just now. "I'm sure dad has a reason. He usually does."

Emily sighs and leans back in her chair. She breaks the silence I've caused; she says, "I've always wished I could do things like that."

"Like what?"

"Like want to build something and then just . . . build it. Not have to order it off Amazon or some shit. Like, a few weeks ago, I went to get my brakes fixed and after it was done they were squealing and grinding worse than before. So I took it to another place and they said the other guys did a 'butcher job.' And that made me wish I knew how to do all those things. To do it right, you know?"

"Yeah, but then you'd have to spend time doing it your-self when you could be doing other things," I said.

"That's fine," she says. "I don't really do anything else. How many times can I look at my phone or watch some new series before I'm content, you know? I want to get my hands dirty for once before I die."

She takes a drink from her Pepsi and shakes a ciga-rette from the pack I took from Dad's carton and smells the toasted tobacco, but doesn't light it. I just watch her a moment. All of these memories come to mind and pass right along like water. I want to tell her so many things.

"You should come out after work with us," she says. "It'll be fun. Plus, you look like you've been sitting right here all winter. You're like a ghost."

I love you, I love you, I love you.

"No, I'd just be miserable if I came out," I tell her. "I'd ruin your night with whatever his name is. Gary."

"Gabe," she says.

"Jade?" I smile a little.

"Cut the crap, Jude. And you won't ruin anything. He's working tonight. So it'll just be us anyway. Like old times."

I look at her, then I look everywhere else. One of those old times comes to me. I had come home from school for the summer, and Emily and I spent every day together. We talked about whatever came to mind; we went to the movies, hung out with friends, all the usual boyfriend-girl-friend stuff. But one night in July Emily came over late to see me, after Mom and Dad were asleep. I met her out-side and we walked down to the dock. We sat there with our feet hanging over the edge and splashing around in the dark water. In the distance there came these fireworks far out on the Lake, bursting brilliantly against the horizon.

Each one exploded like a tiny dawn and illuminated the clouds for a brief second and was mirrored by the Lake all at once. Emily and I sat there watching them, and then we sat there for hours after, neither of us saying a word. She held my hand in hers and let her head rest on my shoulder as we looked out at the Lake and watched the green light of a buoy flashing on and off, on and off, as if showing us what might be just out there, beyond our reach. Or maybe it was just a light, signifying nothing at all. But everything in life seemed immaculate just then: sacred and pure, simple and true. But there was something about that silence though. It felt like a dream, like one of those fictions, and yet this one was real. Simply being beside one another, existing at that same moment, beyond words, was everything. I needed nothing, wanted nothing else in the world just then, as if my entire life was held in that one moment, as if the universe aligned itself, fell into place to show me a glimpse of what was possible. That silence held everything I could ever want.

I go back to that night often, imagining it and trying to transport myself back there again, even for the briefest moment. To feel but a whisper of that love for even a second longer could last me my whole life, I think. I think of it whenever I see her: that silence, the two of us there together and simply alive, truly vulnerable, as if we'd removed our hearts and placed them in the other's hands to carry forever.

I think of it whenever I see her, and I know it will never be like that again. I was decent then, kinder.

"Whatever. Clearly it doesn't matter to you anymore," Emily says. "You never come out anyway."

We sit there listening to the snow for a moment. Not saying anything. Not discussing what we maybe should. Right there before us, the hole in the wall, my mom dying,

Gabe Welch, how I'm in love with Emily, what the hell I'm doing here living like this—in this strange half-life with Dad: We don't talk about these things. But then, I can't help myself.

"Why are you with him?" I say. "I mean, he's nice and all, but, why Gabe?"

Emily stands to leave, but not without a little parting shot: "He just makes me happy, there's no other way to say it really."

"That's good," I say, but I am so far in my own head I'm not sure if I say it aloud or only think the words.

Gabe Welch, of all people. I wish there were something bad I could say about the guy, but truthfully he is a very good and decent man. Quiet, kind, works like a mule, goes to church Sundays with his parents, and is simply pleasant to be around. The only bad thing about him is how he makes me feel when I see him. It is again that game of comparisons. I look at Gabe and I am envious, envious because he doesn't mind living in between. His life has found a strange and quiet harmony with doing and non-doing. He doesn't wish to be any more successful or rich than he already is, he doesn't want to be famous. Really, he has no other ambitions or dreams other than being a good person and doing the best he can with what he has. It's irritating. It all sounds a little too soft-soap, I know, but it's the truth, and that's where the envy comes in. He is sincere and never has to fake it, not like the rest of us. He is perfectly comfortable with not being the smartest, strongest, richest, whatever-est person in the room. And I can't help but envy his manner and ability to accept what is out of his control. He doesn't try to control much of anything (at least from an outside perspective), but instead he accepts what comes to him, and he does so with grace and sincerity.

Gabe Welch and I used to be friends growing up. We would go out on the Lake together, we were on the same hockey teams and all the rest. But just about the time I was taking rowing seriously and saw it could be my path to something great, he began to only do it leisurely; he began to work odd jobs instead of applying to colleges because he wanted to learn a trade. His dream was to own a little custom boat shop on the Lake. And he did it, too. But back then, that was far too blue-collar and short-sighted for me. I was going to the Olympics; I was going to make something of myself.

But it took no time at all for ambition to become pride. And pride comes in legions, it never lets up. It tastes sweet at first, that euphoric sense of false confidence and vague vindication of selfishness, and then it is forever bitter after that first taste. But we keep after it, for another taste of the sweetness that never existed to begin with, hoping to break out of it somehow, only digging ourselves deeper in the process.

"I am happy for you," I tell her. I think I really mean it, too. I want to be happy for her anyway, and the desire alone is enough for now. I hope it is.

Emily stands there in the kitchen, just staring at the snow in the backyard, blanketing the old boat house and dock and Mom's favorite tree, the massive cypress just on the shore. I look at what she's looking at. The room feels heavy; there's something one of us is not saying, but I don't know who.

The winter blows the smell of dirty laundry and empty sardine cans into the house. I look around suddenly, as if for the first time. What a mess. What depths we've sunk to. I look up and see Emily is seeing it too. I see something in her face and my chest tightens.

"Well, I guess you should go if you're going," I say.

She stops pacing in the kitchen and stares at me.

"What? You can go," I say. "I can tell you don't want to be here. I don't either. I get it. Just leave if you want."

She looks at me. "You just left me waiting, Jude. Not one word from you."

"What?"

"Ever since you came back home I've been eating myself alive trying to ask you, so here it is. How could you do that to me? You left me with a promise, and for four years I held onto it. Even after you stopped coming home to see me, even after you quit calling. You made me believe in something that was never real. You let me believe you loved me more than you loved yourself. And that's a cruel thing to do to anyone, Jude." She doesn't cry just then. I can tell she's already cried enough over this. "That's the worst way to break a person's heart. And that's exactly what you did to me."

She turns and leaves through the open doorway.

It's snowing again and the wind blows it into the house where the wall used to be. Everything is cold and settling like fault lines inside me. My shoulder aches in the cold air and I rub at the scar. It hurts. It's never stopped hurting. A Goddamn refrigerator.

THOM

1

Thom Algonquin calls his manager's office and tells Richard he needs the night off. Something's come up. In all his years working for the county he has never called in, never asked for a night off. When his wife died he was scheduled to work that same evening. He had every intention of going in, even after it happened. Better to keep busy, to keep things normal and moving. Jude wouldn't allow it. His manager told him not to come in that night. It wasn't that Thom wanted to work, only that he didn't want to be in the house without her. That quiet. That feeling of eternally waiting for someone who will never come home again.

Thom's thankful that Richard just accepts the request without prying or need for further explanation. Richard sounds almost happy for him. Thom's steadfast devotion to his work and his willingness to work has earned him trust and respect. If Thom calls in it must be something important. And it is.

He drives slow and calm along the Lake access road that runs parallel to the frozen shore. He likes to pretend that to his right lies the infinite, the endless, and the immaculate: there lies the path. That is the Lake. To his left is the world, the everyday and the rest of it—fettered and full of listless ends, where the heart can do all it wishes, but the heart is so confused about everything among the ten thousand paths.

Thom feels something in his chest. A pressure, a tightness, but not that bad kind that comes for a man his age. Not in the heart or blood. It comes from somewhere farther off, deep and deeper still. He slows the truck and pulls off on the shoulder. He breathes, gripping the wheel, staring at the snow and white-gray asphalt stretching out before him. He breathes. The pressure is firm but doesn't hurt. More like someone tugging on his soul than squeezing it. He steps out onto the road and walks toward the guardrail separating road from shore. Ancient rocks line the shore littered with driftwood, water-smoothed and sun-silvered, caught amid the stones and frozen tide break. He looks out to the Lake. Fog and wind drift and stir the powdery snow into a haze, muting the horizon into a faint whisper. The path stretches itself out before him.

For as long as he can remember Thom has been a man living in two worlds: not a man assigned to one and accidentally tangled up in another, but belonging to both at once. He exists in the material, the temporal and fibrous. He holds the moving parts in his tired, callused hands and seeks only to understand them, to know them by the name they call themselves. The other world is the Word, the whisper. It is the language and idea, the intangible: immutable and constant, yet it can never be held, never seen. Not created but existent, it is felt in the soul, among the flesh, but separate in the deep and deeper still. It is *there*, always, constantly and profoundly there. But he can never hold it, never see it. He can walk ten lifetimes and never step an inch closer to understanding it.

This pisses Thom off more than anything. This is what led him to seek God when his wife asked him to; this is why he hopes God might truly exist; this is why Thom curses God at various moments of the day.

In the afternoon silence there comes a moment of still beauty and eerie peace. Snow falls like feathers from a torn pillow before his eyes, flakes mammoth and soft and he feels his tongue twitch and salivate for them. A strange sense of wonder comes to him, but there is a grayness too, a darkness. The distant trees sit jagged and fading across the winter haze, on the far side of the Lake. The cold whispers in his ear like an old lover, reminding him of things he has told himself but doesn't wish to remember just now. There comes a moment, one of new wonder and of old pain. How winter can close such wounds of the heart, and yet place such hooks in the flesh, all at once. Winter has banished all flying things, no hope for summer's blush. There is a focus that comes to him, as his eyes stare into the void, and the void after that. It looks back upon him. There is a warmth within him, of golden memories when his heart wasn't so stiff, when his beard wasn't so feral. But louder still, dripping and seductive, a moment comes and whispers even louder. It is all too much. Too much. All of this world, too much. There comes a whisper of being finished with this world, worn down and enervated by this life. Not sick of or angry at or disgusted by it—simply finished with.

Thom climbs over the guardrail, steps onto the frozen Lake and looks over the silence. He finds a large stone at his feet and picks it up, feeling its weight in his hands. He walks to where he is certain the water is deep and the ice might be thin. On his knees he begins to hammer at the ice, chipping away inch after inch with each steady blow of the rock. "What are you doing exactly?" Joe asks. Thom says nothing. "There are better ways than this," Joe says firmly. Thom breaks the ice with heavy swings of his arm. "What exactly are you doing, Thom?"

The hole is three feet wide, an oblong circle, small but big enough to slip into, soul-sized, heaven-sized. Thom stands upright and stares at the abyss of white stretching out forever before him, encircling all around him. He can hear the lapping summer waves of the Lake, can smell the green grass on the shore, the pine trees bathing in the sunlight, though they are not there just then. Just as he can hear God's voice, as he can hear his wife's voice, only he is completely alone just then, as he is always alone.

This is the quickest way, Thom says.

He steps forward and lets his body slip into the cold blue waters. He feels nothing, he hears only silence. He likes this, and slips deeper into the dark, and into the darkness after that.

2

"What are you doing exactly?" Joe whispers.

Thom slowly sinks toward the bottom.

"You only have a few moments left to get out, Thom."

Thom can feel the blood slowing and dragging along in his veins. The weak thump of his heart out of beat. Sunlight pierces the ice. All else is silent and cold blue.

"Move now, move."

Thom floats suspended like a soul in the water. He feels himself slipping away.

"Move now, it's all right, just rise now."

Thom paws at the water. His body refuses to obey his command.

"Rise now, it's all right, Thom, just rise up for breath again." The voice is no longer Joe's. Thom does not know the voice. And then he does.

Thom hears her voice among the silence, can feel the phantom blade of her soft finger stroking his cold cheek among the still pulse of water. He feels the cracked lace of ice carrying her to him again. He finds her voice among the silence and follows it toward the light bending through the ice.

"Come up for breath now, Thom. Rise. Come up for breath again."

Thom tries to move but only drifts. He wishes to breathe in and fill his lungs with water, to inhale the cold oblivion and sleep forever in her voice.

"The water is not for your lungs, Thom. Rise now."

The light dims and he feels the ice breathing into his heart's blood and into his flesh.

I can't I can't no I can't rise I can't anymore no I can't anymore I can't rise no.

"Come up for breath again now. The water is not for your lungs, rise, rise."

He sees her hand reaching for him and the light fades. Thom reaches up for it. Reaches. And all the light dies in the dark pull of water. He takes a breath and lets the cold water fill his lungs. He feels her hand in his and rises to the warm light.

3

Thom Algonquin awakes to no heaven and no peace. The frozen Lake lies beneath his bones. He coughs up lungfuls of water and drinks the air. He lays supine, gazing up at the low pewter sky moving languid and solemn to some further north. Thom wonders if he isn't dead. He feels nothing but numbness, as if he had not existed for just a moment. Then he feels the burning tingle of lifeblood rushing out to his limbs. Then the cold slap of wind on his wet skin. Then the crinkle of breaking ice on his frost-stiffened clothes as he tries to roll and move.

As he rolls to his side he sees the figure running toward him. The world takes shape. Slowly, things begin to have names. Shore. Lake. Cold within cold. Trees. Endless, vacant horizon. He sits up, a great burning pain aches through the numbing cold that has enveloped him. He feels at his beard. His hand feels only a bush of ice.

The figure comes closer and takes a more solid shape. The word comes. Woman. She runs toward him. He sits up and gathers himself. His body shivers without his command or impulse. It quakes and cavorts in violent fits, each part separate from the whole.

"Don't move," she hollers, almost to him now.

In her arms she carries a blanket. Wool, gray. It looks as if it has been in a car trunk for twenty years waiting for a picnic or campfire on the Lake shore—or for a stranger to fall through the ice and freeze to death. It looks scratchy. His wife would have hated that.

"Stay still," the woman says. "Try not to move too much. You'll go into shock."

Thom stays perfectly still, though his body shivers. She looks familiar. At the moment, though, everything looks so familiar and yet so profoundly foreign. As if he had been in this world his entire life and had only now been alive.

"My God, I thought you were dead for sure," she says. She kneels down beside him in the powdery layer of snow. She is bundled tight in winter garb. Her arms in coat sleeves are wet and icing over where she reached into the water. She wraps him in the blanket, rubbing his shoulders hard and violent for a second. Thom says thank you in his mind but can't remember if he has said it aloud. The blanket is just as musty and scratchy as it looks. "No time to be picky, you stupid bastard," Joe says, impatient and furious. "Breathe now, just breathe and get warm again."

"Thank you," Thom says. "How . . . what happened?"

"I was driving past and I looked and saw you just drop out of sight. So I parked and ran over. Jesus, I thought for sure you were dead. I don't know how I even got you out. I just pulled and pulled . . . I just . . . shit. Fuck, man, this is insane . . . are you all right? Are you sure you're not dead?"

Thom looks at her. She looks cold and familiar. Everything does.

"Do you have, like, hypothermia or something? What happens now?"

"I don't know, I've never had it," he says.

"What are you doing out here anyway?"

"Just out walking."

"And you just fell through? Shit, man, that's . . ."

I hit the ice with a rock to make a hole so I could die. So I could feel something different or feel nothing at all.

"Yeah," he says. "Dangerous being out here." He sees her suddenly and knows her. "I think I've seen you before."

She looks at him.

"I've seen you walking into town I think."

"Yeah, I work in town. At the boat shop. Welch's." She looks at Thom square and as if for the first time. "Are you sure you're not dead? Or that we both aren't dead?"

"No, I'm not sure," Thom says.

She smiles.

"But I'm pretty sure we're still here, and I need to get warm."

4

The woman drives Thom's truck into town. He shivers in the passenger seat but tries to control it, to hold it back, as if it were just a habit he wants to break.

"I read somewhere that you should rub your chest when you're this cold," she says. "It's supposed to speed up the blood flow."

Thom moves his arms inside the blanket draped around him and rubs his chest and ribs. He is unsure if it is this or simply the movement of his hands and arms that is working, but either way, he feels warmer. "What were you doing out there exactly?" Joe says. He sounds pissed off, Thom knows. But Thom doesn't feel like talking to Joe. Not when there is someone else here with him.

"Should I take you to the hospital or something?"

"No, I'll be fine. Just somewhere warm," Thom says. "Where were you heading before this?"

"To work."

"Is it warm there?"

"Yes, it is."

"Just take me there, then." He looks at her a moment, hunched forward, two hands cautiously on the wheel. "What's your name?"

"Freya," she says. She looks over at Thom. "I know. My Dad gave up everything about being Danish except our names." She smiles, and this makes Thom smile.

"You're Danish then?"

"My family is, which means I am too, I suppose. Dad came over when he was sixteen, Mom was born here. Both grandparents were adamant about becoming *real* Americans. So they quit speaking Danish, unless they were yelling at each other, and quit doing anything un-American—whatever that means. Everything except keeping our names super weird."

"Well, for what it's worth, I think it's a pretty name." Thom repeats the name over and over in his head. It's suddenly stuck there, caught in the frozen tangle of his mind struggling to stay conscious . . . Freya, Freya . . . the syllables drip over his tongue as if he'd never spoken before.

Thom looks and sees the soft rise of her belly as she unzips her coat. Five, maybe six months along, he thinks.

"Do you have a name picked out yet?" Thom points his clacking chin toward her belly.

She is quiet and keeps both gloved hands on the wheel, firm and steady, as if fighting the urge to steer into the Lake or move both hands to her warm stomach.

"If it's a girl I was thinking Louise," she says. "Knud if it's a boy." She is quiet, staring ahead at the gray-white world. "If they come at all."

Thom looks at her. "Those are strong names," he says. He lights a cigarette and takes a drag. Quickly, he rolls down the window and tosses it out, suddenly realizing... "I'm sorry, I . . . It's a habit. I always smoke in the car . . ." He empties his lungs, lets the last ribbons of smoke drift out, and rolls the window up again.

"It's fine. Thanks, though."

Freya pulls into the small snow-banked parking lot of Welch's Boat Shop. Thom sets aside the haunting fear of possible pneumonia or hypothermia and wonders what this woman could possibly do at a custom boat shop.

"I'm not a secretary, if that's what you're thinking," Freya says. Thom looks at her, stunned.

"No, no, I didn't suppose . . ."

"My grandfather was a carpenter by trade, and my dad

was a fisherman. But mostly I just needed a job. So I came here because it's all I really know how to do."

Thom nods and gets out of the truck, leaving the wool blanket wrapped around him. The wind off the Lake reminds him of the cold deep in his bones, still rattling and shivering to get warm.

"It's warm inside. You can stay for as long as you need," Freya says. "Do you have someone you can call for a ride or anything?"

"I'll be fine," he says. "What about your car back there?"

"Don't worry about it. I'll get it later on."

She holds the door open for Thom and he walks into the shop. Warmth and the golden-sweet smell of curing wood and raw-cut planks and tools and sawdust fill Thom's nose and stretch like roots down into his soul. He is warm, but not his flesh, not his bones. He is warm in a warmth of being home, of perfect homeness, which is familiar and fragile, which he knows so intimately. He is warm.

Thom has never been in here before. It is a specialty shop for boats, custom building and repairs mostly. Thom Algonquin is among the few residents of Wolf Falls, Minnesota, who does not own a boat anymore. He grew up in boats and on the water, of course. He has owned many boats over the years. He taught his son to row almost before he could swim. But in nearly ten years he has not been on the water—save for his short time twenty minutes ago. He never had any need to come to this shop, until this moment.

He stares at the framed pictures of old fishermen in their skiffs, young men in small sailing dories, held preserved and sacred in black and white, lining the walls. Toward the back of the shop is a large workspace. Here the ceiling rises high like a cathedral's with windows lining each angle of the roof, letting long silver rafters of light in. It is a perfect workshop,

Thom muses. He used to childishly believe—or rather, hope—that heaven was something like this: a perfect place where one could perfectly and entirely do that which they were made to do. It seems silly to him now as he remembers such dreams, but still, he hopes he isn't too far off.

Freya walks to the back of the shop, leaving Thom to warm by the wood-burning stove near the front. Parts and pieces of boats and masts and motors and keels lie lined up on shelves and benches in methodical order all around him. Freya talks to a young man who sands the gunwale of a kayak that sits on a trestle. Thom recognizes him—not him exactly, but the young man's father somewhere in the boy's face.

"Hi there," the young man says, walking over to Thom. "Freya said you fell through the ice? Must be freezing, eh?" He smiles, dusting his hands off on his leather apron. "I'm Gabriel Welch. Gabe. Get warm there by the fire long as you need. Want some coffee or anything?" Gabe asks as he pours a cup from the steaming pot.

"No, thank you. You're Pete's son, right?"

"Yessir," he says, and hands Thom the mug.

Thom holds the coffee in his hand like some foreign thing. He looks at Gabe and nods, ever so slightly. Something sinks in his heart, or perhaps, something lifts. If even for a moment.

"Your dad's a good man." Thom sips and feels the coffee run warm through his chest. "I'm Thom Algonquin. I used to work with your pop years ago. You know my son, Jude, I think."

"Oh, yeah, yeah, how is he? Haven't seen him in years."

"He's doing all right. And your Dad?"

"He's getting by. Retirement's been a son of a bitch. He works here a lot of the time. He'll be in tomorrow, actually."

Thom nods, holding his hands out over the clean cast-iron stove top, spreading and retracting his fingers like slow flaps of a bird's wings.

"Well, just holler if you need anything. Stay as long as you need." Gabe smiles and stands there awkwardly a moment before walking back to his work.

Thom can't help but to gaze innocuously at everything around him. His eyes find and remain on a wall filled with tall shelves holding planks and planks of wood. All specialty and exotic woods, labeled and in order of hardness and color, dark to light. The clean, fragrant order of it all makes Thom almost giddy, a brief respite from the millstone of grief hanging around his neck.

As soon as he feels warm enough, Thom unwraps the blanket, folds it neatly, and lays it on the front counter. He wanders away from the stove and over to the shelf of raw wood. Birch, hard maple, poplar, ash, beech. Hickory and alder; white and red oak. Down through shades of cedar to the darkest walnut, mesquite, and teak. He fills his lungs with their sweet smells; his hands twitch to run his fingertips across their quiet grain. On the far side of the workshop Freya dons a leather apron, ties her hair up, and looks over a set of blueprints on a drafting table. The shop is filled with the sound of Gabe's steady strokes, pushing the coarse sanding block over the raw frame of the boat he stands beside, solemn and contemplative, as if touching some holy relic.

"What do you use for the hull?" Thom asks. "What type of wood?"

Gabe pauses and stands up straight. "It depends . . ."

"What doesn't rot, what would last the longest?"

"A lot of people swear by ash. Strong, good resistance to rot and mold. Others prefer firs, which are lighter on the wallet and good for planking."

"What would you use, say, if you were building a boat for yourself?"

Gabe looks at Thom a moment, thinking. He walks over to the wood and lays both sawdust-powdered hands on a low shelf.

"I've tried most everything, but this yellow cedar is the way to go. Resists decay and rot like a son of a bitch. Tight-grained, so it doesn't absorb much water, if any at all. That makes it lighter when you're on the water. Plus, it's just absolutely gorgeous wood."

Thom nods. "What about for gunwales and frames?"

"Oak is always good. White oak. But I'd prefer cypress, if you can find any. It's become extremely rare over the years."

"You know, there's this old, bald cypress in our back yard, just on the edge of the Lake. It was my wife's favorite tree. They're not supposed to grow this far up the Northern Hemisphere, but it's there. Been there a hundred years or more. She used to sit under it every day. That was her tree, her place."

"It's amazing it's still alive. They say it's the oldest native tree in America. Your wife must love it."

Thom is quiet. He's said too much, or thought too much. He is far away. He floats on the water, weightless and scattered as fine silt. The flesh, poor flesh, is gone. He is soul. Adrift in the silent on-and-on of the ancient tides of the Lake.

"So are you building a boat?" Gabe asks.

Until these words had been uttered to him, Thom Algonquin had never done a single spontaneous thing in his life. Never before had he abandoned control, but this is where the seeking after control had carried him: to slipping into the Lake in winter; to standing here now, in Gabe Welch's shop, at this crossing.

"Yes, I am," he says.

"That's great. They say either you'll never build a boat or else you'll build five. You'll love it that much. It's unlike anything. Building something with your own two hands. Really, it's unlike anything. It's beautiful if you can go the distance with it."

Thom looks at the kid a moment. He nods solemnly. "Beginning to end, about how long does it take?"

"Again, that all depends. On size, plans, how often you want to work on it. If I go five hours a day, I can usually get a small boat out and on the water in four or five months. But that's with other projects going on and little hiccups along the way. There always are, too."

"So, that'd put it done just after the icebreakers come. Spring," Thom says, more to himself than to Gabriel Welch.

"Is it just for exercise or fishing, something like that?"

Thom breathes and lays his hands on the smooth boards before him, feeling the warm grains of the wood against his callused hands. "Something like that."

JUDE

1

A black caribou stands on the edge of the Lake like a mirage
of shadow and shape among the drifts of snow. Slack-jawed
and laconic, he nibbles at the mistletoe growing halfway
up the frost-tipped branches of the evergreens and cedars
along the shore. He's big. A survivor. He sniffs at the wind
blowing in strong over the frozen water, down into America
in lopping steps from Canada. The creature doesn't seem
worried that he has wandered close to people, into the enemy's camp. He stands as if he welcomes death, if death is to
come. Otherwise, he tosses death off with a shrug. He has
only come to fill his cold belly a little bit.

Every few weeks the local news station plays some report
or other about wildlife crossing boundaries from wilderness
into society. A black bear wandered into a 7-Eleven and ate
all the candy bars; a moose walked onto the highway with
her calf and headed north, backing up rush-hour traffic for
three hours and twenty-two miles. There's all sorts of life
everywhere. It was someone's idea to build homes and run
electricity right in the middle of it all. Somehow everyone is
pissed off when things like this happen, and it's always the
bears and deer and wolves that get killed.

I stand on the edge of the yard and watch the caribou
disappear out onto the Lake. Emily's sweet smell still lingers
on the air around me like a dream. I always worry I've said
too much or too little, I never know which. Words have the
power to put out fires or to fracture jaws.

Like the caribou, I would gladly shut my mouth and
whisper to no one for a long while.

2

There's plenty of daylight left before I have to go to work. I follow the caribou's tracks out onto the Lake. He's far off now, a shadow trotting along the treeline, the dark saw blade where the pines make a new horizon.

The Lake freezes a good four, sometimes five feet deep in places. Just to the right or left is the shore: trees, houses, life. Straight ahead is endless white. The Lake is nearly the size of a sea on its own. It's bigger than Vermont, Massachusetts, Rhode Island, Connecticut, and New Hampshire put together. In winter it is a barren tundra of ice and snow and nothingness. Since I was a kid I have always wanted to step out onto the ice and just walk. Walk for as long and as far as I could. It's several hundred miles across, point to point. There are always a handful of morons each year who come from all over and try to hike across and set records. But the Lake rarely freezes over entirely. In spring and summer, it's worse. They try to swim, or paddle board, or canoe across the whole damn thing. Very few make it. It takes a certain level of courage, persistence, and preternatural skill to accomplish something like that. It also takes a willingness to die. None of those assholes have it. They're tourists. All they have is cell phones, and they think they're going to set out and find America. I guess you can't hate them for wanting to be a part of something, though, only for being pricks about it.

The caribou has turned north, and his tracks disappear a dozen yards in front of me. They'll go on for miles following the shoreline. I have half a mind to go and follow him wherever he goes.

Our house looks out over the Lake. It's no mansion, nothing special about it other than its location.

It's one of the last old houses, built to be a home and to survive the winters in this lonesome Northern Hemisphere. Contractors have taken to buying up all the Lakefront properties, tearing down the old homes, and building brand new vacation cabins and mini-mansions and condos that they turn around and sell to non-locals for small fortunes. They're not homes, though; they're not built to last. They serve the simple and immediate purpose of looking pretty for a few months in the summer, and then they go vacant and are boarded up for winter's hibernation. Few of these new-builds make it through winter undamaged. The cheap roofs cave under the weight of snow. Windows crack in the frost. All the cheap pipes freeze and then buckle in the thaw. It's the same with people, too.

Not many are built for winter.

Mrs. Clemens, the pushy realtor in town, has been emailing and calling us twice a week since November. I always read her emails explaining how good the market is and how right now is the time to act. I can even understand her position of wanting to help Dad and me find a home that "better fits our station in life," as she puts it. Her notes are perfectly light-hearted and practiced in their specious brand of sincerity. Try as she will, Mrs. Clemens isn't as altruistic as she'd like to seem to potential clients. She gets twenty percent commission in deals with private buyers and sellers. God only knows what she gets in commercial deals. I don't blame her for wanting to make money. Money and sex are the two founding principles of most people's lives. They are what most people find makes them "happy" or what leads them into despair. If you're making love you're all right. If you're making money, even better. If you are doing both, you're a king or queen in this deranged land. If you're doing neither, well, no one wants to hear about it. Mrs. Clemens's take-home percentages are her own business. I couldn't care any less about how much she makes. I don't care how much Dad makes selling the house, either. The largest part of me that is beginning to consider her offer, which is moving closer to truly wanting to sell the house, is that it might be the tipping point. It might be the one thing that will knock things loose and pull me and Dad out of this, whatever *this* is we're stuck in. It could be that selling the house would breathe new life into Dad, into me. Not that I would move someplace else with him. I don't think I would. But at the very least it would put me at the edge of something, and then I'd have to choose, one way or another.

Looking back at the house from the Lake it looks like a bear's cave, only cold and darkness in the mouth where the wall used to be, where Dad hopes to build a sunroom and catch all the light.

It strikes me just now how I've lived on this shore, on this Lake, all my life. And so has Dad. All the places I would explore as a kid, Dad had already explored decades before. The tides I dove into and swam against, Dad had already fought and swum them. We've breathed the same air for a lifetime now, touched the same ground, looked out the windows at the same trees, at the same jagged shoreline. We've seen the same storms come over the Lake and sat quietly in the same peaceful sunsets. My room was Dad's childhood room. The floors I took my first steps on are where Dad also took his. We've been born and raised in a specific time and place, we've been berthed deep into this landscape, he and I, and we should be deeply connected because, essentially, we've been formed into the same person—at least by our natural environments. And yet Dad is an unknowable man. You could talk to him for a lifetime and never get an inch closer to knowing who he is. Really knowing. His mind is off someplace else. He could tell you he loved you ten thousand times, but you'd rarely feel it. He's been gone too long without ever leaving. He's never done a single thing that wasn't calculated and perfected; he hasn't done anything that he couldn't control entirely. The man has lived an entire life without being alive, I think. Because he isn't living in the past or the future or even the present. He has moved beyond the present moment into the relative specific, that place absorbed in place. He does not see the sun coming down on the room he is building. He does not feel the hammer in his strong grip, does not see the wood he nails into place. He moves past it, so far into the presence of it as a means of controlling the infinitesimal, and in turn, the mammoth of things that could and will go wrong every time. But what does he think about in that lonesome abyss, that silence within the silence? Where does he go off to, and why must he control such meaningless things? I'll live and die never knowing. But to watch him work is like a prayer in itself. To watch him think and move his fingers and disassemble only to build back up again, is unlike anything else. It is like watching him catch fire and not burn up.

Dad will never leave this place. He has been here so long that nowhere else on this earth could possibly make sense to him. It would be outside of his control. And that is something he simply couldn't abide.

3

Twenty-five degrees. Four o'clock. I should be leaving for work.

There is a part of me, some long-lost child maybe, that wants to stay home and wait for Dad to come through the door; to make sure he is all right. To hug him. Talk to him and be normal, pretend we're father and son for a moment.

The other part of me just says, fuck it. Fuck you, old man. If you don't want to call me or see me all day, why should I just wait around? I've spent my life just waiting around for people. It's always been this way with Dad. I don't know why it still crawls under my skin like this, though. Not even the skin, under the meaty folds of my heart, is what it feels like. As if he doesn't call on purpose, doesn't talk to me because he doesn't want to talk to *me* in particular. He's an unknowable man. Fuck that, I say. I don't feel much like talking anyway.

I look back at the caribou for a final second. To be silent, shut my mouth, and whisper to no one. That'd be something.

4

Often I think I love my father.
The rest of the time, I only wish I knew him.

THOM

1

Thom stands in the middle of his back yard staring at the tree in the last light of the afternoon. It stands rooted deep and mammoth in the ancient ground, frozen in hibernation and holding fast for another spring. It seems strange to him that such a thing as a tree can be so involved and present in one's life, that it can play such a profound role. A tree, under which his wife used to sit on autumn evenings and sneak little puffs of marijuana and paint watercolors of the Lake. Under which Thom would stand and watch his son climb higher and higher in the thick tangle of branches. A tree. That stands watching over the house, watching over the Lake, always showing Jude the way home when he went out on the water. That each morning his wife would step out onto the back porch and whisper good morning to, no matter the day or weather. A tree. Under which Thom cried for his wife when no one else was around. Where he slept for three nights, terrified to go back inside the house where his wife would never be again. But she was there in the tree. Was there, would always be among the blue umbrage of its shade, in its spidery branches, her voice whispering among the roots deep within the ancient earth as if to say: I am I am I am. What a beautiful thing, a tree.

2

Thom looks out at the Lake, frozen and still like dead air on a radio. The trees along the shore stand in mute witness, leaning toward the water under the heavy snow clumped on their winter-thin branches. A wind comes from far off, scraping across the frozen water, gathering the cold in its cape. It is an ancient air, a breeze from another time and place. Thom hears the Lake begin to murmur. From the edges the ice flexes on the stones and shale, cracking in places, and freezing stronger again at the broken places in mere moments. The deep waters writhe below the sky like sea monsters, unseen, waiting to awake. Thom watches. He listens. He feels a certain heartache when he looks across the horizon long enough: a heartache that comes only in seeing something so beautiful, so delicate, that it hurts the soul. He felt this way decades ago, when he would play with a much younger Jude in the yard. His blue-eyed boy, so tiny, so pure, wandering around the grass. Thom would watch from a distance as his son flipped rocks and gathered worms in a plastic bucket. Jude would whisper and talk to them, letting out little shrieks as the worms folded and squirmed in his tiny hands, moving between his muddy fingers. "They're dancing, Dada, they're dancing!" Jude would shout, dropping them one by one into the bucket. Thom would watch, and he felt his heart ache for Jude. So beautiful, so delicate. And again, he felt this same sensation whenever he saw his wife. When she came into a room, when she sat on the dock, reading, puffing on a joint she didn't think Thom could see—even in the middle of arguments, he felt it. He couldn't help but be overcome by such a beautiful thing. It was in such moments that he felt the true frailty and fragility of his life. Entirely temporary and slipping away, and yet permanent within the moment. As if time folded in on itself, such as the worms in Jude's bucket, past, present, future, all at once, all things beautiful as they were created to be. The heartache came in the perfect admiration of a single moment's beauty, alongside the knowledge that it would not last. Thom had never been a man to wallow in agitations or anger or disappointment. This came from a strange certainty that such sentiments were useless. No, he rearranged his mind in those times, allowing them to pass through him like breath in order to feel the weight of life itself. And this was because of Helen. His wife was the other half of his heart. He felt her heartbeats in his, as if there were hooks in his heart and lines connecting the two. He was alive, because she gave him life. He carried her heart in his; her very breath consumed his lungs like the breath of heaven.

But now there is only the Lake. The Lake has hooks in his heart. When the summer tide pulsed and rolled endlessly in the soft on and on, he felt it. His soul squirmed and danced as the Lake did. Now, in the winter after Helen's passing, he writhes in restlessness, in search of something he doesn't know, in hope for a belief he can believe in. Now, in winter, his heart remains still, as the Lake is still. Yet something moves down there, deep, deep, in the dark and the darkness after that. Something writhing and waiting to surface, though he knows not what.

The Lake sprawls before him like the Great Beyond. He looks out at the vast desert of snow and feels his heart aching. He misses everything all at once. But he doesn't let himself wallow in agitation. There is work to be done. There are things to be prepared. Things to be put into place. Things to be ended.

He walks back to the house, and picks up his tools. They feel familiar and perfect in his hands. Everything washes away like running water. Across the opening he has punched into the back of the house Thom hammers down the frame for a temporary structure, a room. This will be the workshop. The framework goes up in quick strides, easy as a breath. His precision and focus are pure. He can see only what is at hand. None of it planned out or reasoned through. He has not considered or thought out each angle and has built nothing in his mind. There is only the burning in his hands. This work comes from him hot and spontaneous as a match-head's strike. He can feel himself burst into flames. He feels as if he is traveling a road at night, on the first miles of a long journey. The headlights glow only a few dim feet in front of him, but he knows he can make the entire journey this way, one mile at a time. He has no control, and now he trusts he might have faith again.

By nightfall the awning of the workshop—not a sunroom—has gone up, complete with heavy-weight tarps pulled tight and sealed on all sides. It is a good space. Big enough to do all he needs. He can work in peace here, and from this room he can see his wife's tree, and the Lake just behind it.

In the house Thom gathers all of their dirty clothes and any trash he can find and piles it in the back yard. He douses it all with kerosene and sets it ablaze. The glow of the bonfire shimmers in the winter night. His hands begin to shake, the bats flapping madly about his head. "No drinks now," Joe says. No, not now, Thom thinks.

There's work to be done.

3

Just walking through the doors is soul-crushing. All hope abandon, ye who enter here, he thinks. Thom walks through the entrance of Walmart anyway. There are things he needs at this late hour that can only be found and bought here. Giant walls of special-priced sodas and beers entomb the front entrance like a barricade. Any other day Thom would gladly pick up one of the twelve-packs of Old Milwaukee at the low low price of $8.95 to keep in the back of the truck. But not tonight.

People mill about loading their carts full of *stuff*. Some necessities, perhaps some gifts, but mostly just stuff. Thom has never liked *stuff*. It's not the items themselves, but the seductive aura about them, the little sirens they are, shouting out about how you need them, couldn't possibly live without them. Thom is weak to such a song, and so he tries to avoid most *stuff* at all costs.

He finds the clothing department and gets Jude a few pairs of jeans and packs of white shirts and socks and underwear, all on "special." But they're always on "special." So really, nothing is special anymore. He gets the same items for himself, as if these were their winter uniforms. He gets more than he usually would. There'll be no time for shopping in the weeks to come. Usually he and Jude go to Goodwill or church thrift shops for their clothes, but these will last a little longer, see them through until the icebreakers bring the spring again.

People move and squirm all around Thom. He maneuvers his cart through the aisles, avoiding everyone as best he can. He hears something above him and looks up. Among the metal framework of the ceiling, Thom sees bird nests, and birds fluttering and chirping from perch to perch high above the oblivious shoppers. He stands and watches them fly around, gathering and eating, as if in their natural habitat. And maybe it is, he thinks, in this new creation. There is no "farther south" for them anymore.

He makes his way to the food and buys all of the canned sardines they have in stock. Ever since they have been on their own Thom and Jude have almost entirely subsisted on potatoes, eggs, and sardines. It is not that they can't cook better food, but rather that cooking reminds them of her. Meals were sacred when Helen was alive. Food was something to be cherished, not merely consumed, but enjoyed and gone about with a certain love. Thom eats now only because he must.

He moves numb and demure through the narrow aisles among the people. His eyes carve perfect lines across dirty shelves holding faux bamboo silverware holders, and pink fluffy pillows, and decorative plaster vases with rainbow-colored plastic flowers. Nothing real. Everything touched and dirty and lifeless. Nothing made, only things produced. In the hunting and fishing aisle, he picks up a fiberglass kayak oar. He holds it, feels the dead weight of it. His mind wanders to the foreign machine that vomited it out, to the yearning face of the poor bastard who watched it float down a conveyor belt. The grim face of the next one who slapped a label on it and saw it shipped across the world. He looks at everything individually, every single thing, and his head spins. He steps back and takes all of it in.

There's no life in it, nothing in any of it, he thinks.

He moves down the rows, rings the bell on a little blue bicycle as he passes. He moves along felled forests of white rolls wrapped in cellophane, down rows of green plastic bottles smelling like some advertiser's dream of pine, across rows of video games that seem more horrible than any reality Thom wishes to know. For so long he has distanced himself from this modern life, this everyday *merde*. He floats around like they all seem to do: organisms in an environment; microbes in agar.

Thom has secretly always wished he could become a hero like one of those he daydreamed and read about in novels and comic books as a boy. Not only a hero, but one who takes on an impossible quest, who journeys to the ends of the earth for fire. He has secretly hoped there was something more to this life, some inherent and definite path and purpose among the ever-changing. He stands now gazing at the profoundly unprofound day-to-dayness all around him in the checkout line. Something comes to his mind and suddenly, Joe whispers: "Memento homo quia pulvis es et in pulverem reverteris."

"Quit it. Just be quiet," Thom says. He nods to the woman who looks back to see who was talking.

He tries not to look at any of it, but it rushes toward him from all sides. The names of things, the neon colors flashing, the tastes and smells. Artificial flavors and plastic replicas. Ahead, the cashier calls for a manager, and a groan murmurs through the line before him. Thom holds his eyes on the image of a grizzly bear on a package of beef jerky. He stares at it, looks deep into it. He wonders if there is no such journey at all, no new wonder to be found, not anymore. No heroes left to bring back the fire, but only those to carry the fire that remains, to preserve it and keep it immaculate. There is no journey to the ends of the earth but only across this place here and now. No road to Byzantium, only a pilgrimage through the everyday shit.

And Thom knows this journey is more impossible than

any heroic quest. Impossible, as it calls you not to strike out for glory but to give up and slouch back into hibernation, into that sleepy despair; impossible, as it lures you not onward, *excelsior*, but backward, to all the *stuff*. This checkout stand bristling with its orange foil packets of chips, its rolls and rolls of crystallized dyed corn syrup in waxed paper, holds no more signs and wonders, no miracles to be worked and witnessed. These are the modern solutions to ancient problems. Whoever thirsts, let them come to me and drink, Thom thinks. He scoffs to himself. No, "Come, consume, consume and forget," Thom thinks. The faithful have their faith; the rest only try to carry the tiny spark of the fire and not to let it burn them up. In this perpetual hibernation, all there is left to do is to hold fast for spring.

4

Birds flutter and chirp under the fluorescent lights high above. No southerly migration when all you need is right here, convenient and gathered for you. Thom watches them, entranced, neck bent and eyes gazing heavenward, as if the sun were dancing in the sky. Birds in winter. He stands and watches until the cashier calls *next* and pulls him back to the merde once more. Bird shit covers the bronzed cheek of a pretty celebrity on the cover of a magazine. Thom moves forward in line.

He parks in the driveway and fills his arms with bags. A cigarette smolders on his lips, and he stops halfway through the yard, looking up at the dark house and late December shrouding everything. It all looks different. It has looked different for some time now but Thom has refused to stop and notice this change. His mind begins playing song lyrics somewhere far back. He hears the music. *"You may find yourself in a beautiful home, with a beautiful wife, And you may ask yourself, well, How did I get here?"*

Thom stands in the cold and stares, says aloud, "This is not my beautiful house. This is not my beautiful life. No, not my life anymore at all."

But all things must pass, the freezing water running past it all. There's work to be done.

JUDE

1

A tall pile of pans and dishes, more than usual from the prep shift, awaits me as I come in the back door of the restaurant. Chef must be expecting a big night. A sonorous din of clanking, chopping, and chit-chat fills the kitchen. The front-of-house staff set tables and arrange things for a few larger reservations. The cooks continue their prep and go on talking about anything that pops into their heads. It's mostly habit for them to babble on as they work. For me, all of it is a perfect amount of noise to block everything out.

There is a great amount of time spent waiting around when you work in a restaurant. Waiting kills most people. They—we—have this strange need to be doing something, anything.

After tables are set, glasses polished, menus stuffed, floors swept, cook's line prepared, all there is left to do is to wait for customers. And in a place like Belle Mer, at least where we live, there is no built-in customer base; no one, at least no one outside the coastal big cities that run our country, makes a fifty-dollar steak a regular meal. I've come to realize this is why everyone smokes cigarettes when they work in restaurants. They'd rather breathe smoke than sit there quietly doing nothing. I am only slightly spared from such throes of idleness, and only because there is always something for me to clean, always.

Watching everyone wander about in the meantime makes me think of Dad. He can't ever sit still. He has to be doing something. But his need for action isn't rooted in a fear of or aversion to boredom, I don't think, not like the rest of us. His stems from feeling useless and, at the same time, I believe, he's afraid of confronting his own thoughts, sparks of soul that tend to flare up in such stillness and boredom. I search around in my memories of college, thin pages slipped in between nights out and long days of training on the water: was it Pascal or maybe David Foster Wallace who wrote that "Bliss... lies on the other side of crushing, crushing boredom." If this is true, which I tend to believe that it is, it's no wonder everyone is so miserable all the time. They can't ever make it to that other side of boredom, of sitting quietly, doing nothing. They'd rather smoke or drink or stare at screens or die than to do something like that. I'm no different.

When Dad is working on something his concentration and focus is unwavering and unassailable. He dives headlong into the most menial, boring, tedious tasks and pushes through to that far side. He rides out that tsunami of stillness and boredom and comes to that quiet place waiting for him alone.

Dad once said that most of the world's problems, especially in this day and age, arise solely from our human inability to sit alone in a room for an extended period of time. Just as I was about to call out his hypocrisy when he told me this, he continued, "Me too, I'm unable to do that too. I can't be still two minutes. And that's a big damn problem, when a person can't be still."

I've always wondered why it is such a problem, why is it so hard to simply sit still and focus on something, or nothing, for even a few minutes. It must be that we can't stand what we are left with in our own heads after the noise is gone and we're truly alone. We can't examine ourselves because, if we did, we'd have to reckon with what we actually found there.

2

I push the mop and bucket of soapy warm water into the main dining room and start on the floors. The floor is a rugged industrial slate-type concrete. The owner decided to keep it from the original building he converted into Belle Mer. I don't know why this modern trend of raw industrial interiors has come to be synonymous with elegance and expense. People love that shit, though.

While mopping I listen to music. Lately it's been Chopin, Dvorak, Tchaikovsky. I was never really interested in classical music until college. When I was left to train indoors in the infinity pools, I preferred listening to music than having to go numb as the pool's pumps droned on. The main problem with classical music before was that I didn't understand it and didn't have the patience to sit through an entire symphony. Being born in the time I was, I've been systematically programmed to crave catchy melodies and clever lyrics that relate to what's happening now, to people like me. I've wandered free from that path now. There is this brilliant wave of passion and emotion in classical music. It can begin so soft and serene—boring, even—and the next thing you know, there is this rushing torrent of sound pulsing through you. It's amazing, really, the transcendence music can achieve. It's as if the composer is trying to tell you something and they took years, decades, to try and get it just right. Not just a catchy little shit song, but substance. Something that has travelled centuries to arrive right now to you alone.

Right now, the world is Brahms's Symphony No. 1 in C Minor. Everything else is muted and drifts away. Cold white light aches through the floor-to-ceiling windows that line the restaurant and overlook the Lake. The lights in the dining room are dim and warm and the mix of cold gray and smoldering orange feel perfectly homey. This is why I mop the floors first when I come in. This hour is perfect for the light: the last glimmer before night comes on. The evening and the music are kind the way memory is kind, rubbing out the lazy details, transforming us, inch by inch, rising up like sediment to the stars, if we let it.

Mopping floors has become a rather enjoyable activity. There is immediacy to it, along with an art form, a method that can see you through the misery and crushing boredom of having to mop floors and on into this strange and mysterious state of neither thinking nor non-thinking. There's a stillness that comes over me. A stillness and quietude, even though my body moves. The physical action becomes automatic and repetitive and I find myself slipping entirely over into the movements and then I am nowhere near them at all anymore.

The thing about being a dishwasher is that you don't have to worry about ambitions. There is no more money for working faster, no promotion to aim for. There is only the job at hand, steady and unwavering, and this is one of the reasons I took the job. I wasted too much time on ambitions, on becoming *something*. Competition rots the soul. People like to say it's good, healthy even, but they're only trying to ease their pain, I think. I was, at least. Competition is only false hope, it is the destruction of a moment. It ruins brotherhood—not that I was ever really seeking brotherhood with anyone. But I am tired of chasing that false promise and hope. Tired of playing the game of ambitions as a means of finding happiness, or whatever. But the finish line is never as grand as what we've built it up to be. Once you're past it, all anyone wants to know is when you'll cross it again, when you'll compete again, what comes next? I gave my life to rowing, to competition, and it failed me. It left me with nothing. It only ever takes and takes.

Washing dishes takes nothing from you, asks nothing of you. It gives you back a place that is no place, allows you to exchange somewhere for nowhere, if you can get through to that other side. I'm perfectly happy remaining here for the rest of my life. There's nothing I need to prove to anyone, nothing more that I want or need to do. Here, I won't lose anything. And so here I'll remain. It takes patience to get through the crushing boredom, the misery of it. To accept that you will remain in hibernation for a good while, patience is needed. And it is only recently that I've realized what true patience is. It begins at the edge of suffering, on the brink of losing all hope.

3

On my way home I stop the car and pull onto the side of the road and look out at the Lake. My mind is a fog. My fears move in rings outward in the cold silence. My father, my mother, Emily—they drift with the night wind in some silent on-and-on.

My mother is the cracked latch-work of the frozen Lake. My father, a cloud of sawdust, petitions the Lord with the only prayer he knows by heart.

Nothing is going to change. Nothing is coming to break the fall. Everything sinks a little deeper into the snow and it feels like I am about to burst into flames. I think I can hear Dad already burning far off.

I pull into the driveway and the house is all dark except for the back yard. It is aglow like a bonfire amid the winter blackness. The snow reflects the light and carries it out into the night in every direction. It's a little after one in the morning and Dad is home. He shouldn't be. He should be at work. He never misses work.

THOM

1

The rich smell of coffee fills the new workshop. Thom sips from his cup as he makes a few crude sketches of the boat, a Scandinavian faering in the style of the classic Elfyn. The same boat his father had.

The sketch is rough, but the underlying form is there, taking shape like a fossil in the ground. Some people tend to be romantics, seeing only what there is to be seen, driven by intuition and creativity and passion—no reason that needs to be followed. They might look at such blueprints and mechanical designs and feel nothing—they are just lines and numbers, after all. Give them the thing after it is built, and they will then see the beauty in it.

But not Thom. A set of plans, of mechanical drawings or mold designs, has the capability of bringing him true joy as he awes at what is to come next. He sees the sketches themselves, but he also sees what they represent. He can see the work and sweat and grit that will go into creating it and bringing it to life. All of this, every last detail, is beautiful to Thom.

He consults a manual on building small boats and another on specialty carpentry design. He specifically reviews the chapter on shaping and bending wood. On the paper beside the design of the boat he makes a list of supplies, what tools and materials he already has and what he will need to purchase. He knows everything he has, every tool, and he lists them in order of the most important to this job.

His mind sinks deeper into the vision. He slides from future to past to present, and then moves deeper into the present at hand: he sees the moment, and then ten thousand moments in between this moment and completion. He stops his pencil and sits there perfectly still. He does nothing at all and stares at the place where he will build the boat. He shuts out the cold, the smell of coffee, the brief gusts of warmth from the fire leaking into the tent. He sits there, perfectly still. His mind moves pieces and builds the first parts of the hull. He sits and lets the parts go and they begin to build themselves. He does nothing, thinks about nothing now, letting the far corners of his mind work like a spider spinning its web. He looks insane or like one who is talking with God. He is blank. He sits there for a long time until he feels every part of him settle into itself. This is the only prayer he knows by heart. *O, grant us one more hour to perform our art and perfect our lives.* The preparation and alignment of body and soul, of his entire self, in order to perform a perfect task.

Often he feels like the damned must feel, cut-off and cursed, separated from what is pure and sacred. But in this moment he has found himself in the dark wood, in the middle of his life as he has lost the path, and yet inching just a little closer to paradise. All things push out in rings through time and Thom slips deeper into self-forgetfulness. Into his deepest self. He is there and he isn't. He exists how trees exist, how fish exist.

He rises and comes up for breath again and gathers the boards into their shape on the ground. What was to be part of the base frame of the sunroom will now become the trestles that will hold the boat for several months.

He cuts them to length with the hand saw, pulling clean smooth strokes across the grain. He hammers nails into the joints and erects the trestles. He moves slow and calm, taking care to focus entirely on everything he does.

"It'll take you twelve years at this rate," Joe says. Let it take a hundred and twelve, Thom thinks. Remember what Hadrian said of Rome: Brick by brick, my citizens, brick by brick. And again: Nothing is slower than the true birth of a man.

"So you are reborn, is that it?" Joe chides.

No, only waking, Thom says. I had fallen asleep. This bear is waking from his hibernation.

2

Thom doesn't look up when his son pushes aside the tarps and stands there looking at him. He bends down beside the third trestle, adjusting the slope of its center board to match the others.

"What are you doing?" Jude asks.

"Shaping the trestles," Thom says, still not looking up. "The hull will sit here, and the shape and angle need to match."

"No. I mean, what are you doing, Dad? Why aren't you at work?"

"I called in."

"Why?"

"I have things to do."

"And this is all for the sunroom—?"

"Nope. For the boat."

"What boat?"

"I'm building a boat," Thom says.

"Dad . . . What's going on, Dad?"

Jude wavers on his tired legs, corrects himself. The grief in Jude's voice forces Thom to stop. He looks at his son.

Thom wipes the sweat from his forehead under his wool hat. It is warm in the tent now that he has moved the electric heaters in and stationed them around the large space.

"I've decided not to build a sunroom for now. I am building a boat instead."

Jude stares at him. "What? What for?"

"I don't know. Just felt this pull inside me, a feeling."

"Come on, Dad. You don't listen to feelings. Keep it together, for Chrissake. We have to keep it together and start taking shit seriously, not building Goddamn boats in a tent in the back yard . . ."

"What? What is it you want me to take seriously? What do you want me to do, Jude? Just be at work? Tell me."

Jude is quiet. The blood that rushed to his head finds its way back to the heart, settles. He breathes and tastes the gin from drinking at work.

"I don't want to fight with you, Dad. Not tonight."

He wanders back inside the house. Thom bends down again and continues his work, as if he'd never been interrupted.

He is suddenly overcome by that word: *Fight.* Jude didn't want to fight. Thom and his son haven't fought in some time. Years. Truth be told Thom wishes they would fight, just then. He craves a good fight, to yell and scream until his lungs burst. A fight would mean they were talking, that they cared enough about something, enough about the other, to get angry. Silence, their breed of silence, is death. A fight would be something. But they drift to their own worlds, tearing things apart in hopes of building them up again.

3

Thom sleeps deep and sound on the sofa. He has not slept more than a fitful hour or two in a row since his wife died. Tonight, he has dreamed for eight long hours.

He gets up by ten o'clock as daylight fills the house. It is a different light this morning. Not the cold steel of winter but golden light shining down, not a cloud in the sky to hold it back. Thom stands at the window looking out at the back yard, at the tree standing on the edge of the shore. For a moment he can't recall when he last saw blue skies. It has felt like a lifetime at least. But that doesn't matter. He sees it now.

He goes upstairs and cracks open the door and peeks at Jude. His son is asleep still. Thom showers and dresses in the new clothes. He stands by the sink in the kitchen eating a can of sardines and looks out at his wife's tree. The bats begin to stir behind his eyes as the thirst comes and he looks at the fridge. Not now, he thinks. Later, after things are done.

The sun melts the top layer of snow just enough to glaze everything in a shell of ice. Eighteen degrees, still, by eleven a.m. He lets the truck run for the time it takes to have coffee and smoke a cigarette. He fights through the haze in his eyes, fights through the dull beat of ache in his head, to find the sharp blade of his thoughts. He gathers them close like lost sheep.

He is silent on the drive across town to Welch's shop. Plumes of white-gray smoke drift into the blue sky from the metal chimney. Thom walks in and is taken aback as the warmth crashes over his cold cheeks and nose. Gabe Welch and his father look to the door from the back of the shop. Thom nods, pursing his lips, and walks to meet them.

"Morning, Thom," Peter Welch says. "How've you been? Gabe told me you came by yesterday."

"Holding fast," Thom says. "And yourself?"

"Ah, you know how it goes, same shit," Peter says. "What brings you by?"

Thom takes the detailed list of materials from his pocket and hands it to Peter. "Not sure what you have in stock here, but that's what I need."

Peter Welch unfolds the papers and lowers his readers onto his nose. He looks over the list with his finger. "Yeah, I think we can help with most of it. Pretty good list here. You need all these boards cut to size?"

"No, I'm cutting them myself."

"Well, let's get you set up here."

Peter wheels a flat cart to the back of the shop and Thom follows. "Thanks for thinking of us with all this," Peter says. "Instead of one of the big stores."

"I knew you'd have better quality."

"Do you want all the hardware now, or just the boards?"

"I'll go ahead and take what all you have now. Saves me a trip later."

"Fair enough. I think we'll have to special order these oarlocks. Our supplier dropped the ball on our last order. Put us behind on a lot of stock."

"That'll be fine."

Thom helps Peter load the cart with boards. "What got you the itch to build a boat?"

"Not sure. Been holed up in the house too much, I guess. Just looking for a new project," Thom says. This is all I have left, my last journey for fire, he thinks.

"Are you going to get Jude back in the water?" Peter's

voice peaks a little higher as he stops and looks at Thom.

"I wish. He hasn't touched an oar in almost two years now."

"Damn shame what happened to him," Peter says. "We were all so proud of him, like he was our own. He was, in a way. Hometown boy in the Olympics . . . damn shame."

"Yes, it is."

"What's he doing these days?"

"Working at Belle Mer. Washing dishes."

"Nice place." Peter looks for a few clamps hanging on the wall. "You can have these, no cost. They've just been hanging there."

"Thanks."

"Gabriel talk you into the cedar?"

"Yeah."

"Good choice. Pricey, but you'll see it's well worth it. What are you using for the rest of it?"

"I'm going to use cypress."

"Beautiful wood. I don't think we can get that for you, though. . . . That's tough to find anymore."

"No, it's all right. I got it myself."

"Oh yeah?"

"I'm using a tree that's in the back yard. An old bald cypress."

Peter Welch looks up at Thom. He nods but says no more.

They finish loading the cart and Gabe helps Thom load it all in the truck.

"How much do I owe you?" Thom says.

Peter finishes writing out the receipt inside the shop and hands it over. "Twenty-five hundred, and I'll get those oar-locks to you soon as they come in."

Thom nods and thinks for a moment. "All right with a

check?"

"Sure thing," Peter says.

Thom writes it out, doing the math of bills and mortgage in his head. He doesn't have the money. He can pull some out of savings, but it's not enough.

"Would you mind if I put the date as next Monday?" Thom says. "Just need to move some things around."

"Sure, sure, whatever you need, Thom. We'd be glad to offer you some credit if you'd like. Takes ten minutes to get all the paperwork done . . ."

"No, no, 'neither a borrower nor a lender be' . . . I can make it for today."

"Monday's fine, Thom. Just glad to see you're doing all right."

Thom nods, keeping his head a little lower. "Thanks again, Pete."

"Our pleasure. And get Jude back in that water, eh?" Peter says.

"Yeah, we'll see."

Thom sits in the truck pulling absently at his beard, staring at the air vent, but not at it, past it, at nothing in particular.

"That's a lot of money," Joe says from someplace close. Yes, it is, Thom knows. "Money you don't have, now or next Monday." Yes, Thom thinks. But we'll get it.

There is a call he must make, one he has been putting off for over a year now. "You'll have to talk to her," Joe says. Maybe there's another way, Thom thinks. "You know there isn't. Otherwise you would have done it a while ago." Yes, yes, shut up now, Thom says.

Thom puts the truck in gear and ignores the shudder in the transmission and drives a few blocks across town. He passes the office at first, turns at the stop light, and smokes a cigarette as he detours listlessly through side streets, making his way back again.

I don't want to talk to her, he thinks. "I know, but it's all that's left," Joe says. Thom parks on the street and walks with a lowered head into the office, like a general entering the enemy camp to surrender. He stands at reception, looking around at the dull bland lobby. Chairs upholstered in tacky floral patterns. Magazines neatly arranged on glossy side tables. The stinging smell of chemically imitated strawberries from a cleaner they used on the carpets.

"May I help you, sir?" The receptionist hangs up the phone and looks at Thom.

I don't want to talk to her . . .

"Yes, my name's Thom Algonquin. I was hoping to speak with Susan Clemens, if she's in. About a property."

"Yes, sir," the receptionist says. "Let me tell her you're here. Feel free to have a seat over there."

4

By the afternoon the sunlight is broken up by clouds migrating in vast herds across the sky. A storm builds in the east and blots out the horizon like a mountain range rising out of nothing. It is cold, but Thom cuts boards to length in the tent behind the house. A metal trashcan burns hot with dry logs and dirty socks and keeps the space warm as he pulls the saw. The smoke rises in thin plumes and up through the chimney Thom has cut into the tent. He can hear Jude inside, awake and milling about the house. Thom can feel the boredom, the malaise radiating from Jude's movements. He knows that boredom is the bride of depression. Jude is always bored now. But he tries to keep busy, not really doing anything, but moving just the same.

Thom stacks the ripped lengths of wood on a platform a foot off the ground. It is important to keep the wood dry and moisture to an absolute minimum. The boards will warp in a second if you let them, and then all will be lost. Because of this, Thom has made the workshop more fitting: sealed up the corner seams in the tarps, laid a thick ground cloth, arranged heaters and dehumidifiers in the corners. The cold dry air helps keep things balanced, but he knows the air won't last long.

With the saw in his hand, Thom wonders why he came to love tools the way he does. His father was remarkably un-handy when it came to fixing things or anything mechanical. The parts and pieces always made sense to Thom though. The way Chopin saw a piano and heard music or Keats saw words and knew their poetry, Thom understood the mechanical world without any need of explanation.

Jude has always seen such work and tools as some kind of false testament to manhood, as many do. For so long, handiness has been a qualifier for manliness. Men must do laborious jobs, build things, *provide* with their brawn. But Thom never felt this way. For him it is about the art of the work in his hands: the feeling of holding something in its pieces and putting it back together again, not creating something out of nothing, but caring for the things of this world, fixing them. It is the only connection to life he has ever truly felt.

Jude was born with a different heart. At fifteen years old he was already stronger and taller than his father, standing at a demi-god height of six-foot-seven, two hundred and five pounds: a born athlete and competitor. Jude became obsessed with Greek myths and with the honor that accompanies sport and competition. Thom had also once been possessed by such myths. In boyhood, he too became enamored with gods and heroes and the hope that good would overcome, a faith that the night would not last forever. But slowly they vanished, replaced with gritty realities, ashy little hells piling up: the day-to-dayness, the merde, the dust. By the time Jude needed him, needed to know that such good, such faith was possible, Thom had forgotten it.

Thom has felt guilty for too long about the fact that all his son is and all he loves and knows didn't come from him. The only thing he gave Jude was that initial push off the dock, sending him out into the open waters alone. That, and unfettered trust in his son. Perhaps that was what made the difference.

Seeing Jude on the water rowing and competing was something beautiful. He was a perfect athlete performing a perfect task, doing that which he was made to do. He would wake early every day and be in the water training before anyone else was awake. Thom and Helen would watch from the dock or shoreline under the cypress tree as Jude glided across the water. He trained hard in the Lake. The water was always unpredictable. One moment it was glass, the next, four-foot whitecaps would be crashing down on him and his boat. But always he pushed on, always kept rowing through the tide break and swelling storms. This, if anything, is what Thom gave his son.

Jude has stopped now, though. He has no fight left in him, or if he does, he refuses its call. He is the hero betrayed by the gods. He is Odysseus, adrift, alone. He is Outis. He moves about like a house ghost in these ghostly days; he feels like the damned must feel, cut off from what is sacred and pure, and Thom knows he gave this to his son as well.

The flap of the tent flips open and pulls Thom from his drifting thoughts. He looks up and Jude is standing there. Thom stands up straight and stretches his back. Every muscle is tight from the work. Jude's eyes move about the workshop. He looks and sees it now, sees that he has never really known his father at all, has only ever been at a distance from him.

"You do marvel and wonder, don't you?" Jude says under his breath. "This is the way you look at the world and marvel."

"What?" Thom says.

"Nothing. Why didn't you set up in the garage?" Jude says.

"Needed more space."

"Abandoning the sunroom altogether, then?"

"No, just putting it on the back burner for now."

Thom bends again and continues sawing and Jude watches, as he has watched his father work a thousand times before. "How much is all this costing, Dad? You know our situation."

"All told, it'll be about four grand, give or take."

"What—? Jesus, Dad, we don't have that kind of money, especially not to blow on a Goddamn boat." Jude shakes his head and turns to leave.

"I've got the money sorted out," Thom says.

Jude stops, holding the tent flap open. "How?"

Thom pulls the saw hard for a few strokes. "I went and talked with Susan Clemens."

Jude stares at him, letting the flap close again. "You... you sold the house?"

"Give me a hand here, will ya?"

Jude walks over and steadies the opposite end of the board Thom cuts. The yellow glow of the lights Thom has set up around the high corners shine down on Jude's bare arms, illuminating the black rings tattooed on his forearm. Thom glances at the tattoo and continues to pull the saw.

"Why didn't you talk to me about it?" Jude says. "I could've helped. We could've..."

"It's fine. I got it all handled," Thom says. The saw bites through the final half inch of wood and Jude catches the board. "Stack it over there with the other six-footers." Thom watches him and pulls at his beard. "I made a good deal with her."

"So we have to move out? What about this wall you've knocked out?"

"No, the buyers don't want it until June. We have time to patch it up if we want. But I don't think it'll matter. They're going to tear it all down anyway."

Jude stands there a moment, trying to make sense of this.

"What made you finally do it?"

Thom purses his lips and shakes a cigarette from his pack. "It was just time." He motions for Jude to follow him outside and they step out into the snow. Thom lights up and offers the pack to Jude but he waves it off.

"Are you going in to work tonight?"

"Haven't decided yet," Thom says. "There's a lot to do."

"So, this boat . . . what are you planning to do with it?"

"I'm going to take it out on the Lake. Soon as the ice-breakers come."

"You're going to start exercising now?" Jude laughs a little.

"No, not really. I'm going to take it across the Lake," Thom says.

Jude looks at him. "What?"

"I'm going to row across the Lake. Get as far as Eagle Harbor or maybe a little island on the first leg of it, then go all the way to Whitefish Point."

"You're kidding, right?"

Thom shakes his head.

"That's like three hundred miles, Dad . . ."

"It's been a dream of mine since I was a kid. To just row out into all that water and not stop until I hit the far shore or capsize somewhere on the way. I have nothing left here anyway. Thought now was a good time to just do it."

"Never took you to be such a romantic, Dad."

"Not a romantic. It's just something I have to do. If I don't now, I never will."

Jude laughs and blows warm air into his hands. "This is a joke, right? It's a joke."

Thom shakes his head again.

"Yeah, well, you better cut back on your smoke breaks then, old man."

Thom nods, letting out lungfuls of smoke. "Planning on it."

Jude starts back inside but stops. "You're really doing this?"

"I was thinking you'd maybe want to make the trip with me," Thom says. "The boat'll have two sets of oarlocks, a nice eighteen-footer. It'd be one last good fight."

Jude looks up at the clouds building on the horizon, sweeping across the empty Lake. He moves his eyes down to his father. He doesn't recognize him, not just then.

"No, I'm done with the water, Dad. Done with all that. And you should be too. You need to get your head right and think about where we're going to live."

"You can't carry on like this forever, Jude. You can't just hide out, holding fast for something to come and pull you out of it. You have to do it yourself, son."

"Yeah, thanks for the advice."

"You know what," Thom says, tossing his cigarette out into the snow. "You've only ever coasted on your talent, Jude. That's it. You've been given so much, everything, and you still want more. You think you're something special. Stop it now. Just stop it. You have some grand idea of yourself, of your life, that something brilliant will come along, just out of the blue, and you'll have it all. Stop all this pathetic whining. Get over yourself."

"No, no, you want to get into it?" Jude says. He squares his feet in the snow. His left arm gestures his fury. "I am special. I was given a talent, given a path. You know when I used to see paintings of those Greek heroes and gods in Mom's books, I used to think they were me. And they were, too. I pushed myself, I made something of myself and got to the highest peak, and it was taken from me. Fucking ripped from my hands. And now I'm left here, with nothing."

"No one is special, Jude. Not me or you. No one. We're given things, and we eventually lose them. Such is life, and on it goes. You're no more special than that water, than this ground, unless you wake up and realize you have life. Not life to waste pitying yourself anymore. But real life. That's what makes the difference. Stop all of your bitching and whining for Godsake. You have to pick up the pieces and keep walking, find the rest of it for yourself."

"What about God, won't *God* come and reveal some great path for us?" Jude says, facing his father, his voice tense and mocking.

"No, He's not coming for that. It's already there."

"Fuck that. We're just dropped into this life, and everything is so fucked up. We can't do anything. Nothing good, nothing bad, because none of it matters, does it? Tell me I'm wrong."

"Why didn't we die at birth?" Thom says. "Why didn't we just breathe and expire right then and there . . ."

"Well, why not, if this is what's here for us? All this shit."

"What, should we take all the good life gives us and not worry, and not take the bad too? Life is suffering. Who are you to complain about that? Things happen, Jude. Terrible, horrible things happen. And there's no explanation for it. I'm sorry about what happened to you . . . Look at me, son . . . I'm sorry. I wish I had answers for you. I wish I could tell you everything happens for a reason, that God has a plan, that everything will be all right. But I can't, because I don't believe that. If all of that is true, then let it be true, and it'll find us at some point. But right now you have to pull yourself out of it. That's all that's left. To get back on your feet and keep walking, keep moving."

"So I should just go insane like you and knock walls out of the house and build a Goddamn boat in the back yard? Yeah, you have all the answers."

"I don't have anything. All I can tell you is that I'm sorry, Jude. I wish I were a stronger man, I wish I knew how to be a father to you. I've never known. I've never gotten it right. But I know a hundred apologies won't change a thing unless you forgive yourself, son. Until you can get over your own Goddamn pride, you'll hide out forever. You'll keep pushing farther and farther down to the bottom. It's time to move on, Jude. When the winds have gone, take to the oars."

"What the hell's that?"

"My father used to tell me that."

Jude stands there in the snow, gazing out at the Lake. He turns and heads back inside. "You need to get your head together, Dad, and stop all this. You need to think of what you're going to do when the house sells . . ."

5

The winter evening comes on fast and cold and long, like someone walking through a house shooting out all the lights. Blue skies have dissolved, sunlight and the calm clarity of day along with them. The heavens look blotted out where they hang heavy and swollen with snow. The prayers of the people dangle just overhead, suspended and waiting for God to change His mind. But He doesn't, does He, Thom thinks. We change, us down here, that's all.

As Thom is leaving the county equipment yard, the snow starts. A drowsy peaceful dusting falls over the trees and quiet dark houses. Only the rare set of headlights disrupts the gray-black screen of the world ahead of Thom's plow. In a matter of a few miles he won't see anyone or anything for the rest of the night, save the brave deer or wolf. He'll be alone for miles in every direction. Alone on the winter road, salting and plowing.

Thom takes the next turn and lowers the blade of the plow on the main road leading out of town and toward the highway. He drives past the very place where he pulled over and walked out onto the Lake . . . . It feels more like a dream now than reality. "What exactly were you trying to do out there?" Joe says. Just wanted to feel something different, Thom thinks. "Well, that was a damn stupid thing to do," Joe says.

The road is straight for three miles here and in the dim glow of the headlights and snowfall Thom sees a figure in the road. He comes up behind it, slowing the truck.

The woman walks along the snow-crested edge of the road in jagged strides. She is bundled in a thick winter coat, arms crossed tight in front of her. The fur lining of her hood is dusted with snow and ice. Thom pulls up beside her and she stops, moving her whole body to see around the hood of her coat.

"Freya—?" Thom hollers from the open passenger door. "Get in, come on."

The cold snaps like a bullwhip against Thom's hands and face as he stands there waving her in. She doesn't move at first, as if frozen there on the roadside. She turns and looks far down the dark road before them.

"Come on," he yells over the wind. She moves and walks to the truck. Thom takes her hand and helps her up into the cab. "What the hell are you doing out here? You'll freeze to death."

Freya sits there quiet and shivering, holding her hands and face in front of the heater. Thom pulls an extra coat out from behind his seat and lays it across her skinny legs. The cold radiates off of her and fills the cab of the truck.

"Are you all right?" Thom asks.

She nods, bouncing there on the seat to get warm again.

"What are you doing out here?"

"I was trying to make it to my sister's house before the snow got too bad," Freya says.

"How far is it? I can take you."

"Not too far, about ten, fifteen minutes . . . but you don't . . ."

"It's no trouble, the least I can do to repay you."

They are quiet for a time. The sound of the plow fills the truck in a sonorous drone. The sound of the blade scraping against the ice and road sounds like the sea if Thom closes his eyes. It is this that makes the job more bearable some nights, until the loneliness jabs a little harder at his heart. The loneliness and the silence within it.

"Actually . . ." Freya looks at Thom. "Could I maybe just ride along with you for a while?"

"Yeah, sure. Do you need to call your sister, though? She might worry if you don't show up."

"No, it's fine. She didn't know I was coming over."

The snow passes through the white beams of the headlights in a thick haze. It's dizzying when Thom stares into it. For a moment he forgets everything. His mind wanders. He feels as if he were commanding an interstellar journey to Alpha Centauri, in search of life and resources. He is a child again. He is dreaming. The snow glints like stars ten thousand years dead but still burning, shining against the fading light. The snow holds him in her hands and he feels himself slipping away . . . He steers the truck and comes to himself again. There is only the night and empty road before him, only space and eternity.

If he drove on forever, would he ever reach the end of it? He hopes not; he hopes some things are endless and infinite. He wants to believe in something like that, something pure and endless. He wants to be someone who believes. But the trouble with belief is that you have to believe in it. You have to believe in belief before anything else. Thom knows this. He knows, too, how endless that effort can be.

Nothing is endless, though, is it, he thinks. "No, all things must pass away in this life," Joe says. "There is something wrong with her, though. Maybe see to that instead of the infinite, instead of driving the plow into the Lake."

Thom straightens the wheel and looks over at the girl. He sees the dark shadows of bruises on her cheeks and encircling her right eye. He stops the truck without a word and jumps out. From the plow blade he breaks off a thick piece of ice, breaks it into several little pieces, and wraps it in his handkerchief. He gets back in and hands it to her.

"This'll help," he says.

She thanks him and holds it gently against her skin, turning her face away.

"Is that what you meant the other day? When you said, 'If the baby comes at all.'"

"Yeah," she says. "It's been getting worse. The winter makes him worse. I used to think I loved him, that he loved me. But maybe we just wanted to love each other. We're just all the other has now, only each other. Not love, just fear that the other one'll leave. And maybe I should . . ."

Thom is quiet a moment. "Where's your car?"

"Andrew took it, my boyfriend. He dropped me off on the side of the road and just left me there." She looks at Thom, adjusting the ice on her cheek. "He's not a monster, he's just in a bad place right now . . . ."

"You don't have to explain it all," he says. He is quiet a moment and then looks at her. "But I guess . . . what I know about this kind of thing is that love doesn't do *that* to people, neither does being in a bad place, or whatever. That's the person who does it. It's there in them, and they just wait for the time to let it out. If it's there, it's always there, and it will come out sooner or later. Love, though, it gives up everything for someone else. Love will let all that other shit die away, because when you have love, nothing else is worth the risk of losing it. And you might not believe it. You can go the whole world over, looking for someone who deserves love more than you, because you feel unworthy or something. But you'll never find them. No one deserves love any more or less than you. Love doesn't need a reason. Never did."

Thom turns onto Highway 53, heading for the National Forest. The night is dark, and only the headlights guide the way, just a few feet ahead of them. But he knows that's all they need to make the journey.

"Get some sleep and rest for a while," Thom says. "We can get everything else sorted out tomorrow."

Freya leans back in the seat, balling her legs up close to her chest and pulling her coat over her knees.

"Thank you," she says, her voice soft among the sound of falling snow and the sound of the plow. "No one's ever done something like this for me."

"Like what? Given you a lift home?"

"No, cared about me. Cared if I was all right."

Thom nods solemnly. "Get some rest."

6

Surrounded by the quiet forest, Thom's mind races. The girl sleeps soundly beside him while he lets an old country station play on the radio. Often he feels like he doesn't want to know his son. He's afraid Jude will see the man Thom is if he gets too close. Often, he doesn't want his son to know him, because there is a part of Jude that is still pure, still has time to find redemption, to become a saint. Often, he wishes he could gather Jude in his arms and carry him off to someplace monsters can't touch him. Often, he is too cowardly to even do that. Always has been. Jude carries me now, Thom thinks. And that's the most beautiful thing a son can do for a father.

7

Thom wakes the girl and helps her into the house. It is just after three o'clock. The cold touches everything, permeates everything. He helps her up the stairs, careful to hold onto the railing. He lays her down in his bed, gently pulls the thick blankets over her. She thanks him and is asleep again in a moment.

Thom looks in on Jude, who is asleep and quiet. I wish I could gather you in my arms and carry you someplace safe, he thinks. I wish I could tell you I love you. Thom comes back downstairs, careful to hold onto the railing again in the dark. He sits at the table and drinks a can of beer sitting in the august glow of the workshop lights from the tent outside. He stands a moment and grabs the ax from the shelf in the garage, along with a file, and sits again at the table. He turns on the clock radio and listens to this show where they talk about ghosts and angels and aliens. But it doesn't matter what they say. The voices keep him company. Thom pulls the file across the ax bit in firm even strokes, watching the tiny flakes of steel bend like ribbons and fall to the floor.

"I'll cut it down tomorrow morning, Helen," he says aloud. "In that morning light. I'll cut it down and make something beautiful out of it."

Thom sits at the table and finishes his beer. He will sleep on the sofa for a few hours, and then, when the sun rises, he will go out and cut the tree down.

JUDE

1

I watch from the window. Dad just stands there looking at it. He leans on the ax and looks at the tree as if he's never seen it before. What the hell is he doing? He won't cut it down, if that's what he's thinking. Mom would never forgive him, if she were here. And if he does cut it down it'll kill him. If the tree doesn't fall on him, then his heart will surely give out as he swings the ax. What the hell is he doing out there? He won't cut it down. He won't.

I dress quickly, pulling on a clean white shirt and thick wool sweater and pants. The house smells like bacon, and the scent gets stronger as I walk down the stairs. The front door just leans in the frame now, waiting for Dad to hang it on the hinges. I swear he's finally lost it. I see it now. It's not grief, it's insanity. And I'll be left to wrestle him down.

I stop in the hall leading to the kitchen and just look at her for a moment. Her dark hair bounces just at her shoulders, wavy and tucked behind her ears. For half a second I think it's Emily, I wish it was anyway, but I know it isn't.

"Hello—?"

She turns and looks at me, covering her mouth as she chews a bite of eggs and toast. She tries to speak but stops, chews faster.

"Hi, sorry . . . I just thought I'd make breakfast," she says. "I was pretty hungry."

"Oh, okay, thanks."

"I'm Freya," she says.

"Jude." I look around, wondering if there is anyone else here. "You must know my Dad, then?"

"Yeah, Thom," she says, talking around another bite.

"Yeah, he gave me a ride and let me stay over. I hope that's all right." She chews and eats. "Sorry, I get pretty hungry lately. He won't ever quit in there . . ."

I follow her hands down to the soft rise of her belly.

"Wasn't your name on a sign in town or something? Jude Algonquin, right?" she says.

"It was. They took it down, though."

"What was it for?"

"I was going to the Olympics."

"Really? That's awesome . . . what sport?"

"Rowing," I say, quickly avoiding the rest of this, and I walk to the back of the house. "Sorry, I need to talk to my Dad for a second."

I walk through the tent and out into the back yard. Dad just stands there. Doesn't look at me.

"What are you doing?" I holler, walking barefoot through the snow.

"I'm cutting the tree down," he says.

"Yeah, that's what it looks like. You can't cut it down though, Dad."

"Of course I can. I need the wood."

"I don't care. You're not cutting it down, Dad."

"Why not?" he says.

The snow is almost up to my knees. The cold burns slow against my skin but it doesn't matter just now. "That's Mom's tree," I tell him, even though he knows this. "It's alive and healthy and you can't just cut it down. It was hers."

"I know it was. But the house is sold. The company who bought it will just cut the tree down and pulp it and destroy it. I can't let that happen, Jude." I look at him, my heart racing for some reason. "I'm going to cut it down and make something beautiful out of it."

I see now he's crying as he turns toward me. I can't help

but tear up.

"You're using it for the boat?"

He nods. "There's something beautiful after all this, Jude. There is. And I have to row out to meet it."

Dad lifts the ax to his shoulder and walks through the snow down to the tree.

2

I watch from the window as Dad swings the ax. He's crying harder. The sharp blade bites deep into the bark, pulling bits away and exposing the white fleshy meat beneath. Each swing stills the air and the hits vibrate through the roots and out into the frozen earth. Dad moves like a man out of time. Like a man searching for something, but he doesn't know what.

There is a heavy draught creeping down the hall and filling the house. The girl eats her breakfast at the table now, flipping through one of Dad's woodworking magazines. I can't take the cold anymore. I find the hinge pins to the door in the laundry room.

"Can I get you some breakfast or coffee?" Freya says. "I think I had the last egg. But it looks like you guys have plenty of sardines."

"No, thanks," I say, passing through the kitchen.

Light pierces through the edge of the front door where it leans cockeyed against the frame. The light moves from gray to golden bars. I stop in the hall and let the light lay stripes on my skin. Wind screams like a banshee, fighting its way through the cracks. I'm tired of the cold. I can't take it anymore.

I take hold of the door with both hands, grabbing it in the middle. I drag it out and lift it up onto the hinges. A blade cuts through my shoulder as I lift. The pain cuts, as if severing every muscle and tendon all over again. I can't help but scream out. The door falls against the frame and I fall backwards to the floor. Everything fades, moves ten feet away in a haze. Only the pain remains. It's deafening, numbs everything else, as if focusing all of its power on my shoulder alone.

"Are you okay?" Freya runs over and kneels down beside me.

"Just grabbed it wrong," I say through the desperate urge to scream out again. "Heavier than I thought."

It's only now I realize that Dad replaced the old door with a thick, oak beast of a door. How could he even lift it? What the hell was he thinking? Is someone coming to kick the door down? No one needs a door like this.

"You're lucky it didn't fall on you," Freya says. "My cousin had a door fall on him and it fractured his skull. He's a little off now. Says strange things."

She helps me stand and I gather myself. Half-dazed and nauseated from the pain, I watch as she angles the door in the frame, lifts it up, using the corners to balance and get it up on the hinges and secure it in the jamb.

"Here, I'll hold it in place if you get the pins in," she says.

I gather up the pins that went rolling down the hall and fit them into the hinges, knocking them into place with my fist. My right arm hangs at my side, limp and as if cut off from the rest of me.

"Thanks," I say. "I could've gotten it myself though."

"Clearly you couldn't," she says and smiles. "A little help isn't the worst thing. I'm stronger than I look . . . and you're weaker than you look."

"It's just my arm. I hurt it in college."

"Let me get you some ice for it."

I follow her into the kitchen and just watch her. She seems more comfortable in the house than Dad or I do.

"So, why are you here again?"

"Your Dad let me stay," she says. She fills a dish towel with ice and twists the end, forming a ball. "Here, hold it on the joint there."

"Thanks."

"My boyfriend likes to keep things interesting," she says. "He kicks me out every once in a while, and then we make up and all's well again."

"He kicks you out?"

"He's not a bad guy, not a monster. Just has his issues sometimes . . ."

"Well, he doesn't sound like a good guy either."

"We all have our little hells we create for ourselves," she says. "We hate them, but we'll never leave them either. It's how it goes. It's almost addicting, you know. Like how depression is addicting. This is just my little hell."

She stands at the sink looking out the window. I look past the tarps flapping in the breeze and watch Dad swing the ax. The top branches sway a little more with every swing. He doesn't let up, not to rest or to catch his breath. He cuts away at the thick trunk, one swing at a time.

The first crack cuts through the breeze and screams out across the morning light. Dad swings hard, driving the ax bit deep. Another crack of wood and the wind grabs hold of the branches. Dad gives one last swing and then runs back into the yard. We all watch the tree lean, slowly bending. Then all at once it falls fast to the powdery snow. The ground shakes and the tree's ancient weight rolls like a storm wave through the ground, splitting Dad's heart in two where he stands, splitting mine where I sit inside the house. It tears down the last bit of Mom we had, a bone at a time, a root at a time. I see Dad staring at the felled tree and crying. His flannel coat lies at his feet on the snow, and he is drenched in sweat from the work. His mouth moves as if he's talking to someone who isn't there. I cry as I see him cry.

"That's a beautiful tree," Freya says.

"It was," I tell her, wiping my eyes.

"It still is. He'll make something beautiful from it. He told me about it."

"There's nothing beautiful left for us to make. Only to cut down."

"Maybe so," she says. "But not him, I don't think. There's always a little beauty left. Just takes a spark to get it going."

Dad drops the ax and falls to the ground, hanging his head in his hands. I watch him. I want to run out to him, to hug him and lift him to his feet. But I stay in the house and let him be, adjusting the ice on my shoulder.

3

Emily sits on a bucket as I work through plates. I have a system. Glasses first, silverware and kitchen utensils next: these can all go into the dishwasher. Plates and other dishes need a good soak first. All the hand-washing I save for last, so I can take my time with it. Even just sitting here, Emily disrupts the quiet of the work, though. She doesn't say much, but I can't help wanting to look at her, wanting to tell her so many things.

She scrolls through her phone aimlessly, a sojourner adrift in a virtual world, trying to wade through the ten million voices shouting out to her. Knees close together as she leans on them in rapt boredom. She is the last server left for tonight. The others are either up at the bar drinking with the cooks or have long since gone out to other bars or back home. Drinks and more drinks, the nature of these people: trying to find a short-cut from verisimilitude into transcendence. Not Emily, though. She has always seemed comfortable and content with wherever she is, with whatever state of her life unfolds before her.

"How many tables are left out there?" I ask.

"Just one five-top. They're cashed out but still sitting there, just camping," she says. "They finished their wine like an hour ago, but they keep talking and talking."

The dishwasher stops and I lift the handle on the box. It's a good machine they have here. A Noble HT-180 High Temp washer. It can clean upwards of fifty racks an hour, if I am able to keep up with it, and it uses less than a gallon of water per rack. A few weeks back it was using too much water and the pressure had gone haywire. I had to take off the cover and get into the motor and water pump system. Somehow the pressure valve had corroded and was raising the pressure too high and letting too much water flow each cycle. Wine glasses were popping like firecrackers each time it ran. I'd open the machine to a tray full of shattered glass. I replaced the valve and pump, adjusted the pressure settings, and even cleaned out the deliming mechanism. It runs like a dream now. Dad would have been proud of me, but I never told him about it. I'd never fixed anything in my life despite all the times he'd tried to teach me. I feel proud of that fix, though.

Clouds of hot steam billow out as I lift the lever and the door rises. Water drips and runs down the stainless steel trough and into the sink. I give the plastic tray of silverware a good shake and lay it out to dry on another rack.

In the big double sink I keep one side filled with hot soapy water for the pans and trays. One at a time I pull out a pan and work the Brillo pad across the metal. Bits of food and grease spiral down the drain in the warm water. I try to focus on the task at hand, focus myself entirely like Dad does, but I can't stop glancing over at Emily every few seconds.

"You don't have to wait back here," I tell her. "Go have a beer if your table's cashed out."

"No, I'm fine," she says. "I like watching you work. It's kind of calming with the water running. Plus, it's warm back here."

I start another cycle of plates in the machine. The motor runs, turning gears and churning water like an outboard motor on a boat. If I close my eyes and drift, I'm on the Lake. It doesn't last. I glance at Emily again, at her legs pulled close into herself. I suddenly wish it was summer. To see her legs gleam a soft olive in midsummer light. I wonder what that makes me. Some kind of sick bastard hashtag of some kind, because I wish to see her legs. But they are beautiful legs. Simple admiration of the human body has been lumped in with creeps. Because they let creeps run rampant too long. Too fucking long they have. It blows my mind how disgusting people can be. The depths a human being can sink to are appalling. They'll follow their appetites into death.

Emily's legs are only a part of a different whole that I am now longing for. I wish to lie beside her. To hold her. Kiss her and then hold her for a long time after. That human touch, to sit and listen to those human sounds we make together, just lying there, alive together. I wish for a lot of things and yet I tell her nothing of them. Those thoughts belong to one of those other lives. There's no fixing the way things are now. Nothing is coming along to wake me up and split the universe open for me. Nothing can come from nowhere. Perhaps it'd be better to be no one then, a nobody from nowhere. And then it could all end and begin again.

I dive my hands into the hot water, feel its sting, and start on another pan, letting Emily wash out of my mind.

"I think Cherry and the others are going to Golden Hours," she says. "Half-priced whiskey."

"Cool," I say. I don't want to go. I don't want to see Cherry and everyone. I don't want to drink half-priced whiskey. Sometimes I wish I could just not exist, just for a moment.

"You're coming out with me, Jude."

I set the clean sauté pan on the plastic rack to dry, take another out of the water, and start scrubbing, hoping all the noise will fall away like running water.

"Jude—?" I look over at her. She halfway smiles. "You're coming out with us. You owe it to me."

"I don't know. I have a lot to do still."

"That's fine. I'll wait with you."

"Why? You can just go if you want to go. I'll try and come out."

"No. You'll wait forever and then make up some excuse why you can't come. Or you'll just not text me at all." She smiles deeper and narrows her eyes playfully, as if she were reading my thoughts. Maybe she is. When you've known someone long enough, it isn't difficult to read their mind.

She drops her phone into the pocket of her server's apron and walks out to the dining room to check on her table.

4

It's almost midnight by the time I finish with everything. Everyone except Emily and Chef Adam have left. The restaurant is all dark, only one light left on over the bar where they sit. The smell of food lingers warm and fragrant in the air. I suddenly remember that I haven't eaten dinner. My only hope of eating dinner has to come before I start work. Otherwise, after a night of scraping plates and smelling food cook, you're sick at the thought of taking a bite.

As I come through the dining room I realize I could leave and sneak out the back. Just text an apology later, say Dad needed me for something. For all I know, he very well might.

"Are you all done?" she hollers from the bar.

Shit. I don't want to go. "Just have to roll the trash out."

"I'll help," she says. She takes a last sip of her beer and walks to the kitchen where I stand holding the door open for her. I wave at Adam, letting him know I'm leaving. He'll sit there watching television and drinking for a while longer.

Emily zips up her coat and rolls one of the heavy trash cans out into the alley. I maneuver the other two through the door and follow behind her.

"God, it's freezing," she says. "Why do we still live here?"

I can barely hear her over the thunder of wheels rolling over the salted pavement. When we get to the dumpster I toss the bags over the top with my left arm and stand there a second, feeling the night wind come walking off the Lake. It's a little warmer than usual, which in any other month would be fine. But in winter, it means more snow is coming. I stand and bask in it a moment longer and my face goes numb, my blood a cold blue under my skin.

"Look, I really just don't want to go. I'm not feeling too good," I tell her.

"Too bad, son. You're coming."

I stack the empty cans and roll all three back toward the alley. Emily follows close behind in a suspicious manner, as if she were my guard, I her prisoner, ready to spring at any moment.

"You know, since you've been back, we haven't hung out once, Jude. Not once."

"We see each other every day at work."

"That's work," she says. "We used to be friends. We used to talk and laugh."

"We used to do a lot of things, Emily. But we can't repeat the past. It's done and gone. I'm not the same old Mr. Sunshine anymore. You're different too. People change. It's fine. But it's not the same anymore, is it?"

"'Can't repeat the past? Of course you can,'" she says. Her words linger on the air, vanishing a moment later in the wind like ghosts. "Can we please just go and have a damn drink together, Jude? Let's just go and talk and pretend like we're friends. Can we? Please?"

I look at her as we stand freezing in the alley. I want to say so many things. "Yeah, we can," I say.

"Good, thank you. You drive."

She runs back inside to get her purse and I sit waiting in my crappy little Toyota. I swear it's warmer standing outside. There's the thought to call Dad, let him know what I'm doing so he doesn't worry. He's probably already out on the roads in the plow though. Plowing and salting in the winter's night.

There's no good reason for it, but I feel upset with him. Maybe it's that he just keeps going on how he does.

Pretending things haven't drastically and profoundly changed. As if he doesn't want to stop for fear of what he'll find. I have long worried what Dad would do if Mom died first. He doesn't know how to take care of himself. Cigarettes and cans of sardines and black coffee. It's hardly a life. And just living here in this empty Northern Hemisphere, it's too much for him anymore. The winters alone are enough to kill a person, but I guess Dad's different. He's a grizzly bear. He's only ever known this land, this Lake. He's only ever lived in our cave of a house. He won't deal with what comes next, only put his head down and drive deeper into winter. He'll never quit. I think he hopes to die before spring. Maybe that is what upsets me. That he leaves it to me to care more about his life than he does. I'm left to be the hunter that drives the bear out of hibernation.

I don't want to talk to him. I send a text instead. That's enough for now, maybe more than he deserves.

Emily gets in the car and her sweet perfume fills the cold air.

"Jesus, it's freezing," she says, breathing heavy and rubbing her thighs for warmth.

"Sorry, heat doesn't work too well."

We drive across town slow and cold, tires crunching over ice and salt and snow. In the orange glow of street lamps December holds everything in its frozen fingers. All is still and trying to hold out for the thaw. I feel at once calm and yet perfectly strange. Cold and warm at once. I pretend I'm taking Emily on a date. Pretend that we're in love and will be for a long time. I pretend that we're happy and it's all going to be all right, and it's a pretty thought, as we move along silently listening to the radio struggle through the static.

Golden Hours is perhaps the shittiest bar in town, but it's

warm. It's crowded tonight, so we park on the street outside. We can hear the noise even before we get out of the car. It's one of two or three places open this late. Emily and I step out onto the brick sidewalk, step through inches of wet snow towards the neon OPEN sign glowing for us.

A raucous din of voices and music and caroming pool balls fill the bar. All is dimly lit and warm as low lights shimmer off the mirror behind the bar. Emily takes me by the hand, guiding us through the crowded room over to where Cherry and a few other servers from the restaurant stand huddled at the elbow of the long wooden bar. The bar shines in the light, polished smooth by decades of heavy minds leaning on elbows. In unison they all pick up a shot, tilt their heads back, and drink. Emily moves into the middle of them, smiling, laughing. She orders us a drink. I take a seat away from the crowd and sit beside Derek. Emily passes me down a whiskey and ginger ale and bitters, and Cherry whisks her off to talk.

"What the hell are you doing out, Jude?" Derek says.

"Just tagging along. Emily talked me into it." I look over and see Cherry sitting on some guy's lap now. "You come with Cherry?"

"Nah, fuck that, man. Done with that shit." He takes a long drink. "She can do what she wants. Long as I don't have to deal with her crazy shit anymore. Done with it."

Derek's wooden leg dangles in the darkness under the overhang of the bar. His eyes remain adamantly fixed on the TV behind the bar as Cherry laughs loudly across the room. He drinks with solemn purpose, careful not to so much as even glance in her direction.

In the center of his chest Derek has a big sprawling tattoo of the Sacred Heart of Jesus that endlessly points to itself. The thorn-pierced heart and Jesus's face look out from where his shirt is unbuttoned too low for this weather. He has a smiling Buddha tattoo covering his forearm, a few lines from the Upanishads on his ribs. As if he were spreading his faith to have a place in one of their afterlives and to gain some blessings and graces along the way, just in case one of them turns out to be the right one. And across his knuckles, the old sailor's words, *Hold Fast*.

"So, you and Emily, eh? Thought she was dating someone?" he says.

"She is. Gabe Welch. We're just friends, you know."

Derek's face is as calm as a Zen disciple's in mid-meditation. Some people have this incredible ability to truly not give a shit. Derek is one of them. Some part of him might care about what Cherry does. He's been in love with her since middle school. But when you've lived the sort of haphazard, gritty life that Derek has been allotted, you learn what things to care about and what things to simply let go of.

It comes down to the soul, I think.

There's a certain depression, one that's more like a species of despair, that empties the soul, blanches it clear, and leaves it hanging, like a plastic bag on the rocks of the creek. It's there, though, only it has become so overfilled that it has emptied itself. Despite the faiths illustrated on his skin, Derek is too tired to give breath to a belief, too worn down to petition the Lord with prayer. But still the desire is there, that hope for salvation, for love, for truth. Sometimes that desire to believe in something might just be enough. These are the new martyrs. No more burnings at the stake, no beheadings or crucifixions. But those who simply hold fast to that tiny possibility of hope, of love. That's all it takes. A desire alone might be enough to see you through. No one gets it right. But maybe the desire to be better is a strong enough plateau from which to leap.

5

Bars are breeding grounds for this day-to-dayness that tends to leak into the rest of life and out into the world. The day-to-dayness, this apathy, atrophic and sickening; an ideal of material and ambition as a means of satiating that pit knotting in the gut like snakes. The day-to-dayness, that rush of everything that makes you blow a car horn when someone doesn't go fast enough at a light; that strange need to fret and worry over retirement plans and stock portfolios and vacation homes; that haunting void that lurks in the silence, in the benevolent nothingness that greets us soft enough, but which we fear like some monster. It can begin in a place like this.

There are other places for its origin, but I have come to find that bars are the most productive. First, no one is their true self in a bar like this. If you run across someone who says they are, it's better to have that drink elsewhere, unless you'd like to sink into their little black void with them. People are only bloated versions of themselves, usually waxing philosophic or drunkenly poetic, masquerading as someone they wish to be or saw in a movie. Second, despair tends to find its host in bars. The dark seeks dark. It attaches itself with its fangs and holds on for as long as it can. And third, bars create such a noise that one forgets about silence. A noise so great while you are there in it, and then one so soul-emptying afterward that flaps about your head like a bat for days after. Until that next numbing, everyday something comes along to feed it just enough that it knows it's hungry.

For the moment I try to remove myself from the room,

try to be like Derek and not exist for a little bit, even in the middle of this crowded bar.

It doesn't work. Gabe Welch walks in and stands respectfully and stoically by Emily's side, holding her hand. She glances at me for the briefest of moments. All in a moment, there is so much said. It's impossible to drift away into silence completely, just as it's impossible to be present in the moment when you hate the moment you're present in. But, as in rowing a boat, when an opponent knocks your oar or encroaches on your water or takes a cheap shot that tries to hit your hand and fingers with the blade of his oar, you do not take offense. You don't first assume he was out for you maliciously. But, thereafter, you do regard him with a wary eye. Not in anger or nearing revenge, but in simple avoidance. It's open to us. Anger is a simple emotion. It is easy to become angry, to indulge that appetite. One slides into anger as easily as a dream. Anger takes everything if you let it.

Dad always told me to never let myself be swept off my feet. When a stray impulse or desire shows itself, stand away from it at first. I have tried to do this but almost always fail miserably. I am no stoic. I am flesh and blood and dirt. I tend to lose my breath when I see Emily. I lose my soul a little more each time I bite my tongue and she slips a little further away. When the glass sliced my shoulder, when I realized I could no longer navigate this world, when I realized it was not the land of endless potential I had so romantically imagined for myself, I fell away from it. I find myself euphorically happy and confident at times, at others despairingly lost and hopeless, and never over some particular thing. I ask myself whether this is the brokenness of being alive or merely of living in a broken and disconnected time. There must be some connection, some place neither too close to the sun nor frighteningly dark and lonesome. There must be.

I look at Derek and can't help but wonder if he's found some piece of it, a piece of that peace. Or maybe he just has a desire to find it.

To have such a desire is to be onto something, to be closer to that which we search for in the banal day-to-dayness, in all of our ceaseless doings. But to silence such desire, to dress it up or numb it, that is the beginning of despair.

Fuck. I wish I could stay out of my own head, even for a Goddamn minute. I wonder what Dad or Derek think about.

Emily and Gabe walk over. She has a look on her face like she wishes to apologize, but she doesn't say anything.

"Hey, man," Gabe Welch says. "So funny, I see you here now, and I saw your Pops earlier today."

I forget my anger suddenly, forget the churning pit of angst in my gut. "You saw my Dad? Where?"

"Yeah, he came by the boat shop this afternoon."

"Why'd he do that?"

"He was asking me about different types of wood. What was best for dampness, what protected against rot and sun exposure."

"Oh, yeah. He's building a sunroom onto the house," I say.

"That's cool. This wasn't for a sunroom, though. This was wood for boats."

"Boats? Why was he asking about that?"

"Sounded like he was building a boat, or wanting to," Gabe says.

"Lord, he's bringing you in on this now, eh?"

"Sounds like he knows what he's doing. You know, the winter can get the best of us, never a bad time to build a boat and get out on the water," he says. He politely excuses himself and steps aside to order a beer.

Emily taps my arm, mouths the words *I'm sorry*.

I nod and take a drink.

The room stirs with life. Talk and laughter and music. I think I would even enjoy it, were I living one of those other lives.

I can feel despair coming on like a fever the longer I'm here. It starts with all this self-pity and wallowing. It makes me disgusted with myself.

"What are you doing?" I turn and see Cherry standing beside me. Emily and Gabe have moved across the room. "You look like you're about to burst into flames or something," Cherry says.

"No, just thinking," I say.

"About Emily? Man, you need to get over it. You already messed that up. Either fix it or get over it, you know?"

"I am. I'm fine, Cherry."

"You don't look fine. You need a drink and a couple of these." She knocks a few pills out of a little pouch and into her palm. "Cherry's little pharmacy," she says, smiling and zipping the pouch closed. She holds her hand out to me.

"No, I'm fine, thanks."

"You don't even know what it is," she says. "It could be an Advil for all you know."

"Is it Advil?"

"No. Klonopin." She smiles.

"I'm fine. Thanks."

She takes the three in her hand and finishes her drink with the pills. I see Derek looking around the room for her. He stands and walks to the door with a cigarette dangling in his mouth. I follow him.

Emily grabs my arm and stops me as I pass. "Where are

you going?"

"Just going out for some air."

"Don't leave, Jude. I'm sorry, I really didn't know he was coming."

"It's fine."

"Don't leave yet, all right?"

I nod and follow Derek outside. He hands me a cigarette and we stand there in the freezing cold. Snow swirls like insects in the glow of street lamps. It's ten degrees out, twelve-forty a.m. the sign at the tire place across the street flashes.

Derek moves side to side, kicking his wooden leg out every couple of seconds.

"Did you think we'd still be here at this age?" I ask him.

"At Golden Hours?" he says, his voice wavering drunkenly.

"No, like, here in town still."

"Yeah, sure." Derek spits and it almost freezes on its way to the sidewalk.

"Really? You never wanted to go someplace else?"

"Like Saint Paul? Or Chicago?" he says.

"Sure, or anywhere. Doesn't matter. Just someplace not here."

"What would I do there?"

"I don't know, man. Anything you want. It's just a thought."

"When I was a kid I wanted to be a fireman."

"Really?" I can't help but glance at his wooden leg and picture it blowing up into tiny pieces again, the joint of his knee charred black, everyone clapping far off, thinking the fireworks had begun. That smell—it smelled for months after. Followed him around everywhere.

"Yeah, I wanted to save people, put out fires and shit."

"Why don't you still do it?"

"I'm missing a leg, man." He kicks out at the cold air, spits again.

"Yeah, but you could do something else, instead of being a line cook."

"What's wrong with being a cook?"

"Nothing, just, like . . ."

"You're a damn dishwasher, Jude."

"There's nothing wrong with being a cook or a dishwasher, all right? It's fine for right now," I say. "But I don't want to do it forever, I don't think."

"You could. Steady work. Pay isn't too bad," he says.

"There's got to be something else, though. I don't think my purpose in life is to wash dishes now. I tried to convince myself maybe I'd just keep doing it forever, that I didn't need anything more, but, I don't know now . . . I feel weird, man."

"That's not a good enough purpose? You think you have some grand purpose in this world?"

"No, I'm not saying that. Just . . . there's got to be something *more*."

"Like what?"

"I don't fucking know."

Derek looks at me. "Didn't you already go and do something else? Follow your destiny and shit, like you always said? You were a damn Olympic athlete, man."

"No, I just qualified. I never got to go."

"So the hell what? You made the damn team, you were good enough to go. That's not good enough?"

"No, I didn't get to compete. That's the dream, that's the whole point of it. To compete against the best."

"Yeah, that sucks and all, but still. You did something almost no one in the world gets to do. You've felt sorry for yourself long enough, though, man. It's time to move on, or just shut the fuck up about it."

I look at him. We used to be close friends, close enough to talk like this. But that was back then. "What?"

"For like a year I've watched you mope around, sinking in your own bullshit like there's a brick tied to your ankles. You look miserable, you're miserable to even be around, Jude, and that says a hell of a lot. I know some real losers."

"Whatever, man. I don't need this shit . . ."

"I'm just being honest 'cause it's clear no one else has leveled with you. You intimidate a lot of people. Big guy like you, tall, powerful, people see you and figure hey, he can take care of his own issues. So they let you get away with whatever." He tosses his cigarette, kicks out his leg. "But that's just why you need to get over yourself. People always think there's some great thing coming to save them. That some brilliant sign will appear in the sky and show you the way. Fuck that. If you wanna leave, then leave. If you hate your life and your job, then just quit for Chrissake. But don't sit around judging the rest of us, feeling sorry that you didn't get to have your precious little dream or some shit. You're here now, Jude," he says, and hits me in the chest. "So *be* here now. Be a dishwasher, be whatever the fuck, who cares? But be a better person. Be a better friend. We used to be friends and you know, I try to hang out with you, try to talk with you, and not because I really want to, but because I care about you, man. I really do. But you act like no one else even exists. You're so fucking selfish sometimes, man."

"Derek, I'm . . . I'm sorry, man . . ."

"No, don't apologize…" He looks out across the street at the sign showing the time. "Shit, man. It's been a rough night. Half-priced whiskey always gets me." He spits and looks back at me, pulling the door open. "Just be better,

Jude. That's it."

6

For the better part of a week Dad didn't go to work. He spent daylight hours cutting up the tree by hand—no power tools, no life in it, he kept muttering. Sawing up the pieces didn't take all that long, but he spent hours and hours gathering every last leaf, every tiny piece of bark, every broken branch, collecting every little mote of sawdust that he possibly could. He gathered every last part of the tree and lost none of it. Dad, the Good Shepherd. He lost none of the tree that was given him.

The work he could not do himself in the tent, he took to an old friend who owns a sawmill. On a Friday they loaded the thick straight logs onto a truck, and Dad drove the tree to the mill. His friend let him cut the logs himself because Dad said he'd never be able to forgive the man should something fuck up. He couldn't bear to carry something like that around. Not now. He did the work himself and saved every piece of scrap and sawdust. The boards were cut perfectly.

The house took on a different aura, too, in the following weeks, one of quiet, of stillness, though Dad worked in his tent all day long and on into the night. Cutting and building, fitting a thousand tiny pieces together to create something new. Something beautiful, he keeps saying.

Freya has stayed on in the house for almost two weeks now. She sleeps in Dad's room and he sleeps on the sofa downstairs. I can't sleep at all lately. I'm out of place, as if the world I thought was stopped and ended had just started anew without me.

The two of them work diligently in the tent, day after day, and I'm left to read technical manuals at the table and go to work in the evenings. Dad offers me a place in the tent at least once a day, but I won't take him up on it. I have no heart to indulge in his delusion that building a rowboat that will somehow solve all of our problems. Fucking insane. Dad is too far gone for me to pull him out of the water this time, drag him out by the hair onto the shore and help him get his breath again. I am resolved now to take care of myself. Nothing is coming, after all, nothing coming to knock us free of the rocks, nothing coming to save our lives. Nothing that isn't already here . . . .

The thing I am most troubled by is how can I possibly tell Dad I am leaving when the house sells. How can I break it to him that he'll be alone? How can I live with myself thereafter? Not that I know where I'm going, just that I am. That I have to.

And I am going—when the house is gone and the ice-breakers come. For some there is hope to be found in remaining still, in holding fast. For Dad, this is so. For me there is only going now. Like he said, there is only to take to the oars when the wind has gone.

7

I watch Dad work for a little while and it's like watching him burn right in front of me. He's feral and wild. He's lost it all now, I'm sure of it, what little of his reason he had left. Only Mom could pull him back now, but she's gone. And I'm tired of trying to save him. I have my own life to save.

I get in the car and drive, telling myself I'm going nowhere, but I know exactly where I'll end up. Emily knows how to pull me back, how to cut me down and level me out.

Emily's mom, Beth, answers the door. She smiles wide and opens her arms to me.

"Oh, Jude, it's good to see you," she says. She wraps her arms around me and my eyes follow the cigarette burning between her fingers. I bend my shoulder away from the inch of hot gray ash. My shoulders have a good four or five little circular scars from hugging Emily's mom. I've ruined a lot of good shirts hugging her. "Why don't you come around anymore?"

"Well, we . . ."

"I know, I know you two don't date anymore, but that shouldn't keep you from coming by," she says.

"Just been busy," I say. "But I'll try and stop in sometime."

Emily's mom is thin and always made-up, as she likes to say, even though she never goes anywhere. She hasn't left the house since Emily was five or six, not even to get the mail. Emily's dad used to do everything for them until one day he just got tired of Beth's "illness." He left for work one morning and didn't come home. Emily was maybe fifteen or sixteen then.

Beth spends all of her time making artsy jewelry that she

sells on the internet. She sits at the table in their kitchen, watching soap operas that she records on VHS tapes and keeps stacked and organized in the closet, surrounded by dozens of little plastic drawers and containers filled with beads and metals and gemstones, snipping wires and bending them into earrings or necklaces or whatever. She sells thousands of the little things. Amazing what can be done in desperation.

"Come sit down and talk," she says. "Emily! Jude's here!" she calls up the stairs as we pass. I feel like I'm in high school again. Everything comes rushing back. Maybe I shouldn't have come. "So how are you holding up? I'm so sorry about your Mom passing. Just tragic." She puts a hand to her heart as she takes a long last drag of her cigarette then stabs it out in the half-full ashtray.

"Thanks, yeah it's hard, but Dad and I are holding fast."

"You know, I heard they took your sign down in town. I couldn't believe it. I called up everyone, even called the mayor's office and gave them an earful. Those arrogant fools. Heathens, that's what they are." She stands and pours me a coffee, adding cream and sugar without asking.

"It's all right. Guess it had to come down sooner or later."

She sets the coffee in front of me. "That's what I always liked about you, Jude. You're so level-headed."

The coffee tastes like the lukewarm milk at the end of a bowl of Lucky Charms. I take small sips, not wanting to be rude.

"Hey, Jude," Emily says coming into the kitchen, singing my name like the Beatles song like she used to. "What are you doing here?" She walks around the table, putting her hair up. She takes the fresh, unlit cigarette from her mom's hand and throws it in the garbage without skipping a beat.

"Just driving past and thought I'd say hi," I say.

Beth lights a new cigarette and sits down across from me. She glares at Emily for a moment, an unspoken battle in a daily war. She picks up a pair of needle-nose pliers and bends a piece of sterling silver into a large hoop.

"I need all those to go out today," she says to Emily. She points her cigarette in the general direction of a massive stack of little earring-sizes boxes. All of them are neatly wrapped in brown paper and stacked against the far wall.

"Wanna go for a walk?" Emily says, waving her hand dramatically in front of her face to ward off the smoke.

"Jesus Christ, get over it," her mother says. She looks at me, shaking her head. "It's my one vice, Jude. Least she could do is not give me a hard time."

Looking at her pretty, made-up face, I wonder if each little wrinkle hidden under the powder and blush represents all the smokes she has in a day. For a moment, I wonder when it is we convince ourselves that our vice is our virtue.

"A walk sounds nice. It's cold though," I tell her. "And don't give your mom a hard time."

"Thank you, sweet Jude," Beth says.

"Hard time nothing. I'm trying to save her life," Emily says. She walks out to the hall and I follow, saying goodbye to Beth.

"Your mom looks like she's doing well," I say, once Beth is out of earshot.

"I guess. Some days I think she's better, and then I realize it's just the same. She just breaks down and has these crying fits that last for days."

We walk down the sidewalk and out onto the road in her neighborhood. The cold is everywhere, gray and damp, but not biting. We walk and all I want to do is hold her hand.

"I don't know if I can do this anymore, though," Emily says. "I can't just stay here taking care of her like this."

"It must be hard. You'll be made a saint one of these days."

"Saint, hell. She's my mother. But I don't know . . . I feel like I need to start my own life, you know?"

"Yeah."

"I can't just care for her like this forever. I can't. I'll go insane, Jude."

"Well, why don't you do something?"

"Like what?"

"Move out, get your own place. Tell her you can't keep on like this."

"Of course, I would. I feel so guilty even thinking about it, though. I'm all she has. Like fucking literally. She has no one else. I can't just up and abandon her. I couldn't live with myself."

"I know, but I don't think that's your guilt to have to bear. I think she has to take some responsibility. You have a life too."

Emily is quiet and sighs. I follow the little puffs of air leaving her mouth and vanishing before us. "I don't know. I keep thinking of maybe going back to school. Of finally going to college."

"You should. That'd be great."

"I'd go far away, though. That's the thing. I'd want to go somewhere far from here . . . I can't do that to her." Emily looks over at me. "Why'd you come over? You weren't just driving past."

"I don't know. I just wanted to see you. Maybe I shouldn't have."

"No, I'm glad you did."

"Dad is just . . . I don't know what's wrong with him. He's going all manic and crazy building this Goddamn boat. It's like he's had a nervous breakdown or something.

Nothing else matters except the boat. He's stopped going to work even."

"Why does that bother you?" Emily says. "Just let him do what he wants."

"No, it's more than that. He's selling the house, too. Which is good, I guess. He needed to."

"Really?"

"But he's not doing anything for it. It's like he doesn't think he'll be alive in a few months or something, and so he's not planning what he's going to do after. Not that it matters, life plans or whatever. I don't fucking know. It's just not like him. He always plans everything. He doesn't just up and sell everything and build a boat and cut down a tree . . . He's not himself."

"What about you? What are you going to do when it sells?" she says.

"I don't know. I can't stay with him like this, though. Might get a place in town or something. I always thought I'd go somewhere else, but there's nowhere else to go. It's all the same in the end."

"Jesus Christ, why do you always have to be so drippy and mopey, Jude?"

"I'm not drippy."

We turn and head back toward her house. A light snow falls on us. It's cold, but I don't want to go back inside. I don't want to stop walking beside her. I could walk on with her forever. I look at her and take a long breath.

"You know, I never stop thinking about you," I tell her.

"I don't believe that for a second," she says.

"No, really. I'm not being sentimental, and I'm not playing around. I miss you, Emily. I miss being with you. And I'm sorry. I'm sorry for everything I did and said wrong. I'd take it all back in a second if I could. If I could do it all over again, I'd take it all back . . . ."

"But you can't," she says. "I miss you too, Jude. But don't do this, all right? I think it's better how things turned out. We would have just ended up hating each other, and I could never live like that."

I walk her back up to her porch but stay on the sidewalk.

"Are you coming in?" she says.

"I think I'll head out," I say, and walk down the driveway to the car.

"Jude," she says from the doorway. I turn and look at her. "What is it that you miss about us? That'd make you say all that?"

I stand and look at her for a long moment.

"I miss how everything melted away when I'm next to you. How nothing else mattered and how hopeful the world seemed. I miss how I lose my breath when you walk into a room, how my heart beats like it's alive, really alive, when you're beside me. But mostly, I miss holding your hand when we walk. I miss that most."

She looks at me and a faint smile comes to her lips. "Those are good things to miss," she says. I nod and stand there in the snow.

"Yes, they are," I say.

8

"I think she's going to stay with us for a little while," Dad says. He sits at the table, flipping through a manual on building small boats as he eats a can of sardines. His beard and face are powdered pale with a fresh dusting of sawdust.

"Why? She doesn't have a place to live?"

"No. Not anywhere safe. And her baby is due in April. She'll stay with us till then."

"That's two months. We need to be getting the house packed up and things ready to move, Dad."

"Plenty of time for all that."

As he speaks I can't help but feel like I'm talking to a stranger. He looks like my father, the voice sounds the same, but the tempo of speech and the words are not his. Something has changed.

"Since when are you a guy who brings pregnant girls to live with us?"

"Since she came into my life," he says. "Freya saved my life, and so I'll do what I can to save hers now."

"What are you talking about? What's going on with you, Dad?"

He looks at me. "For too long I've cursed and blamed God or anything else for my losses, for every problem in my life. But I've come to realize that my complaints and disgraces have been my own doing and are mine to bear away. Any little bit of light and hope that comes my way is from the Divine, just keeping me afloat. I will waste no more breath on blaming other things. And I think you should consider doing the same."

He stays quiet after this and finishes his sardines.

"Whatever. I'm late for work." I stand and pour a cup of coffee. "And you know, you should probably go to work too, Dad. You haven't gone in a week."

"I'm taking a temporary leave," he says.

"Leave? For what?"

"For things to be done. I have almost two months of vacation days and sick days saved up. So, I'm using them."

I look past the wall at the tent out back. "How's the boat coming along anyway?"

"She's taking shape," he says. "Might be the most beautiful thing I've ever made."

"And you're still going to row out to Whitefish Harbor, across the whole entire Lake?"

"Yes. And my offer still stands, if you want to come along with me."

"You know how insane this all is, right?"

"It's good to go insane a little bit," he says. He stands and walks to the tent. "It's good for the soul to lose your mind every now and then."

9

Late February. Twenty degrees. This is a dead dark month, and the winter crawls impossibly slow toward spring. It feels like it'll never come.

I haven't spoken with Emily since I went to her house that day. There's this haunting feeling in my gut that she's avoiding me. Maybe she is. I've made it all that much more complicated between us. She cut her shifts back because her mom isn't doing well, she said. Beth was in the hospital for something and now she's back at home, worse than before. Part of me wishes Beth would just go ahead and die. That seems the only way Emily can finally be free. And I wish for that most of all, that Emily is happy and can live. Free of all the shit. Free of me, if it's to be that way. But in truth I don't want that. I want to live the rest of this life with her. That's all I have, really. Just that tiny flicker of hope that we might end up together somewhere down the timestream. And either way I have to tell her that. I have to tell her I still love her.

10

Dynamite Derek is sitting on a crate in the alley behind the restaurant when I walk up. He scrolls idly through his phone. Must be one of his low days.

"Hey, man." I stand beside him. "You okay?"

"Yeah," he says, listless and mute-tongued.

"There any reservations on the books?"

"Couple. It's the dead season now though, man. March *Sadness* started early."

"It'll pick up again. Always does."

Derek slides his phone away and sits hunched over his knees.

"Sure you're all right?"

"Just some shit with Cherry."

"What happened?"

"She got all messed up again last night. I had to go pick her up from some guy's house over in Two Harbors." Derek is quiet a moment. "It fucking kills, seeing her like that. It's like I lose a little bit of myself each time. Like she does this to herself just to hurt me or something. Or to prove I don't love her or won't come and get her, to prove she doesn't deserve love."

We're both quiet. He is probably waiting for some sort of advice, but I'm no good in situations like these. I'm no good with advice. I never have an answer to much.

"That's rough, man," I say.

"Part of me wants to get her out of here and get her off all that shit. Then I try, and she destroys me a little more. And I'm just left to say fuck it all. Just let her get swallowed up in it all, down to the belly. A woman that'd take the last bits of your soul and heart when that's all you got left, that's nothing but cruel."

"Well, man, if you love her, just keep going. It's always worth it in the end."

"Yeah, until it's not anymore," he says.

Chef Adam opens the kitchen door and calls Derek inside.

I follow him in and go to the dish pit and hang up my coat and slide the rubber apron over my head. I work through the dishes from prep and see the servers walk in and out as they get the dining room set, but Emily isn't here tonight. She must have switched with someone. I try not to think about it and focus on scrubbing pans instead.

In a matter of an hour or so the restaurant is at capacity. The kitchen is going like mad and the servers run around in the weeds, cussing everyone and everything under their breath. The dishes pile up, but I work steadily through them, keeping pace. Every stack of plates I load and clean, a server sets another stack on the metal trough. Busy nights are best if you want to get lost in the running water. I don't have to look up for hours. Everything becomes repetition, everything drifts. The balanced chaos around me mutes out that deafening silence.

I glance over at Derek. He's on grill tonight. I watch him sear steaks. He stands there over the flames and smoke, completely focused on his work. He needs the chaos, too. Just that little bit, right on the fringe of losing all control. That's enough to mute everything out and distract the heart for a little while. It lets you not exist, just for the moment.

11

The fire wakes me up. It climbs the cold night air like a forlorn lion, pawing vagrantly at the darkness in sabbatine, golden waves. I get up from bed and stand at the window looking out at the fire Dad left burning. It is two-fifteen a.m. and twenty-four degrees. I can see my breath in the darkness. Dad and Freya are asleep in other rooms and my mind is off to the races. A long night with nothing to think about. Nothing I wish to think about. I pull on a thick wool sweater, one of Dad's old Irish fishing sweaters, and I light a cigarette out my window. I fill my lungs with the smell of cold and snow before the smoke.

Through the frost and cold, headlights cut across the darkness and brush across the windows and the far wall of my room. I squint in the lights and back away from the window. Everything is illuminated for a moment. Dad must have gone to work after all and is getting home early. That would be good. It would mean some things haven't been lost. Some things are still as they've always been.

I watch the lights settle and see it's a car, not Dad's truck. The voice is deep and muffled from inside my room, all bass and guttural tones. I peek out around the window frame and see a man standing there in the pale glow of headlights. He shouts up at the house, at nothing I can see or hear. Just shouting and screaming out.

It's not Dad out there. He's younger, this guy, stout and pacing in the snow, shouting. I watch him and finish my smoke as he comes up the driveway and stands on the porch.

"You better get out here!" he shouts. "You little bitch, you better get out here!"

He punches the door hard, and then he takes a step back and drives the heel of his boot hard into the wood. I see why Dad bought that door now. It doesn't budge.

"Get the fuck out here!" he screams.

I go down the hall and downstairs and stop on the landing. Dad is already there in the darkened hall. He listens, calm and sentinel. He looks up at me a moment then back at the door.

"What's going on?" I whisper. I hear Freya in the kitchen, nervously walking around, biting at her fingernails.

In the dark Dad looks like a bear, ready to meet the hunters coming into his cave.

On the porch the man screams and hits the door again. Dad laughs a little to himself. "Red oak," he says, nodding to me.

"Should we call the police?"

"No, he's just drunk," Freya says.

"I hear you, I know you're in there!" the man screams outside. "Get out here, Goddamnit!"

Dad waves her back into the kitchen. "You stay back," he says. His voice is level and calm. "Jude, you come here behind me. Don't say or do anything. Either of you. Just stand there and let me talk."

I walk behind him and he turns the locks on the door, loud so everyone can hear. He flips on the porch light and opens the door.

Dad stands there looking at the guy. It's as if my old man has grown seven stories tall, wild and feral. He's terrifying. The young man's rage quells a moment as he sees Dad. He must have thought he'd be opening the door to some young asshole Freya's been sleeping with.

"I'm looking for Freya," the guy says. "I need to talk with her. Is she in there?"

"It's two-thirty in the morning," Dad says. "Nothing needs to be said right now. Nothing worth saying, anyway."

"She in there?" the man says, his anger finding a second wind.

"She is, but she's resting right now."

"She needs to come out here or you need to step aside, old man. I don't know what the fuck is going on, but she's coming out here and leaving with me."

"That's all fine," Dad says. "But . . . what's your name?"

"Andrew."

"That's all fine, Andrew, but right now Freya is resting. She's going to rest here tonight, and then tomorrow, when things are clearer, we can sort it all out. But if that's not good enough for you, we can sort this out in the yard there. And I'll tell you this, son. You take that path and, no matter what happens next, you'll be crawling out of here. Your choice."

I peek over Dad's shoulder and watch the guy stumble down the porch steps. He paces on the sidewalk and then turns toward Dad, as if accepting his challenge. The guy takes a step toward Dad, starting for him, and slips on the ice. He falls flat on his back, his head knocking against the cement with an echoing *clonk*. He squirms to his feet and walks half-drunk, stagger-stepped, back to his car.

Dad closes the door and we all stand there in the darkness. Freya comes up and hugs Dad, crying into his shoulder.

"Go and get some sleep," he tells her. "He won't be back tonight. We'll sort it all out tomorrow."

She goes upstairs and I follow Dad into the kitchen. The glow of the fire out back flickers against the walls.

"You wouldn't have fought him."

"Probably not. But he didn't know that," Dad says.

"Why didn't you just let them talk? It's not really our place to get involved."

"Of course it is. That asshole is a bully. And I can't abide that shit. When it comes to keeping that girl safe, it is my place. Yours too. It's always our place to protect those who can't protect themselves."

Dad walks to the tent flap and lifts it.

"Dad," I say, and he stops in the doorway. "Are you not going to sleep?"

"No. Going to work for a little while."

"Mind if I watch for a bit? I can't sleep either."

He looks at me in the warm glow. He nods and walks into the tent and I follow him.

12

When I was maybe five or six years old, Dad took me to the Natural History Museum in St. Paul. We walked all through the exhibits and eventually came into this great hall where the sea life displays were. Sunlight poured down from the windows four or five stories above us. Everything shone golden and illuminated and immaculate. I wandered away from Dad, lost as I was in the wonder of everything, and found myself staring up at the great Sperm Whale exhibit in the center of the hall. It was life-size and weathered and aged, and it stretched massive and giant for fifty feet across the room. You could see the outline of its bones on one side of it and the ribs curved up into the air like arches in a cathedral or a boat half-built. Its jaws were open wide, bearing all of its sharp teeth, perpetually hunting and devouring everything it could. I stood there before the mouth of the whale, frozen with fear, certain it was going to wriggle to life and swallow me whole. I am not sure how long I stood there, but it felt like a lifetime, that I had lived and died and had been born anew in that instant.

With eyes raised to the giant beast I suddenly felt Dad standing beside me. I slid my hand in his, and we stared up at the whale. He didn't say anything. He just stood beside me, as if he knew how terrified I was. But the fear vanished with him there, as if him just being by my side protected me from all harm. Just his presence was enough to make me feel safe, that it was all right to be swallowed up if he was there with me. We said nothing, my hand in his, and stood looking far into the dark jaws of the whale, deep into the dark belly, calmly waiting for catastrophe, waiting to be swallowed up.

13

The boat sits upon the trestles in the tent. The wooden frame of the hull curves up in a smooth wave. It looks like the bones of a great buffalo, picked clean and left to return to dust among the weather. Only Dad has salvaged the bones, the forgotten things; he has shaped what was lifeless and inanimate and brought life to it. From a thousand forgotten things he has made something beautiful. The tent is warm and sweet with the smell of cedar planks taking their shape. The cypress boards cure under the glossy sheen of clear varnish. The workspace is clean and everything is in its appointed place. For the moment I set aside the pointlessness of this quest of Dad's, the delusion he continues to prolong and shape. For the moment, I only wish to be a son; I wish him to be a father.

"This is beautiful," I say.

"It's coming together, isn't it? Freya's helped quite a bit."

"You think she'll go back to him? That guy."

"Probably. But I just wanted to give her a chance to think through some things." He climbs up onto the stepladder beside the boat and works the boards over with a sanding block. His eyes are focused on his hands. He looks rested. Still wild, still feral and unkempt, but rested and prepared to work for a long time.

"How are you doing, Dad?"

"Me? I'm holding fast," he says.

"No, don't give me that shit. I mean really, how are you?"

His arms stop for a brief second, and then continue working the sanding block, rounding off the edges of a board. "I miss your mom. A lot. Sometimes it'll hit me so hard that I can't breathe. That I don't want to breathe again. All the things that I've done all my life don't really make much sense anymore. Almost feels like I'm just moving along in the dark in someone else's life. But I try to keep going, keep moving."

I look up at him, somewhat taken aback that he's answered so honestly. I don't know what to say.

"That what you wanted to know?"

"Yeah, thanks."

"And what about you?" he asks.

"Yeah, I miss Mom. It's been a strange year."

"Yes, very strange."

I watch Dad work for a while. He moves about the boat doing various tasks that seem pointless on their own, and yet come together after I watch long enough. I feel a little bit of what Emily was talking about, about how she wished she knew how to do things. I wish I knew what Dad was doing. That would at least give us some starting ground, a little push off the dock toward conversation and connection.

I have always found it so weird when people say they are best friends with their parents. I've never understood that. It's as if they are completely denying the deeper bond that is there. The only reason I am here and breathing is because of this man. That in and of itself deserves something more than friendship. Dad is a strange man, and I am strange now too. And it seems our connection in life is something more than friendship, more than being simply father and son. He has lost his breath, and I am losing mine a little more each day. He is moving along in the dark, and I can feel my eyes closing each moment.

"The hulls seem a little high," I say.

"I made them that way. And the keel a little deeper. It'll keep the rougher waters out, but won't lose any speed. That gives the oars a better angle to get a full reach and pull. You can go twice as far with half the strokes."

Dad crawls on his belly and turns onto his back under the boat. He holds a flashlight up to the hull, checking his planking and the drying glue.

"And the planks, are they supposed to be sticking out a little, are they warping?"

"It's called *clinker-built*," he says. "You overlap the planks to give it extra strength and seal up the seams. It allows the vessel to bend and give in the water without breaking the seams or planks. It's the Scandinavian method of boat-building. Dates back to the first century, and some of those boats are still in perfect shape. It's how Viking long ships were built. They were masters."

"How do you know about all this? When did you learn it all?"

"I studied it. Researched it. Thought for a long time about it, but also I learn as I go along. I take my time. I make sure every tiny thing is perfect before I go on to the next thing."

His cigarettes are on the table on top of the large boat plans. I knock one out of the pack and light it.

"I've been thinking, Dad . . ."

"Yeah—?"

"About when the house sells . . . I was thinking I might get my own place in town. Look for some better work."

"I can probably get you on with the county if you want. It's hard work, but it's steady, and the pay isn't terrible."

"Sure, that might be something good to look at."

"You want to stay on in town?" he says.

"Yeah, maybe try to get my own shit settled finally."

"That's always the goal, isn't it? The balance."

"What are you going to do, Dad?"

He's quiet. He works as if I weren't here, as if there were no one else in the world. He works like he is alone and yet like someone is watching.

"Not sure," he says. "Gotta get through this first. Then the other things will come."

The sound of the sanding blocks in Dad's hands fills the tent like the sea. The water tosses us around and we drift, longing for sleep and dreams among the crashing waves.

"Do you think we'll ever get through this?" I say.

He works a moment longer and looks at me. He moves his mouth to say something, but holds the words in. He nods, simply and far away. Only nods. And I think I believe him.

"Give me a hand here," he says. "Grab those clamps there."

I grab them and crawl on hands and knees under the belly of the boat and lie there beside Dad and we work together for a long time, quiet and too tired to sleep. I believe him now. There is something coming, if we can go out and meet it. Something beautiful, maybe.

14

The sun rises over the Lake. The cape of winter sweeps white, gradual and waking. Adrift in the on-and-on of a brief journey between the here and the there. We'd give anything for a chance to do it all over, wouldn't we? We'd kill or give up our names for such a chance. I think we really would. But generations arrive and dismantle, and the Lake remains on forever, sky-tinted and earth-ebbed, perpetually on and on. The sun, it rises and it sets. And there is nothing new. Nothing that hasn't always been and will always be.

Dad is ablaze and cutting across the darkness, ready to emerge from his cave.

And we are adrift like dust.

I sit on the roof of the boat house on the dock and watch the sun climb with her rosy fingers across the heavens. The green pines feel the coming of spring. I wait for it to come. I wait for the Lake to speak to me. The Lake is quiet and says nothing.

It never has. And I believe it now.

15

I drive across town in the first breaths of morning. Fog hugs the earth and casts a haze upon everything. I've always found something hopeful about fog. It suggests things aren't always so harsh and certain. That nothing is as it seems or as we want to see it. There is hope in that. Hope that things can change.

Through the dim light a herd of runners stay close to the shoulder of the road. Red safety lights shine on their arms or around their waists like rosary beads twisting between fingers. Just seeing a team, I feel a strange loss run cold through my veins. That loss of something I once held so dear, that I once partook in and gave my flesh and soul to. Sitting in the cold sigh of dawn, I feel like a ghost must feel, like the damned. Separate and severed from that which was so sacred.

Out among the dark shores and on distant islands I imagine ancient ghosts walking under the canopy of cedars and pines. The forest's thawing comes through the window and everything smells like gin and tonics, floral and smoky and half-frozen in a daze of euphoria. There are ghosts out there in the shadows of the morning. Dad always used to say he lost his ghost out there in the forest somewhere, among the quiet trees, on some forgotten island he rowed out to, or maybe just there, where the Lake ebbs and kisses the slimy shale and tide-smoothed stones like old lovers. Lost and still missing. He always used to say you have to go out and find your ghost before you can make it to heaven, if you can make it the distance. The Ojibwe tribes of this Northern Hemisphere believed that. They believed we have two souls, one of which travels at night and lives in dreams; it goes out in search of other spirits for connection and awakening. That soul separates from the flesh and bone when you dream or die and you have to go and hunt it out before you can begin your journey to the "good land."

But I don't have the heart to be a hunter. It's a lonely business, hunting and talking to ghosts.

There are whispers of summer in the air, of spring and aurora borealis. I feel I've been here before, in some other life, one I wasted before I ever knew it was over. Saw it all firsthand and paled in its blush. And then again, nothing is ever really wasted, nothing ever quite gone.

It feels as if all those ghosts push through the fog and lingering snow like a caravan of carnival folk, surrounding me and pushing closer to see something they can't ever understand. The forest smells of gin and fire. My ghost must be out there somewhere too, white as the soft bone of birch. Lost in the time it took for me to fall to the earth. But I don't have the heart to go out and row with Dad to look for it. Not yet.

No, not just yet.

16

Freya sent me to pick up a few things from her apartment. I did what I could to get out of it, but Dad gave me this look that I haven't seen since I was in high school, and she assured me Andrew wouldn't be there.

I steer into the other lane to give the runners plenty of room as I pass. They are bundled in winter hats and navy track suits with their high school emblem stretched across their backs. I miss that, I do. Being a part of something. It's so far gone now, though, and all that's left is the bitter aftertaste.

Freya's house is a little brick ranch situated between other houses that look identical, save the color of doors and shutters, and perhaps in summer the landscaping, but everything now is covered in the thinning snowmelt and fog. It's a rental house, like all of these must be. The disregard for upkeep and dreary outer aesthetics that seem contagious on the block give off that air of desperation and listless discontent; the landlords won't be coming to fix anything until it becomes an issue of lawsuit, and the tenants won't call the landlords for fear they'll come inside and disrupt their malaise-choked lives and perhaps see what they've been doing in their little caves.

There's no car in the driveway and no sign of anyone inside. I don't pull in, but instead park along the street of the neighborhood, a few houses away. It is still somewhat bizarre and confusing to me why Dad has taken Freya in like this. We can barely take care of ourselves. Perhaps it is simply that comfort of feminine presence nearby, or maybe just anyone at all nearby. Anyone other than me or him, a last lifeline to pull us out of the waves. Just having someone else there could be enough to force us to be different, even if for a moment. But if he's thinking he can become a savior or play Jesus, he's more gone than before. No one can save anyone else. No one gets any of this right. The only thing we can do is maybe push someone a little further along, but that's hardly salvation. I suppose it is something, though.

Before I can get the key in the side door I hear someone coming through the house. I balk and step back down the icy steps. The yard is wide open and empty and there's nowhere to run. Indecision keeps me standing there before the door too long. Fuck.

Andrew is standing there in the doorway suddenly, pulling on his coat on his way out. He stops and is as shocked to see me standing there as I am to see him. There's a cut across his left eyebrow, dried and crusted over. His curly hair is a knotted, tangled nest like overgrown brambles. He's a big guy, not quite six feet, but stout with a wrestler's build. I've always hated wrestlers, their propensity for fury and quick inclination to fight and go for the legs: my height does nothing in those circumstances. The few times I've ever found myself in confrontation, usually my height and size have been enough to make the other man back down before it comes to anything. Wrestlers are something else entirely, though. He looks around behind me a moment.

"Can I help you?" he says.

"I'm, uh . . ." I'm fucked. "I'm here to grab some things for Freya . . ." I say.

"Who the hell are you?" He comes down the steps, staring me in the eye.

"I'm Jude Algonquin."

"Are you the one she's staying with? You stole my girl?" He squares up, and a rage boils through his hangover.

228

"No, not at all. Look, I really don't know what all is going on, man. She's friends with my Dad or something. She just asked if I can grab a few things for her, is all. I'm not stealing her or anything like that. I swear, man. I'm just trying to help."

"Yeah, well, you're helping rip my life to fucking shreds."

"I'm sorry. Look, I'll just come back another time . . ."

"No," he says. He breathes and wipes at his beard-stubbled mouth and chin. "How is she?" he says quietly.

"Good, I guess. I don't really know. I'm trying to stay out of all this . . . whatever it is."

He looks at me, chewing at his bottom lip and half glaring. "What all does she need?"

"Just a few things, clothes and some random stuff."

He nods and walks back inside and I follow him in.

"I'll get it if you just want to wait here," he says. I read the list from her text message, and he goes off to a back room. I look around at their place. It's bare and half empty. No pictures on the dirt-tinged walls. The carpets worn and shadowed from feet trekked across them day after day. A lamp and side table broken to pieces in the corner where Andrew must have thrown them. Bottles of beer and soda and little piles of stuff everywhere: on counters and ledges and on the arms of the furniture, moved from one place to another in a perpetual journey, but never finding the place where it belongs. Unopened mail and trash and clothes and random possessions everywhere and always within arm's reach. But somewhere through and under all that, there is a homey touch. A place that is well lived in and protected. Though poverty and misfortune and whatever other name despair might call itself abounds and reeks, it is this homey quality that fights on, that struggles through; that hopes hope might be that thing with feathers, capable of winged flight, potent to carry them off to a better place.

Andrew comes back out, and I move my eyes to the blank walls and away from the scatter of stuff. He stands there before me and looks around at what he knows I must have been looking around at. The duffle bag on his shoulder has the scratched print of WOLF FALLS WRESTLING in thick white font on the side of it. He slides the strap off his shoulder and hands it to me.

"I put a few things extra in it, and her vitamins," he says.

I nod and hold the bag by the handles.

"So, you're sleeping with her?" he says.

"No, no, nothing like that. I promise you. I'm not, man."

"Is she sleeping with someone else?"

"Not that I know of. No one's been to see her as far as I know."

He's quiet and looks around. He looks like he wants to say something, make an excuse for the untidiness or something, but doesn't. "You know life just gets hard sometimes," he says. "I have some issues I'm dealing with. I only just got out of the Marine Corps a few years back, but some of that shit never dies, you know."

"You were in the Middle East?" I ask.

"You can't ever un-see any of it. You can't ever get back who you used to be. Just stuck with the monster you are. Forever stuck with it. And . . . it just gets all mixed up sometimes, you know? It takes a lot not to end it all every day. A lot. And you'd think I could come back and get settled and shit, but I can't keep any work more than a few weeks without fucking something up. I feel like I'm already damned or something. I know I am. Some sins are unforgivable. And I've sinned every one of them."

His eyes well with tears but his voice remains steady, trained and unwavering in its steadfast evenness.

"I'm sorry," I say, and the very words sound so idiotic as I utter them. As if my little apology means anything to this man. "I can't even imagine . . ."

"Can you do something for me?"

"Sure."

"Can you tell her that I'm sorry? And that if she wants me to go, I'll go. Tell her that if she doesn't want me to be around when the baby comes, then I'll give her that. I will. I don't want her to be anything like me. I hope she's like her. And if the only way is for me to go, then I'll do that."

"Yeah, I'll tell her. Do you want her to call you?"

"No, only if she wants to. But I'll be here, tell her."

I nod and walk to the door and he follows behind me. As we come outside I linger for a moment as he locks the door behind him.

"Do you need a lift somewhere?" I ask.

"No, I'll be all right. It's my penance," he says. I look at him as he pulls on a wool hat. "I wrecked the car last night and walked home. I gotta go and see if I can get it driving and fixed up for her."

We walk to the end of the driveway and I head for my car but stop. "You know, she loves you," I tell him. He turns and looks at me. "She's said it just about every day."

He stuffs his bare hands into his coat pockets and nods solemnly. "Thank you," he says.

"My dad always said that there's never any point in waiting around for things to change, no point in wanting to be better."

"Then what is there?"

"There's only changing those things. There's just being that better person. Nothing's coming to do it for you, you know."

"I'm not sure I'm even a person any more. I'm just

a monster most of the time and all I can hear are those screams and voices and shit. It's constant and permanent as hell."

"Yeah, well, 'be not afeared, this isle is full of noises, sounds and sweet airs that give delight and hurt not,'" I say, though at the moment I don't know why.

He stares at me a moment. "What the hell is that?"

"Nothing, it's from . . . doesn't matter. I'll tell her what you said."

He nods and walks off toward the road.

17

It has been almost a month since I last heard from Emily. I've seen her at work a few times, but she doesn't come and talk to me much, and the invitations to Golden Hours after work have ceased. Not that I want to go out at all. It was a nice excuse to talk with her for a few minutes, though. I can't help feeling like I've lost her completely, because I only partly told her the truth, because she is the one choice that I have failed to choose.

Love is a lonely hunt when one has a fragile heart. And Emily has such a heart, one that I broke in my hands, and I'm still holding the thousand pieces. If only I had a manual for such a fix. If someone could give me the words, any words, and the way: that would be something. Dad would know how to put it all back together. But a heart is so easy to break and shatter, and yet so resistant to mending again. It's always easier to tear down than to build up. Good wine loosens sadness from the heart, the poet Li Po wrote. Dad might say Old Milwaukee works better. I'd agree I'm sure, but I am sick of drinking. Sick of wandering through its fog, never able to align thoughts or find the tempo of the heart. Good wine might loosen the sadness, but from there it floats, until it can take hold somewhere else again. Usually by the time it returns it has grown claws.

Now, I think all I want is to tell her I love her. I can live with a lot of regrets, a lot of things I've done and things I've failed to do. But never telling her—that's one thing I couldn't ever live with.

No work today, the first time in a few months. Freya's due date is only a couple weeks away. She stays on in the house with us still. Andrew goes with her to all of her doctor's appointments, though. I told her what Andrew said as I promised, but I'm not sure what she did with the information. Maybe she is waiting to see if his words are true. Perhaps she is waiting to see if he'll come for her again and make it all right and knock things into place: to see if he'll come, not in desperation or wrath or fear of loneliness, but out of love and love alone.

Perhaps Emily is doing the same.

The great dynamo of sounds and furies from the tent has ceased for a moment. In the kitchen Dad has the coffee maker in a dozen pieces. He works over each little part with an old toothbrush, scrubbing and cleaning. The heating coil and electric wire in the back have already been taken apart and await the rest of the machine.

"What happened to the coffee pot?"

"Wasn't getting hot enough," Dad says.

"I thought it was hot enough. It was working fine."

"It was inconsistent," he says. "The water needs to be at a certain temperature to soak the grounds and drip down evenly. That, and there was a build-up of calcium and old grounds clogging the water flow."

"It's not like we're making expensive coffee or something. It's *Folgers*, Dad. Three bucks a can."

"Well, it'll taste even better now. And it'll be hot."

"I wanted some coffee now, though. And now I can't. There was nothing wrong with the machine."

"Yes there was. It wasn't working how it should. No reason to be lazy about it. It only takes a few minutes to care for things, Jude. Patience."

I grab my coat and walk to the door.

"Where are you headed?" he says.

"To get some coffee."

"Are you working tonight?"

"No. I'm off." I slide my arms into my coat and look at him from the hall. "I was thinking I might go and see Emily."

"Really," he says, not looking up. "Think that's a good idea?"

"Yeah, we're still friends."

"Isn't she engaged to that Welch boy? Gabriel."

"No, they're just dating."

"You sure? Freya was saying that Gabe Welch got engaged a few weeks back."

"No, no, she would have told me . . ." I say, standing there, watching him work. "Emily would have told me something like that."

"I could be wrong," Dad says. "How is Emily, anyway? Been a while since you two dated."

"She's fine, I guess . . ." I feel my heart pushing up out of my throat. She would have told me.

"Have you thought any more about that job for the county?" Dad says. "Steady work. It's a good job."

"I don't know. Not sure I want to spend my life working some county job." Dad looks up at me, but I'm far away. "Sorry, I didn't mean it like that. I . . . sorry, I need to go."

"Well, just let me know then. It's a good job," he says. "Say hi to Emily."

THE ICEBREAKERS

1

The ice's strength comes from the edges, like that of a dome or the arches in a cathedral. By March the layers of snow have melted away, the thin waters freeze again, and the ice appears from under it. The ice is a deep onyx black, not void of color but somehow holding all color at once, as if the kaleidoscopic prisms of sunlight millennia old were trapped in the water, melting and freezing over once more. The Lake reflects the sky like a great mirror, and the world is infinite in these moments.

Both the strength of the ice clinging to the bedrock shores and the cold water beneath keep the ice from breaking. It is thin now, barely two inches in some places, still two or three feet thick in others. The black ice holds a hypnotic and siren-like lure to it. One wishes to stretch out and lay on its still, smooth surface and bask in the cold and the light. But more than its luster the ice's song is unworldly and euphoric. It is a melody so strong that one might walk out onto the ice and remain in the melody until they fall through in the thaw and hope to freeze and become a part of the song again.

In the earliest breaths of morning, just before dawn, Thom Algonquin stands on the end of the old dock. The sky hangs low and heavy as the steel blue belly of a whale. The snow remains only along the shores of smooth bedrock. Before him, the black mirror of ice stretches out as endless and immaculate as eternity. Smoke rises far out on the ice and creates a new horizon, one almost touchable. In the faintest thaw, the smoke rises like spirits of ancient people whom only now the Lake gives back to the land and air.

Thom steps down onto the Lake. He feels the sheet of ice flex and bend under his boots. His steps are wide and sure, cautious, having heard every story of the Lake all his life: the ships capsized and swallowed down in its darkest depths; the souls of those fallen through the ice or carried off in the riptides and never found. The Lake never gives up her dead.

He walks out onto the ice and amid the thawing silence he stops and listens as the Lake sings under his weight. Like some mythic creature waking from its hibernation in the dark fathoms deep, the moans pulse and rise through the ice like a newly beating heart. The ice, bending and flexing in the cold and thaw, shoots off high-pitched sonorous tones like the eerie vibrations that screech through the black void of the cosmos. The ice bends and tightens, crackling like a fire that never burns, each cold arm holding up the other for as long as it can. It grows weak and breaks at the thinnest parts when the wind warms over the smooth surface. And when the air grows cold, the ice freezes again and becomes stronger at the broken places. The small cove where Thom stands echoes with the sound of the ice writhing and pre-paring to break. Thom stands and imagines such a creature turning on its belly below the ice, waking slow and gradual to a new life in a new world. He stands there and wonders if its great claws might burst through the ice and pull him under, deep into the darkness. He feels nothing. The wind swirls the smoke in a violent torrent and conducts the hori-zon into a great wall of mist and cloud.

The icebreakers will come any day now, Thom knows. The ships will set out from the harbors to cut through the thinning winter and release the waters. They will set free the spring and end all hibernation, and the world will take shape again. Soon, the silence will be gone, and motor boats and great freighters and every machine will roar forth from the silence, and Thom will take to the water. To Eagle Harbor the first day, and then on to Whitefish Point. Three hundred and fifty miles all told. "You might die, of course," Joe whispers in Thom's head. Of course, but let death be as it is, he thinks. I wish Jude were coming with me. "It is for him, after all, that you're doing this. Don't forget that," Joe says. I haven't, Thom says. But it's for me too. For both of us. To break us out of this, whatever it is, one way or another. "And death is a way," Joe says. Yes, one way, Thom says. But not the only way. "And if he does not come for you, what then?" Joe says. Thom looks out at the Lake and listens to its haunting sounds, its voice calling out to the sky it holds up. "He will come," Thom says. "He will come for me. Once more to the Lake. He'll come once more."

From the Lake, Thom looks back at his old house; the tent standing there in the cold winds, attached to the back wall like some foreign thing, and the lights glowing faint within. But within the thin walls the boat lies on the trestles. It is nearly finished and will soon touch the water. He sees it in his mind from afar, and it is beautiful. And the thought of it makes him think of his wife.

"It will be beautiful, Helen," he says. "Not a day goes by that I don't think of you, not a day I don't miss you. I think I've made something beautiful, though. If you could help me this once, please, just let it be beautiful."

2

Easter comes on the second day of April, and Freya feels the nameless weight of the child moving within the warm rise of her belly. She sits up in Thom's bed, looking around for Andrew though she knows he isn't there. She has retreated into herself, into this house like a ghost, and has pushed him too far away, now, when she needs him most. But she knows that's how love is. Freya wants, at least, to believe this: that love, the version of love in this life, is human, and this is why it can be so harsh, so messy and gross at times, why it slouches toward the savage, why it cripples and crushes when you're not paying attention. It is strange as being human is strange. Its loveliness is fleeting, lasts only until we put our filthy hands on it and begin to choke all we can from it. Still, the splendor and the fury of love make it truly beautiful.

She struggles to stand from the soft mattress, bending her back and extending her legs to balance the weight on her hips and back. She stands, and then it comes. The first pain stabs through her gut, shooting out in every direction like a wildfire before it dies off again. She falls back to the mattress and catches her breath. Slowly she stands again and goes to the bathroom. The next pain comes and bends her in two, drawing her to her knees as she screams out in agony. Between her moans and the gasps for breath she hears nothing in the house. No one downstairs, no one coming to help her. But she'd never expected anything different, never expected a savior. And without such expectations, she's never waited for one.

She screams again and rises to her feet as the lining of

her amniotic sac ruptures and pours down her legs. Her hands push against the walls along the hall as she walks, half leaning towards the stairs as if the world were crooked on its axis. She screams, and her voice echoes through the empty house, wild and feral, primal as the grit of her bones and the breath of her soul.

She stands at the top of the stairs and holds onto the railing, leaning over the top step. Sweat beads and drips from her face and splashes on the old carpet. She steps and her hand slips on the railing and her balance is lost. She falls three steps down, catching herself again, holding desperately to the railing. She breathes deep through her nose and lets it out in a harsh blow from her lips. The pain in her knees is diminished and muted by the contractions. She screams and rises up and comes careful and slow down to the landing.

Her whole body shakes as she makes her way to the kitchen. She leans on the table, breathing, breathing, in and out, count to ten, in and out, breathing. She reaches her hand under her large t-shirt, an old Nirvana shirt of Andrew's that comes almost to her knees, and she checks her cervix, feeling the width with her fingers. She pulls her hand back and stares at the blood and fluid dripping down her chipped lime-green fingernails and streaking across the white calluses on her palms. "Couldn't wait, could you?" she whispers. She looks around the room for something, but doesn't know what.

She grabs her cellphone and begins dialing as another pain surges through her legs and up through her back, webbing out into every muscle and nerve. She falls to her knees and tries to scream, but the pain mutes any sound. The breath leaves her lungs and the pain crushes down on her. Her knees slip in the blood and fluid on the tile, steadily dripping from under her shirt. She tries to stand but her feet slip out from under her. Freya hits her head on the edge of the table and falls to the floor, and the pain and the light fade away and the world slips into darkness around her.

3

Thom looks out at the frozen Lake. Soon, he thinks, I will row out and greet my departure. Either to live or to die, one last good fight, and which of these is better, only God knows. "And which is it that you hope for?" Joe says. I hope only to wake up, Thom thinks. Only to awake from this great sleep. And in this, my reach might be greater than my grasp, but if it weren't, what is heaven for?

4

Thom's foot sits heavy and firm on the gas pedal as he tries to wipe the blood from his fingers. The belly of his gray sweater has turned almost purple with blood after carrying the girl to the car. The tires grip firm on the road where the salt is spread thick, and they slide, fishtailing for brief moments, as they hit patches of lingering black ice. Freya lies half-conscious on the seat beside him, blood running down her pale legs and pooling on the floorboards. Thom's face is stern and focused on the road. He doesn't look at her, doesn't glance. He doesn't want to see her yet, as if a look might shatter hope and the worst become real. He won't look at her.

He has been here before.

The feeling of loss pushes up through his chest, clawing at the back of his throat. *I feel like the damned must feel, cursed and cut off from what is sacred and pure . . . .* It was the weight of his wife lying in his arms that made him cry. Every ounce of her, limp and listless; all of her seemingly pouring into him. Her spine bent and broken, her eyes closed tight in that dark hemlock sleep, her soul returning to the silence at its source. Lying there in his arms, it wasn't her anymore. *Not a day goes by I don't think about you . . . .* She was gone and only the flesh remained. It wasn't her anymore, yet she somehow remained with him, and that was strangest of all.

"Stay with me," Thom says. "Stay with me, we're almost there."

Freya moans beside him, writhing deliriously as the pain pulses through her. Her blood-stained hands hold the shape of her belly in protection and love. She is, already, a mother:

even in pain, even now in this place somewhere between life and death, she is a mother. She is a wolf, defiant in the face of all darkness.

The little red pools of blood splash over her toes on the floorboard. Her feet slide back and forth in the sticky blood as Thom takes a turn a little too fast.

"That's a lot of blood," Joe whispers. Too much, Thom thinks.

"Stay with me now," Thom says.

She goes out again as he pulls up to the door of the emergency room. He doesn't bother turning off the truck or closing the door; he runs to the other side and gathers Freya up in his arms. He feels her whole weight lying on his bones. *Not a day goes by* . . . "Stay with me now, we're here, I got you now, we're here, sweetie."

Everything goes numb and muted in the frantic air of the hospital. All eyes turn to the sight of him and then the figures rush toward where he stands holding the girl in his arms. He watches mouths move but hears nothing. The bright fluorescent lights glare down on him, revealing every drop of blood. He stands there caught in the chaos, a scrap of gossamer blown in storm wind. He wishes he could not exist, briefly, just for a moment. He wishes he could save the girl, as he was unable to save his wife or himself.

Thom knows none of the answers to the questions asked of him. He lays her on the gurney they've rolled out and can only repeat her name, saying, "She's pregnant, she's pregnant . . ."

A team of people take her through the doors, and a nurse keeps Thom in the waiting room. He stares at the doors, stares past them.

"Is she your wife, sir?" the nurse asks.

"No, my wife is dead."

"And do you know her age, sir?"

"Will she be all right?"

"We will do all we can, sir," the nurse says. "Do you know if she's taken any medications or . . ."

"You can't let her die," Thom says, his voice on the brink but not slipping over. "I promised I'd keep her safe, save her life. Please, please don't let her die."

"We will do all we can, sir. Come with me and have a seat."

5

Jude pulls up to her house and sits there for a moment, thinking. The midmorning stirs in languorous and sabbatical quietude. The sunlight burns away the lingering fog and mist rising from the still-cold ground. It is cold. Thirty degrees at nine o'clock. But it is not a winter cold. It is one that holds out hope for a little warmth, for a glimpse of early spring. Jude doesn't want to go in. If I stay here, then nothing can happen, he thinks. There will be no news to pierce his heart, no change that will come and snuff out what bit of hope he clings to. By simply going in, he opens up the possibility of everything changing and never being the same. This is something he feels he can't live with.

But man is a strange creature. Not knowing often leads through floundering and ignorance into despair, but it can also lead to hope.

"Shit," he says aloud. He rubs his unshaved face, and the beginnings of a beard prickle against his hands. He checks his reflection. He looks like his father: younger, but turning feral and wild as an animal.

"I have to know," he says, and he gets out of the car in a quick rush of desperation.

There is no answer after the first knock. He stands on his tiptoes to see through the little square windows at the top of the door. He knocks again, and then he sees her come. He paces in wait, wiping his lips as he stares at the cracked cement porch below him.

"Jude—?" Emily opens the door and stands there looking at him. "What are you doing here?"

"I was checking up on you. I haven't seen you in a while;

you haven't been at work."

"I know, I had to take off again. Mom had a bad episode last Monday."

"I'm sorry," he says. "She okay?"

Emily shrugs, her arms crossed in front of her.

"I just wanted to say too, that I'm sorry about that last time we talked," he says. "I was out of line, telling you all that. I shouldn't have said it."

"It's whatever."

He looks at her hands, but they are tucked under her arms.

"And I heard. . . I guess I have to know if it's true," Jude says.

"If what's true?"

"Did Gabe Welch really ask you to marry him?"

Emily stares at Jude a moment, and then her eyes move past him. The silence seems long enough to live and die in.

"Did he?"

"Yes," she says.

Jude purses his lips, his jaw flexing as he bites down on his teeth.

"Well, uh . . . that really sucks," he says. He can't keep his eyes from welling up, can't keep the lump from growing like cancer in the back of his throat.

"Jude, I . . ."

"I am happy for you, though, Emily. I am. He's a good man. I couldn't ask for anything better for you."

"It's not that simple, Jude."

"No, I lost my chance. I woke up this morning and knew I had to come and tell you something, but it doesn't matter now. The gods don't favor indecision or cowardice." Jude walks down off the porch. "I'm sorry for all my shit, Emily. And I really am happy for you."

"Jude, hang on." She steps outside and closes the door behind her. "What did you have to tell me?"

Jude turns and looks at her. "That I love you, Emily. I always have. I've never stopped loving you."

"I love you too, Jude." She looks out at the morning light, holding back her own tears. "But sometimes that's not enough. Sometimes we're stuck in love, in the feeling of it, but there's no life to it beyond the feeling. Sure, we love each other, but it's a blind love, and that can't last, Jude. That is a selfish love, and I need more than that. You, too."

"Yeah, I guess so." He walks back to his car and opens the door to get in.

"I didn't say yes to him," Emily shouts.

Jude looks at her over his car. "What?" he says.

"To Gabe. I didn't say yes. I told him I needed some time."

"Time for what?"

She walks down to the driveway. Jude turns back and walks toward her.

"I got accepted to school," she says.

"You did? That's great . . . but wait, so you're not getting married?"

"No."

"You broke up with Gabe, then?"

"No. I just told him to wait on proposing. I'm not ready for all that. And now, everything is changing."

Jude wipes his face and lets out a long slow breath.

"I'm moving to Denver," she says.

"Denver—?"

"Yeah, I got accepted to the University of Colorado."

"When are you going?"

"I'm, um . . . well, I'm actually leaving next week to get set up for the summer term, start catching up on all I've missed." She looks at him, biting her lips as the morning breeze brushes her hair across her face.

"Next week? And you were just going to leave and not tell me that?"

"I didn't know how, Jude."

"No, no, fuck that. I know I don't deserve anything, really, but you should have told me at least."

"I'm sorry, Jude. But I'm taking your advice. I'm moving on with my life. And honestly, it doesn't concern you one way or another anymore. You've made that clear."

Jude bites down on his teeth and feels the muscles working like snakes in his jaw.

"I can't do this anymore. I can't live here and wallow and become some sick version of myself. I can't spend my life being a mother to my own mom. And I didn't tell you because I knew if I did, I wouldn't go. I would stay here because I love you too, Jude. I want to be close to you. It's terrifying to even think I'll be a thousand miles away, I'll be fucking alone. But it doesn't matter. I have to go. I have to, Jude."

He is quiet and walks back to his car.

"And you know, you can't just keep on like this either," she says.

"Like what?"

"Keeping me in this in-between place, saying you love me and miss me, but not doing anything about it. That's cruel to do to someone, Jude. And that's your problem. You're half-hearted, in everything. I used to be afraid that you'd hate me if I didn't talk to you or something. But now, I wish you hated me. Or I wish you actually loved me. Because either way, you'd be making a choice, you'd show me something fucking real for once, instead of protecting your precious little ego. But no, you stay safe and sound in your little cave. Not saying anything real. Not doing anything but hiding and looking out for yourself."

"Yeah, well fuck me then, right? I'm the monster."

"See, even now you start to get all self-pitying. You never do anything real, Jude. Do something!"

"Fine, here's something," he says. He gets in his car, slamming the door hard, and drives fast back out to the road. He glances only once in the mirror and sees her sitting there on her driveway, her face in her hands. He presses the gas down harder and keeps his eyes on the road.

6

Thom sits in the waiting room, watching the television that hangs above a boy whose arm is wrapped in a makeshift sling. Thom has waited here all morning. Andrew arrived shortly after Thom brought Freya in, and he stands outside now, pacing in the cool midmorning air. Thom stands and goes outside for a cigarette.

"Any news?" Andrew says.

"No, nothing yet," Thom says. "How are you holding up?"

"I don't even know. This is . . . I mean, if she dies, I don't know what . . ."

"No, don't even start thinking about all that," Thom says. "It does no good. Right now you must have faith."

"Faith? Faith means shit right now. This is reality. It's life and death, and that's all."

"No, faith is everything," Thom says. "I didn't used to put much stock in faith. Problem is, you have to have faith in faith, you have to believe in belief. I used to think it was important only to know things for damn certainty. And that's a lonely life. But faith, it's unknowable, it's never certain. If it was, it would be something else. It's all we have for those things we'll never know, those things that aren't for us to know."

"Thanks for the lesson, but for now, I only want to know. And what I know is that my girl and my child might be dead and I can't do anything about it. And faith means shit right now."

"You only ever have power over your mind, over your own will, not anything else."

"But what is this? Why would this happen to her? She's pregnant, for Chrissake. I'm the one who deserves something like this. Not her. She doesn't deserve to die now, not like this."

"I'm so sorry, son. I stood where you are standing when my wife died. A freak accident. She was healthy, kind, gentle, she was wonderful. And still something out of our control came. It always comes. You can spend a lifetime wondering why this happens, or why that. But there's no point. Even if you had an answer, there's nothing to be done with it. 'Death smiles at us all, and all a man can do is smile back.' Marcus Aurelius wrote that. I think none of us deserve anything at all, good or bad. But things come to us anyway. All that can be done is to smile back."

Andrew sees the doctor coming out of the swinging doors and he rushes inside. Thom tosses his cigarette and follows him in.

"How is she? Is she okay?" Andrew asks.

"She's out of surgery and in recovery now," the doctor says. "She's stable and the baby is a healthy boy."

Andrew crouches low, sighing with great relief into his hands. Thom touches him on the back and looks at the doctor.

"Right now, though, we are trying to keep her stable," the doctor says. "She has a concussion and has not fully awoken. We gave her a transfusion for the blood loss. Her vitals are good right now, and we are moving her to another unit for observation."

"Can I see her? Or the baby? I just need to see them with my own eyes, please, ma'am."

"Once we have her moved, you will be able to see her. I can take you to see the baby now, though."

Andrew looks at Thom, and the old man nods

reassuringly.

"I'll wait out here for you," he says.

"Thank you, sir."

Thom walks back outside and takes out his cell phone. He calls Jude, but there's no answer, only a beep. "Hi Jude, it's Dad. Just letting you know Freya's had the baby. I'm here at the hospital now and just waiting on some things. I, uh . . . well, that's all. No need to call back."

He slides his phone back into his pocket and sits on the bench outside the door. Around him the morning takes full shape and color. The fog horns blow from the icebreakers on the Lake as they cut through the lingering winter. The noon church bells from the nearby Saint John of the Cross toll through the clear air. They sound a little longer than usual for Easter and he sits and listens, quietly reciting a decade of Hail Marys to himself.

"Those were your favorite," he says aloud. "You've helped me now, and so I can say these prayers for you, Helen. I can get over my own stiff heart and say them now. I'd say ten thousand more if it meant I could see you again."

7

Jude Algonquin sits at the bar of Golden Hours, slowly sipping on a pint of porter. He stares at the television but doesn't watch. The actors on some show move across the screen. The wall-mounted set is an old one with a curved screen, prone to warping and jumping. Even when the picture comes clear, the staticky faces seem alien and deformed to him. Everything does. Or maybe it's just me who is deformed? he thinks.

He feels his cell phone ringing but doesn't look at it. If it's Emily, he doesn't trust himself not to answer. He needs silence. If it's anyone else, there's nothing to say anyway.

A few stools down, a hefty man eats his lunch and drinks bottles of Old Milwaukee as he reads a book of poetry.

"That any good?" Jude asks.

"Charles Wright. He's great," the man says. He slides the book down to Jude. He picks it up, looks at the cover, and then turns to a random page and reads quietly:

> *I'm starting to feel like an old man*
> *alone in a small boat*
> *In a snowfall of blossoms,*
> *Only the south wind for company,*
> *Drifting downriver, the beautiful costumes of spring*
> *Approaching me down the runway*
> *of all I've ever wished for.*
>
> *Voices from long ago floating across the water.*
> *How to account for*
> *my single obsession about the past?*

How to account for
these blossoms as white as an autumn frost?
Dust of the future baptizing our faithless foreheads.
Alone in a small boat, released in a snowfall of blossoms.

Jude closes the book and slides it back down to the man. "I never read much poetry before. I studied the classics in college. That and history were my majors."

"Yeah, well I've always wished I were a poet," the man says. "'Poetry expresses the universal, history only looks at the particular.'"

Jude finishes his beer and orders another. The bartender takes the two empty pint glasses. The man looks over at him.

"Trying to forget something?" he says.

Jude looks at him and twists his pint glass in anxious circles on the bar. "Something like that," Jude says. "First one doesn't count, my Dad always says. Things get a little loud sometimes, though."

"You know, one time I climbed Mount Hayes in Alaska," the man says. "Not the highest peak you can find, but it's one of the hardest climbs there is. I spent two weeks out there alone, trying to get to the summit. And when I finally did, I realized something."

"What was that?"

"You carry everything with you to the top of a mountain, everything. All you came to forget, all you're hoping to find. You drag it behind you wherever you go. And for so long I only ever wanted to cut it loose, you see. To be free of all that crap. I thought if I could do this one great thing, it would change everything in my life."

Jude looks at him, waiting. Finally he asks, "Did it?"

The man laughs, picking up his book again. "No, it

changed nothing. It only changed my perspective. Life's easy for someone on a mountain, as they say, but the real work is coming back down and learning how to carry all your shit."

"Yeah, if that's why we're drinking at noon I guess we still have some learning to do," Jude says, laughing a little.

"Yeah, some of us do," the man says, finding his page again. "We'll never stop trying to get it right."

8

Andrew comes back out and catches Thom before he leaves. Thom pulls on his wool hat and stuffs his hands into the pockets of his flannel coat.

"How's she doing?" Thom asks.

"She's stable now and resting," Andrew says. "She woke up for a second, and I got to see her, but she's pretty weak still."

"And the baby?"

"A little boy. Knud."

"I'm happy for you, son. Take care of your family. That's all that matters. That's all now, remember that."

Thom turns to leave, and Andrew calls to him.

"You know, it was the baby at first, when she first got pregnant," he says. "I didn't know how to handle it. I had just gotten laid off, had no money, only a shitty little house, no car. I was afraid."

Thom stands and looks at Andrew a moment.

"I didn't know how I could possibly take care of anyone when I couldn't even take care of myself. It just came out of me like a monster. But I'm not a monster. I love Freya. And now I love my son. I guess . . . I just want to say, thank you, Thom. Thank you for everything you've done. I know I don't know you, but I can tell you're a good man. I can only hope to be a good man one day."

"We try to control all the little things, don't we?" Thom says. "All those things we think are important. I used to do that. But we can no more control our little hells and catastrophes as we can gravity, or defy the fact that fire burns, or anything else. All we can control is ourselves.

There's no other way we can get any freedom from these things in life, these laws or whatever we might call them. There's no freedom from them, there's only freedom within them. Trying to keep a grip on things we can't ever control is a slow death. You have to let go. And don't talk of being good. That's useless."

"What is there, then?" Andrew says.

"Just *be* good." Thom nods to him and extends his hand and they shake. "Take care of her, son. I know you can."

9

That following week, Thom works through the night, attaching the oarlocks to the gunwale of the boat. He fastens them securely and gives them a hard tug to make sure they keep in place. Freya had done fine work in shaping the cypress wood and building the gunwales. She worked on the seat and footrest as well, adding in a special net to support his back for the lean into each row. With all the hardware fastened tautly in place, he moves next to the wood finish.

The night is cool but has no bite to it. Thom rolls up the flaps of the tent, so that he's covered from above and the fresh air flowing all around him. Lanterns light the tent, and he works in their warm glow, painting a third coat of lacquer on the hull and along the bow and stern. Evenly he paints in smooth, slow strokes, being sure to cover every inch of the wood. He has kept the boat's woodgrain natural except for a single white stripe across the middle. He measures out the lines and tapes off the edges. The white paint shines in the light, drying fast. Thom steps out of the tent and smokes a cigarette while the wood dries.

He walks out into the back yard and his eyes slowly climb skyward. Above him the northern lights dance a silent waltz across the heavens. He looks beside him, unconsciously. He looks for his son and wishes he were here just then. "And where is your son, where is Jude?" Joe says amid the darkness. He is far off now, Thom thinks. Adrift. "And still you do not go out and get him," Joe says. How can I? He moves farther off when I do, Thom says within himself. "And so do you," Joe returns.

Thom's mind floods with memory. He is standing beside

his father. He is ten years old on a cool October night. His father woke him up and brought him out to the Lakeshore to see the aurora borealis for the first time. Together they gazed in mute wonder at the color and light, the great symphony conducting itself in the heavens. Then as now, Thom felt unworthy to be witness to such a thing. He felt too ignorant and unclean to even gaze up at the lights.

"What makes those colors? What makes the shine?" he asked his father.

"Does it matter?" his father said. "All that matters is that we are here, that we are seeing it with our own eyes. Such things are as close to heaven as we can get."

"But what makes it happen?" Thom asked.

"That is the wrong question," his father said. "One day you might ask the right question and the answer will come."

Thom didn't know he wasn't talking about the lights. It irritated him to see something and not know what made it, what caused it, brought it into being, painted it across the sky. It was then that it began: his obsession with fact, his fear of not knowing. He equated ignorance not with bliss but with unworthiness, with laziness.

"And do you know the right question now?" Joe whispers. Yes, Thom thinks. And it is that which is unknowable. But I don't like that. I never will. "Does that even matter?" Joe says. No, I don't think it does, Thom says. Though I wish it did.

He walks back into the tent and works until dawn, finishing all that needs doing and cleaning the tent.

10

In the morning, Jude comes out with coffee and sits silently as his father works.

"Busy night?" Thom asks.

"Yeah, didn't get in till almost two," Jude says. "Just went right to bed."

"I figured as much. Rest is good."

Jude stares at the boat sitting up on the trestles, as if only just now seeing it.

"My God, Dad . . ."

"What is it?" Thom says, not looking. "The coffee cold again? Goddamnit, that machine. I swear I'm gonna take it apart again . . ."

"No, no, Dad, the boat," Jude says.

"Oh," Thom says, following Jude's eyes. "See something wrong?"

"No, it's beautiful. I mean it, really. It's one of the most beautiful things I've ever seen."

"Yeah, I think it might be," Thom says. "I put some part of my soul in it."

Jude walks up to the boat and gently touches the smooth grain of the hull. The color is rich and draws out every line, every perfect imperfection of the wood. Every inch is precisely sanded. The clinker sides of the hull, evenly spaced, rest atop each plank like overlapping rose petals.

"I knew you'd make something nice, but I never imagined this, Dad."

"Yes, a perfect vessel."

"Is it finished?"

"Almost," Thom says, and he walks over to the table and

pries off the lid of a little can of black paint. He stirs the paint and stands at the portside stern. With the brush, he pulls the paint in smooth strokes, giving name to the boat he has built.

"*Helen*," Jude says. "For Mom . . ."

"Yes, for her," Thom says. "It needed a beautiful name, and that one is perfect. A name that will launch this one last ship." Jude watches him paint the letters in the slow lull of morning. Thom looks at his son. "How's your girl? You get to see her?"

"Yeah . . . she's not my girl, Dad."

"Well, you love her, don't you?"

"That doesn't mean anything. And it doesn't matter anyway. She's left."

"Oh yeah? Where'd she go?"

"She left for Denver a couple days ago. For school."

Thom stands and stretches his back, nodding to his son. "I'm sorry, Jude. That's tough."

"Doesn't matter anymore. Probably better she's gone."

"Yeah, true. Don't want to be distracted while you're washing dishes," Thom says.

"What's that supposed to mean?"

"Nothing at all," Thom says. He crouches, focusing on his hand as he pulls the brush.

"So when are you going to put it in the water?"

"Tomorrow," Thom says.

"Just to test it?"

"No, tomorrow I'm rowing out across the Lake."

"Dad . . ." Jude stares at his father. "Please, please don't do this. Take it out for a while, all day, I don't care. But please don't do something so stupid as rowing that far. It's not safe, it's fucking insane."

"Well, that might be. But I'm ready for it, and that's

what I'll be doing."

"So you don't care what I think? You're just going to do whatever the hell you want, like you've always done?"

"I've planned this out, Jude. It's something I have to do."

"Dad, you will die if you try to do something like this. The physical strain alone is crazy. Not only that, but—you know the Lake. It can turn in a second. There's still ice lingering, not to mention the spring swells. Not even I could row through all that."

"Jude, death comes to everyone, one time or another."

"No, no, don't give me that shit. You know exactly what I'm saying."

Thom finishes painting the name on the other side and replaces the paint lid, hammering it back in place. He sits on a stool near Jude, wiping his hands on a rag.

"You know, back in December, I was driving the truck out near the national forest, and I came up on this wolf in the road. It was eating on a hunter it found in the woods there. He'd been dead a week before that. But I came up on him and reported it."

"Jesus, I didn't know that. Why didn't you tell me?"

"Point is, death comes to us, and usually we're too afraid to be aware of it coming. We cower even at the thought of it. But the sight of that, it's been eating away at me."

"What, that life is short? Use your time wisely and all that shit? Come on, Dad."

"No, not that. Only that we are fragile. We're dust. We want to know how and why these things happen. I've always needed to know. Why Mom had to miss that top step, why you hurt your arm, why any of it. And I've tried to control everything I possibly could because I could never control those other things. But you know, I'm tired, Jude. I'm tired of trying to play God and Maker. I'm tired of holding onto grief and anger. Life is only a series of little deaths and greater births. I'm ready for some part of me to die, and rowing out is the only way I know how to do that."

Jude stares at him, grinding his teeth as he tries to settle his blood. "Yeah, well, I'm not coming to rescue you, Dad. You're on your own here. Be as selfish as you want, I don't care anymore."

He turns to leave and Thom calls his name again.

"Jude—?"

He turns back to his dad.

"I'm sorry about Emily, I really am."

"Thanks," he says, and he walks back inside the house.

After all is clean and the final bits of paint are dried, Thom Algonquin sits on the old dock and watches the evening take shape across the water. He hides a cold can of beer in his hand and sips from it with slow satisfaction in honor of his work.

"Tomorrow," he says aloud. "Tomorrow we awake and row out to meet it."

11

Jude sits in his bedroom, staring at his cellphone. He has typed, deleted, retyped, and deleted the same message a few dozen times. He throws the phone, where it hits the far wall. The sound pierces his ear: the sure sound of glass cracking. "Motherfucker," he mutters to himself. He doesn't check his phone. He lies in bed and can't sleep. His mind is off to the races.

He stands and navigates through the pitch-black halls. He knows these floors well enough. When he comes to the stairs, he stops. He widens his eyes, and he can't help himself. He cries. As if from the black, the darkness, the nothing, he cries and sits there on the top step, touching the floor as if to hold his mother's hand. As if to hold anyone's hand, just to feel something against his own skin, to hold a hand in his own. He moves down the stairs like a child searching for a parent after a bad dream. Bravery flowers forth only in forward motion, not daring to look behind or beside for fear of ghosts. He can hear his father before he sees him. Thom lies on the sofa, sawing whole trees in the calm depths of a much-needed sleep. Jude stands in the bare living room and watches his father sleep. How can he sleep? he thinks. While I'm wide awake, while everything crumbles around us? Thom lies still and tranquil in the immaculate hemlock of dreams and nothing at all. He doesn't exist just then, and Jude is left to take a step toward him, then move away, then one closer, convincing and admonishing himself at once to wake his father, to cry into his arms and feel those safe arms wrap around him. Just this once. Just to feel something different for a moment. He moves away again. How could he disrupt such a sleep?

He sits in the darkness across the room and grabs his father's sawdust-powdered book on building small boats from the table. He looks at the drawings in the darkness as his eyes adjust only enough to make out whole blocks of words, but it is language without meaning. He touches his father's handwritten notes, feeling their impressions on the page with the dishwater-softened pads of his fingers.

"I think I have to go away, Dad," he whispers. "I can't do it anymore. I'm tired, too. I'm tired, Dad. How is it we get so tired?"

Jude looks out at the black night where the Lake sits in solemn quietus. He cannot see it, but he knows it is there. He closes his eyes and hears the waves lapping against themselves, against the ancient stone of the shore. He lets the water pull him down; he sinks deeper. *I'm starting to feel like an old man alone in a small boat.* He sinks down in the water and floats in the silence. *Dust of the future baptizing our faithless foreheads.* His father close by, just there across the room: that is enough to sleep on. Enough, enough for right now.

12

Thom awakes before dawn and looks at his son sleeping on the floor across the room. He is quiet as he stands from the couch and walks across the room. He bends and picks up his son. Jude stirs slightly as Thom struggles to his feet under the weight. But he gathers his son into his arms, as he has done a thousand times before, and slowly, quietly, Thom carries him back to his bed.

The breeze from the Lake comes into the house, past the tent, and blows the flaps around like flags of courage and hope. Thom dresses in clean pants and a white shirt, pulling a thick wool sweater over the rest. He eats at the sink, though he isn't hungry. You'll need your strength today, he tells himself. He takes the bag of supplies he has already packed and checks the contents again. A blanket, change of clothes, extra socks, a tarp, flare gun, filet knife, fire starters, some canned foods, and two gallon-jugs of water. Along with the bag he carries his father's fishing pole and reel in a leather case, should he get the craving for walleye. He pulls on his wool hat as the morning holds the chill of lingering winter. He walks the supplies down to the dock and sets them there on the old wooden planks. He comes back to the tent, gathers the oars into his arms, and walks them down, laying them carefully on the dock beside his supplies.

Inside again, he looks around one last time. He has everything he needs, and wonders, if this is true, what purpose does all of this other *stuff* have?

He writes a quick note and leaves it on the table for Jude.

Went out on the Lake, headed out Eagle Harbor way first. I'll be back by Thursday or so. Sardines in the cupboard. Love you.—Dad

In the predawn grayness he delicately slides the boat off the trestles and lays it on the brown grass. He has built it to be strong and durable against the waves yet light enough for him to carry alone, though with some struggle. Carefully Thom slides the stern into the water along the dock, tying the line to the hook at the far end. He sets his supplies down into the boat, along with the oars, and stands there a moment.

He stands before the boat and before the Lake like a lamb before the slaughter, or the sheep before the shearer. He breathes in the mist of the morning air and holds it deep in his lungs. Aloud, he speaks softly.

"Saint Thomas, I know I don't deserve any intercessions. I don't deserve much of anything. But you've always been my favorite. You're a doubter, as I am a doubter. Until I can hold it in my hands, until I can know its quality and weight, I can never have faith. So I ask now for a prayer. Show me something real, just this once. Let me know just one time that something is real beyond all of this. Yes, blessed are those who believe without seeing. But I am far from blessed. I feel cursed as the damned, fey and cut off. But pray for me now, Saint Thomas, a fellow doubter. Pray for an old man just this once. Send me a little faith."

Thom makes the sign of the cross, and this makes him think of his wife. A face that launched a thousand ships, he thinks. But this is the last ship to launch. He climbs off the dock and steps down into the boat. His nerves run like wild horses in his veins, his heart beating quick but steady. He unties the line and pushes off from the dock. He takes off his boots, lining his bare feet in the footholds and aligning his back. The seat before him is empty, and he imagines for a moment climbing out and waking Jude. But he doesn't. He sets the oars in their locks, adjusting the leather straps around his wrists, and he pulls the water with the oars and lets the small boat drift out into the Lake. He waits, drifting, watching as the house fades into the mist. And then he leans forward, reaching the oars back, and pulls the water, feeling its power and resistance all through his arms. He smiles in the cold air as waves lap against the port side and splash against his face, taking his breath away for a second. He pulls again, and again, and soon the house has vanished in the mist, and the shore fades, and there is only the sound of the boat on the Lake. There is only Thom and the Lake now, and he pulls the oars in smooth, even strokes out toward the sunrise.

13

He stays near the shore coming out of the cove. The waves rise up, only two or three feet high, but enough to rock the boat and make each stroke harder. Thom feels a surge of fear pulse through him for an instant. The thought comes to him that he should return, that Jude was right, that this is a foolish, moronic thing even to attempt. The boat remains steady in the water, though, and he breathes, trusting in his craftsmanship. He passes through the set of waves, and the water settles, and the oars cut easily through the cold blue water again. He breathes and calms himself. Don't start with those thoughts, he tells himself. Soon as you do, you're lost. Keep your head on the task. No further.

"But perhaps you should row back," Joe says. "Perhaps you're not ready for this."

Quiet now, Thom says. Don't start with those thoughts.

The wind is steady and blows with a firm hand all around him. The boat moves perfectly in the water, gaining speed and balanced neatly on the waves. Thom pulls the oars with even strength but no harder than is needed. He knows what is coming: the fatigue, the hopelessness, the futility of the whole bloody thing, and he will need his strength when this stage comes. For now there is only the sound of the water and the wind combing across the surface. Clouds are gathered to the north, white and rising like mountains. He looks along the base of them, squinting in the light. There is no darkness to them. He is thankful for this.

No storm is coming today, but that could change. For now there is no storm, he thinks: so row on, old man, keep going.

The boat bounces in the hypnotic rhythm of the tide. Thom can't help but smile like a young boy. It has been years since he was last on the water, even longer since he was out here rowing. At the moment he doesn't know why he stayed away so long. The beauty is endless. The beauty is truth, he knows. Thom's veins pulse with the electric thrill of rowing, of being tossed by the water and being helpless against its strong arm.

Off the shore of an island, Thom rests a moment, letting the tide carry him. He drinks from his bottle of water and watches a heron swoop low across the water and settle among the reeds and cattails along the island shore. When did he last see a heron, when did he last see any flying thing?

"Good morning, sir," Thom hollers out to the bird.

"You're going to start talking to birds now? You're going completely insane," Joe says.

Talking to birds is more sane than talking to you, Thom says.

In a few hours Thom cannot see the mainland at all. Islands pop up out of the mist here and there around him, but there is no more fixed country to be seen. He is alone in his boat.

The bow rises on a wave and crashes down again, soaking Thom's back in a frothy spray of ice-cold water. He wipes his cheeks on his shoulder and shakes his head at the cold shivering down his spine. He pulls the oars harder to get past the set of waves. The wind picks up and cuts sideway across the Lake and across the boat. Thom looks all around him at the whitecaps appearing and vanishing everywhere. Calm down, wind, he thinks. Don't start this now, just stay calm for a little while.

"The sky is clear, though. It is only wind," Thom says.

"But the wind could be pulling a storm behind it," Joe

whispers.

A storm is not likely, Thom tries to convince himself. The sky is too clear.

But he knows the Lake. He knows she can turn at any second, her temperament placid one moment, wrathful the next.

Thom holds the oars out of the water and watches the tide. The boat moves fast on the waves, tacking eastward in the ripping pull. The wind carries him now. He lowers the oars again, pulling hard and even.

"We might make it past Eagle Harbor today at this rate," he says aloud. "If the waves carry us and the weather stays clear."

"Yes, *if* the weather stays clear . . ." Joe whispers.

Thom pulls hard for a few minutes more, then lifts the oars onto the gunwale. He unstraps them from his hands and drinks water as he looks over the map of the Lake. He checks his watch and does a quick equation. In two hours' time, he has gone nearly fifteen miles. That's fast, he thinks. The tide is doing most of that, though. We can't lose it now.

He folds the map back up and puts it in his bag. He takes another sip of water, closes the cap, and slides his hands into the leather straps again. He leans in, pulls the oars hard for a few rapid strokes, and then slows to a steady pace. He pulls with his legs and back, saving most of the strength in his arms and shoulders for high tide. A song comes to mind suddenly: he can hear Joe singing it, somewhere far off. Thom joins in, aloud:

"*Farewell and adieu to you fair Spanish ladies.*" Thom feels in his open mouth the cold spray of the Lake even as the heat of the song pushes out. "*Farewell and adieu to you ladies of Spain, for we've received orders to sail for old England, an' hope very shortly to see you again. Farewell and adieu to you fair*

Spanish ladies, farewell and adieu to you ladies of Spain . . ."

In the northeast the clouds billow up slow and silent, high in the bright heavens. The clean white slowly churns into gray and then into dark blue as they come over the forests and nearer the Lake. The wind gathers from this distance. The clouds turn in on themselves, and churn. The wind picks up; the tides shift. But the storm is hours off from where Thom rows, and he cannot see these clouds. He rows on and sings parts of old songs and laughs at himself. At the moment, he can't recall ever feeling as alive as he does just now.

14

Jude awakes in his own bed. He lies there a moment, slightly disoriented, wondering if he didn't walk back up here in the middle of the night, half asleep. He stands and walks across his room and picks up his cell phone. The screen is cracked sideways across the phone, the fissure shaped like a bolt of lightning. There are no notifications or news updates. He rubs his tired eyes, sitting hunched over the edge of the mattress. There's a noise from downstairs, like footsteps, and then pans clanking around on the floor. Jude listens a moment, looking toward the door.

"Dad—?" he calls out.

The footsteps continue and then go away again. Jude pulls a sweater on over his t-shirt and walks languidly through the dim hall and downstairs. The pans clank again from the kitchen.

"Dad, what're you doing? You're so loud." He comes into the kitchen and stops in the doorway. He stares blankly at the wolf as his heart rate quickens. The wolf looks at Jude and then continues scavenging any scraps from the over-turned garbage can. Its long pink tongue licks the empty sardine cans. A pan of bacon a few days old lies licked clean in the middle of the floor.

Jude doesn't move. He watches the wolf and recognizes it as the same gaunt, mangy creature they saw in midwinter. Wind from the Lake blows into the tent outside and comes in cool gales through the house.

"Jesus," Jude whispers. "How many more of you can smell the garbage?" He tries to calm his heart and breathes slow and even. "Go!" he shouts, clapping his hands together.

"Go, go! Get out now, wolf, go!" He claps over and over, stomping his foot to scare it off.

The wolf looks up at him solemnly, licking its lips. It works on another half-eaten can of sardines and then moves toward the open back wall of the house.

"Go, go on, wolf!" Jude shouts again. He makes for the wolf with a stutter of loud steps across the kitchen. The wolf runs past the flapping wall of the tent and out into the back yard. Jude catches his breath, feeling his pulse surge up through his neck and into his head.

He picks up the trash scattered across the floor and tosses the pan into the sink. He sees the wolf sitting in the middle of the yard, looking at the house as if patiently waiting for another meal.

"Dad—? Are you home?" Jude walks to the tent and lifts the flap to see if his father is working out there. His eyes widen as he sees the empty trestles. The boat and oars are gone and only the Lake breeze pours in.

He rushes back into the house and sees the note on the table.

"You asshole," he whispers. "You just left, you just went and left like that."

He walks back to the tent and looks far out to the Lake, as if he might see his father's boat drifting and moving among the waves just there. The wolf runs away from the house a few yards and then stops again, sitting and staring at Jude.

"There's nothing here for you," he says to the wolf. "Go on, there's nothing here anymore."

He goes back inside and smokes a cigarette from his dad's pack. Something stabs in his gut. A knot forms and tightens and he takes quick puffs from the cigarette.

Something's not right, Jude thinks.

He looks out at the Lake through the kitchen window,

past where his mom's tree once stood. The water oscillates and ebbs in fast currents, blue and clear as the sky above it. Off to the north the clouds build like a secret militia, armed and ready to march toward the open waters. Jude watches the clouds a moment. He picks a point in the sky just above them, holds his eyes there, and in a matter of seconds he sees the clouds build higher and higher, turning and rolling in on themselves like waves.

"Shit," he whispers. "You didn't check the weather, did you, old man? No, why would you?"

Jude picks up his phone and checks the weather through the crack. Clear skies. Forty-five degrees now at ten a.m. Forty-nine by noon. He scrolls down and sees the clouds on the screen go dark, the little images of lightning bolts and animated winds.

He drops the cigarette in a dirty pan in the sink and runs outside to the dock. Only as he reaches the dock does he remember the wolf. He looks back at it. The wolf watches him with a sentinel stare but doesn't move. At the end of the dock, Jude looks out at the water as the tide carries cold wind over his body. The wind is heavy and cold and the dark smell of a storm hides in its tendrils.

"Shit," he whispers. "Where are you now, Dad?"

He dials 911 but deletes it again. There's no emergency, not yet. Just something stupid is all. He looks up the number and calls the office instead.

"Jude Algonquin," he says. "I was wondering if there is anyone patrolling the Lake this morning?"

"Yes, sir, we have a few units on the water," the officer says. "Is there something you need?"

"My dad rowed out onto the Lake this morning and I'm not sure where he is exactly, it's been a few hours. But is there someone who could maybe look for him out there?"

279

"Is he in trouble? If this is an emergency you'll need to call 911, sir."

"No, I don't think so. I just don't think he knows there's a storm coming."

"Where was he headed?"

"I think towards Eagle Harbor, or out that way at least."

"I can let a patrol boat know he's out there," the officer said. "What is the HIN number on his vessel?"

"There isn't one. It's a rowboat," Jude says.

The line is silent for a moment. "He's rowing from Wolf Falls to Eagle Harbor?" the officer asks.

"Yes."

"Jesus, that's almost a hundred miles . . ."

"Yes, I know. That's why I need someone to look for him."

"Is he lost out there?"

"No, for Chrissake." Jude rubs his eyes, calming himself. "He went out on the Lake just to row. But he doesn't know there's a storm. He's in his sixties, sir, so I'm just worried about him. Is there any way a patrol boat could go out that way and maybe look for him?"

"I'll put out a message to keep an eye out, but if he's going to Eagle Harbor you'll need to contact the local authorities there, sir. That water is their jurisdiction."

"Are you fucking kidding me . . ." Jude whispers, holding the phone away from him.

"Can you describe the boat for me?"

"An eighteen-footer, Faering-style rowboat."

"Is there a name?"

"*Helen*," Jude says.

"If you can stay on the line a moment while I type this up, sir," the officer says.

Jude stands in the open tent, crouching low among the

bits of sawdust on the ground cloth below him. He picks up the little grains of dust, lets them blow from his hand in the wind. The wolf lies down in the grass, watching him, as if waiting for some command.

"Are you still there, sir?" the officer says. Jude says nothing, staring at the Lake. "Mr. Algonquin? Are you there?"

"Forget it, I'll go and find him."

15

His father always said that the Lake has a mind of her own. She does whatever she wants whenever she needs. And all you can do is abide her, to endure and keep rowing, because she does not listen to petitions. Thom remembers the story of Nanabozho, the Ojibway hero. His father had told it to him, and he told it to Jude many times. Alone and rowing among the waters, Thom tells the story aloud to himself.

"One day when the great hero Nanabozho returned to his lodge after a long journey, he missed his young cousin who lived with him. He called the cousin's name but heard no answer. Looking around on the sand for tracks, Nanabozho was startled by the trail of the Great Serpent. He then knew that his cousin had been seized by his enemy. Nanabozho took his bow and arrows and followed the track of the serpent. He passed the great river, climbed mountains, and crossed over valleys until he came to the shores of a deep and gloomy Lake, called Spirit Lake and also the Lake of Devils. The trail of the Great Serpent led to the edge of the water. Nanabozho could see the house of the Great Serpent at the bottom of the Lake. It was filled with evil spirits who were his servants and his companions. Their forms were monstrous and terrible.

"In the center of this horrible den was the Great Serpent himself, coiling his terrifying length around the cousin of Nanabozho. The head of the Serpent was red as blood. His fierce eyes glowed like fire. His entire body was armed with hard and glistening scales of every color and shade. Looking down on these twisting spirits of evil, Nanabozho swore that he would get revenge on them for the death of his cousin. He said to the clouds, 'Disappear!' And the clouds went out of sight. He said, 'Winds, be still!' And the winds became still. When the air over the Lake of evil spirits had become quiet, Nanabozho said to the sun, 'Shine over the Lake with all the fierceness you can. Make the waters boil.' In these ways, thought Nanabozho, he would force the Great Serpent to seek the cool shade of the trees growing on the shores of the Lake. There he would seize the enemy and get revenge.

"After these commands, Nanabozho took his bow and arrows and placed himself near the spot where he thought the serpents would come to enjoy the shade. Then he changed himself into the broken stump of a withered tree. The winds became still, the air stagnant, and the sun shot hot rays from a cloudless sky. In time, the water of the Lake became troubled, and bubbles rose to the surface. The rays of the sun had penetrated to the home of the serpents.

"As the water bubbled and foamed, a serpent lifted his head above the center of the Lake and gazed around the shores. Soon another serpent came to the surface. Both listened for the footsteps of Nanabozho, but they heard him nowhere. 'Nanabozho is sleeping,' they said to one another. And then they plunged beneath the waters, which seemed to hiss as they closed over the evil spirits.

"Soon the Lake became more troubled. Its water boiled from its very depths, and the hot waves dashed wildly against the rocks on its banks. The Great Serpent came slowly to the surface of the water and moved toward the shore. His blood-red crest glowed. The reflection from his scales was blinding—as blinding as the glitter of a sleet-covered forest beneath the winter sun. He was followed by all the evil spirits. So great was their number that they soon covered the shores of the Lake. When they saw the broken stump of the withered tree, they suspected that it might be one of the disguises of Nanabozho. They knew his cunning. One of the serpents approached the stump, wound his tail around it, and tried to drag it down into the lake. Nanabozho could hardly keep from crying aloud, for the tail of the monster prickled his sides. But he held fast and was silent. The evil spirits moved on.

"The Great Serpent glided into the forest and wound his many coils around the trees. His companions also found shade—all but one. One remained near the shore to listen for the footsteps of Nanabozho. From the stump, Nanabozho watched until all the serpents were asleep and the guard was intently looking in another direction. Then he silently drew an arrow from his quiver, placed it in his bow, and aimed it at the heart of the Great Serpent. The arrow pierced deep into the serpent's chest. With a howl that shook the mountains and startled the wild beasts in their caves, the monster awoke. Followed by its terrified companions, who also howled and wailed, the Great Serpent plunged into the water. At the bottom of the Lake there still lay the body of Nanabozho's cousin. In their fury the serpents tore it into a thousand pieces. His shredded lungs rose to the surface and covered the Lake with whiteness. The Great Serpent soon knew that he would die from his wound, but he and his companions were determined to destroy Nanabozho. They caused the water of the Lake to swell upward and to pound against the shore with the sound of many thunders. Madly the flood rolled over the land, over the tracks of Nanabozho, carrying with it rocks and trees. High on the crest of the highest wave floated the wounded Great Serpent. His eyes glared around him, and his hot breath mingled with the hot breath of his many companions. Nanabozho, fleeing before the angry waters, thought of his Indian children. He ran through their villages, shouting, 'Run to the mountain-tops! The Great Serpent is angry and is flooding the earth! Run! Run!' The people gathered up their children and found safety on the mountains. Nanabozho continued his flight along the base of the western hills and then up a high mountain beyond Lake Superior, far to the north. There he found many men and animals that had escaped from the flood that was already covering the valleys and plains and even the highest hills.

"Still the waters continued to rise. Soon all the mountains were under the flood, except the high one on which stood Nanabozho. There he gathered together timber and made a raft. Upon it the men and women and animals with him placed themselves. Almost immediately the mountaintop disappeared from their view, and they floated along, adrift and cold on the face of the waters. For many days they floated. At long last, the flood began to subside. Soon the people on the raft saw the trees on the tops of the mountains. Then they saw the mountains and hills, then the plains and the valleys.

"When all the water had at last disappeared from the land, the people who survived learned that the Great Serpent was dead and that his companions had returned to the bottom of the Lake of Spirits. There they remain to this day. For fear of the great hero Nanabozho, they have never dared to come forth again."

I should have told you more stories, Jude, Thom thinks to himself. I should have done much more than I did.

A succession of four and five-foot waves rolls swiftly toward Thom. He hears the winds pick up and looks over his shoulder. He steers the boat straight into them and rows hard, then lifts the oars. The waves break over the boat. The cold waters spray across his back and his face. He rows harder through the rest of the waves, the boat bouncing madly, but holding strong, remaining balanced.

You can take whatever comes, Helen, Thom says. You are strong, and you were built to endure.

Thom feels the pain and fatigue squeezing his shoulders and tightening every muscle in his back. He arches his back; he stretches. He swings his arms around, one at a time, to get the blood moving.

It is already afternoon, he thinks, and we set out before dawn. Now is a good time for a rest.

"You'll lose all the water you've crossed, you'll drift in the tide," Joe says.

Then let us drift, Thom thinks. My arms are stiff now.

"Don't think those thoughts," Joe says. "Now is no time to think those thoughts."

Thom grips the oars tight in his cold hands and pulls the water again, and again, and again. He tries not to think about the pain, about the waves bombarding the boat. He tells himself they will stop soon, that it will be easier then, but the waves do not subside. They are swelling and coming faster now. The winds whip all around him. He looks up at the sky and sees the blue is gone, the light dimmed, and the great gray belly of clouds hangs low and conspiring above him.

"Clouds, depart," he whispers. "Winds, leave me. Water, be still."

But the clouds gather, the winds blow harder, and the water crashes again and again against the hard wood of the boat. Thom looks by his feet and sees the water is up to his heels. He rows hard, grunting and pulling as the pain surges through his arms and down into his back. The Lake does not give up her dead, he thinks.

"What exactly are you doing out here?" Joe whispers

somewhere far back in his chest.

But Thom only rows harder.

"Out here, alone on the water," Joe says. "You'll die out here, and the Lake doesn't give up her dead. What exactly are you doing out here, Thom?"

Thom looks over his shoulder and sees a great wave swelling just before him, eight, ten feet high. Thom steers the boat headlong into it, rowing harder and harder, then braces himself. The bow rises and the wave lifts it high, nearly vertical for a moment, and Thom holds fast to the gunwale. The boat crashes hard on the backside of the waves. Cold water drips down his face and the wind whips harder. The waves settle for a brief second and Thom turns and examines the boat. He finds no cracks, no damage. He looks all around him for a shore, but there are no islands. The Lake is everywhere and he is alone amid the endless drifts and waves. From the north he stares at the gray wall of rain moving swiftly toward him.

Thom holds still, watching. The rains fall hard and fast and the clouds churn with dark power. He reaches over the side of the boat and dips his hand down into the water. He makes a little bowl and drinks from the clear Lake. Everywhere around him, whitecaps break and churn, wildly random, as the winds shift. He takes hold of the oars again and pulls the water, singing aloud as he rows for a shore that he cannot see.

"Farewell and adieu to you fair Spanish ladies, farewell and adieu to you ladies of Spain..."

Thunder rolls across the northern sky, just behind the winds. A few dozen yards before the little boat, the wind meets the tide and a wave swells, growing, growing: seven feet, nine, growing and sliding towards the boat. Thom knows something is coming, but he doesn't look. The wave swells like some ancient serpent rising from the depths of the Lake. Twelve feet, fifteen feet, eighteen feet high, moving closer. Thom rows and sings and doesn't look at the wave. He holds fast and rows harder. The bow rises up again, and Thom tries to pull harder through it. The boat lies tiny and near-vertical on the wave. Thom looks far below him as the Lake lifts him higher and higher, and he sings louder as the winds rage in a dark fury all around him. Thom looks at the wave. It looks as if it is smiling at him. He loosens his grip on the oars and watches the water. All he can do is smile back at the wave as it rises up and holds there, breathless and infinite, waiting to break over the boat.

16

Jude runs along the shoreline and searches through neighbors' boathouses. Nearly everyone has lowered their boats from their dry docks or brought their boats out of marinas and put them in the water by now. There is a proper way to do something like this, to knock on a door and tell them what has happened and see if they would let him borrow their boat, or even drive him out onto the Lake. But no one would go out in the storm that's rolling in. That, and no one would lend their boat to a stranger so desperately standing outside their door.

Jude climbs into the stern of a bass boat. All the equipment has been taken out by the owner, but a single outboard motor remains. No key needed. Jude checks the gas tank, and it's near full. Rain comes quick and pelts the metal roof of the boathouse. The water grows rougher in the dock. The boat sways side to side as Jude walks to the bow to untie the ropes. He pushes off and lets the tide pull the boat out of the docking. The rain falls hard and cold as he comes into the open air. He jerks hard on the pull cord. It takes three pulls to crank it. He lowers the trim and turns the boat, steering out into the open water.

The waves are rough, and the boat is tossed around on the whitecaps as Jude steers the tiller. The hull of the bass boat is low and shallow and the waves splash over the sides on each break. Jude turns the gas and goes faster and slows, faster, and slows again as the waves force him to a slow, languorous speed.

"Come on, you sonofabitch," he shouts at the motor, at the Lake. "Come on now!"

The rain pelts hard as sleet against his skin, the wind carrying it fast into his eyes and against his cheeks. He is nearly soaked through and peers out ahead of him in short turns, shielding his eyes and face from the rain. The waves roll, violent and random without rhythm, without melody to their breaks. The boat slams hard into each break, and Jude fights to keep seated. He loses grip of the tiller twice. Each fall of the bow against the waves jerks the motor and pulls hard at his right shoulder. The pain is sharp at first and slowly numbs in the rush of adrenaline. He moves carefully to the starboard side and takes up the tiller with his left hand.

His mind swims to his father. He sees his father in the boat he built with his own hands. He sees him being tossed around helplessly among the waves, but too prideful to turn back, too stubborn to quit now. He sees his father crying out for help from the cold blue water. Crying and crying and completely alone on the Lake. Jude feels his heart in pieces, disassembling, ripping within his chest. He sees his father and feels pity for him. He sees him, and he knows they are the same.

Minutes feels like hours. The rain slows but remains, steady and constant. The waves rumble and push out in every direction. He turns the tiller harder and the motor whines in screaming bursts as it cuts through the water and rises out again with each wave. In an hour Jude is soaked through with rain and the Lake. The cold works on him. He feels it heavy on his skin and soaking deeper to the bone. Only the violent trill of his heart keeps him warm. The sound of his father's voice keeps him moving across the water.

For two hours he is headed southeast across the Lake in the direction of where his father might be. He hasn't been on the water in two years, but everything comes back to him. Even in the gray and the mist, he knows exactly where he is.

In the hazy distance and waning afternoon light, Jude stares at the empty horizon. It moves as he moves. It moves with the rain and the waves. The Lake is as endless as a desert, and islands appear and vanish as hopeless as mirages. There is only the sound of the Lake, the sound she makes as she turns and writhes with a life and power millenia old. And somewhere, just beyond it, he hears another sound, a silence there amid the noise. There are the human sounds he makes, as heart beats and lungs expand, collapse, expand. He hears that human noise he makes and it folds into the Lake, like parts of a symphony coming together. The Lake reaches out her arm and touches his face, and the cold water drips across his pale cheeks. He can taste the Lake on his lips and remembers her sweetness, her largesse, her cruelty. He drives on as the storm tosses him alone about the small boat.

Just ahead, no more than half a mile, he sees the orange rocket stream of the flare screaming toward the black belly of the lowing storm just above. The flare bursts bright against the thunder and fades again. Jude's eyes widen as the rain hits his face. The smoke trail of the flare still hangs, steaming, in the distance, a little further south. He turns the tiller, twisting the throttle hard and holding it down.

In the waning light, Jude sees the boat adrift in rough waters. He slows and steers across the waves, losing sight each time he rises and falls on the water.

"Dad!" he shouts out into the storm. "Dad! Where are you? Dad!"

He drives closer and then cuts off the motor. He leans over the starboard side, screaming and scanning the waves.

His father's boat is overturned, his gear scattered around the water, half-sunk and slowly being pulled down to the bottom.

"Dad! Dad!" he shouts again.

A few hundred feet away he sees his father's arms waving, sees his father's head bobbing in the waves as he clings desperately to a life jacket. Jude pulls the starter, but the motor only sputters and dies. He pulls the cord again and again. Nothing happens.

Jude crawls on his knees to the bow, steadying himself against the rocking boat. Along the deck, he finds a long paddle and pulls it out. He leans over the side and paddles with the waves toward his father. "Hold on, Dad! Hold on!" Jude screams out as he pulls the water, cutting through every wave and inching the boat closer.

A great wave swells and crashes over Thom. Jude holds his eyes on the point in the water. He doesn't see his father for several seconds. He paddles harder, harder. His Dad comes to the surface again, fighting the water as he gasps for breath before the Lake pulls him down again and again. Jude paddles faster and comes alongside his father. He gives one more pull on the water and then leans far over the starboard side.

"Grab on, Dad! Grab the paddle!"

Thom reaches, but the waves pull him back in the current. He reaches again and kicks his feet against the water. He lets go of the lifejacket and swims the few feet and grabs hold of the paddle with both hands. Jude pulls him close and grabs his father's wrists. He pulls him up onto the gunwale, lifting with his whole body. They roll onto the deck, and Thom coughs out lungfuls of water. He drinks at the air, rising to his knees.

"Are you okay? Dad, are you all right?"

Thom nods, breathing and looking around madly in the darkness.

"We have to get the motor started," Jude yells over the storm.

"No, I'm not leaving the boat!" Thom shouts.

"Fuck that! We're going, now!"

Thom moves to the side of the boat and nearly jumps over before Jude grabs hold of him. Thom fights and tries to throw his son off of him. Jude wrestles his father to the deck, screaming out against the raging storm.

"Give it up, Dad! It's gone!"

Thom swings his elbow and knocks Jude off of him. Jude grabs him around the waist and wrestles him down again. For a moment, he is taken aback at his father's strength: something primal in it, something bearish and violent.

"Get off of me, damnit!" Thom shouts, and Jude crawls off of his father.

"It's gone, Dad, let it go."

"No, it's not. We can save it. We can tow it in with us."

Jude sees the desperation in his father's eyes. He has never seen such fear. He looks out at the overturned boat floating dead among the waves. The cold waters lap against his mother's name, turned upside down, black paint luster-less in the gloom.

"Okay," Jude says. "I'll swim and turn it over and tie the rope." He grabs a lifejacket from a compartment below his feet, along with a rope. He ties the rope crossways around his shoulder and over his chest. "You hold on to me and don't let go!"

Thom nods, wrapping the rope several times around each hand.

"Jude!" he shouts through the pouring rain. "Let me go instead!"

"No," Jude says. "Just hold the rope."

Jude jumps into the water and floats on the surface. The water rushes into his face over and over. He swims hard across the rough water and reaches the boat and holds on at the stern. He takes hold of the gunwale with both hands and swims on his back, kicking his legs madly as he pulls the boat close to his father. He feels the rope around his waist pulling and giving extra strength. He climbs back into the bass boat and he and his father keep hold of the *Helen.*

"We'll flip it quickly and try to get it over," Jude shouts. He counts back from three and, bending over the gunwale, they lift hard on the rowboat. The water holds it down against the surface, sucking it into the Lake. "One, two, three . . ." They shout and lift again. The boat comes about and starts drifting away. Thom reaches out, grabbing hold of the bow. The *Helen* starts to pull him back into the water. Jude grabs his waist and eases him back into the motorboat.

"Tie the rope on and I'll get the motor started," Jude shouts. He moves to the stern and takes hold of the pull cord. He jerks the line, and the motor sputters and dies. He tries again and again, but the motor won't turn.

"It's flooded," Thom shouts.

"No, I'll get it," Jude says. He pulls over and over on the cord. The motor's response grows weaker and weaker until it makes no noise at all. "Come on, come on, you piece of shit!"

"Jude, it's flooded! That's only making it worse."

"Then what the hell are we supposed to do? We can't sit out here any longer."

Thom looks through the rain and thinks a moment.

"We can row in," he says.

"We can't fucking row in this."

"That's the only way." Thom unties the rope from the

bow of the *Helen* and reties it to the front of the bass boat. He climbs down into the rowboat, and his feet splash into the foot of water it holds.

"Come on, Jude!" he shouts. With his hands he tries to bail out as much of the water as he can.

Jude stands in the other boat, helplessly looking around at the Lake, as if expecting someone to come and save them any second.

"No one is coming, Jude. We're on our own and we have to row in."

Jude grabs a bait bucket from the livewell and two oars and climbs down into the rowboat. The two of them work hard and fast to clear the water out. Thom secures the oars in the locks, struggling as the waves rise and nearly tipping them over again.

"You take the portside, and I'll take starboard," he shouts. Jude sits beside his father and together, they stab the oars deep in the water and pull together in perfect rhythm.

They move out across the water with the bass boat in tow. The waves toss the other boat side to side, pulling hard against the work that they do.

"This is impossible," Jude says. "We can't get anywhere. That boat's too heavy."

"Row harder," Thom says. "Come on, heave . . . heave . . ."

They row through the waves as the rain pours down sideways on top of them. Every direction looks the same in the heavy gray gloom. The storm is nearly on top of them; only in the cracking flashes of lightning do they see any direction. Again and again, they pull hard on the oars. They hold fast against the swelling tides, against the violent random pulse of waves hitting them from every side.

Suddenly, Thom begins to laugh. He laughs hard and

belly-deep as he pulls, reaches, pulls again.

"What? What's so funny?" Jude says.

"This is crazy," Thom says, and laughs harder. "Look at us, just look at us!"

"Why did you do this, Dad? Why would you ever do this?"

"I had to do something," Thom says. He pulls hard on the water and lunges forward again. "Besides, it got you back in the water, didn't it?"

Jude looks over at his father, wild-eyed, and Thom starts laughing again. He stops rowing for a moment and throws an arm around his son. He holds him for a moment. "I knew you'd come out eventually. It's good for the soul to go a little insane every now and then."

"I almost didn't come," Jude says. They stop rowing, catching their breath and letting the tide pull them along briefly.

"I knew you would. You wouldn't let your old man drown."

Jude smiles, and then he laughs, and they laugh together, harder, rowing through the storm, calm and patient, as if there will be no end to it.

17

It is pitch dark when they reach the shore. Not a far shore, not something beautiful, but the same shore they've always known. The rain has subsided to a gentle drizzle; the thunder echoes somewhere far off like the hooves of wild horses gone over the hills, moving on to someplace else.

Jude steps out onto the dock and reaches down to help his father out of the boat. Jude ties up the bass boat and guides the *Helen* to the grassy shore. Together, they pull the rowboat up onto the grass. They sit there before the Lake, silent and breathing.

Thom laughs for a moment, and then holds a shaking hand to his eyes. He cries hard and holds his face in his hands.

"Dad—?"

Thom breathes deep and cries, and Jude puts his arms around him. Jude holds his father, like a father holds a son, and wants to tell him it'll all be okay now. But he says nothing. Nothing needs to be said. He cries as his father cries, and they sit there in the darkness, watching the green lights of the far shores ache through the mist. They sit there side by side, as if with the oars in their hands and rowing on endlessly, berthed back again to the same shores they've always known.

18

Jude wakes up on a Thursday morning to the sound of a hammer. Each hit vibrates through the house and echoes off into the far corners. He gets up and comes down the stairs. Golden light pours through the great hole in the wall his father knocked out. The tent is gone, as are the boat shop and all the tools. Jude can only see his father's boots on the top rung of the ladder.

He walks outside and looks up at his father repairing the gutters.

"A little early to start hammering," Jude says.

"No, there's work to be done. That storm did a number on the downspouts."

Jude looks out at the crystal blue waters of the Lake. An aureole of light shimmers through the mist around the dock. In the far corner of the yard, down near the shore, Jude sees the wolf lying in warm light.

"You see that?" Jude says. "See him over there?"

Thom turns and looks over his shoulder. "Yeah, he's been there all morning."

"Should we call Animal Control?"

"No," Thom says. "He's no bother. I gave him some food earlier. I think he likes it back here."

"It's a wolf, though."

"Yeah, but he's just looking for a quiet place. And he can stay here long as he wants."

Jude sits on a pile of fresh pine boards and looks out at the Lake. "Dad?" Jude says. "What are you going to do about the house? It's supposed to sell next month. It's all torn down."

"Then again, maybe not. So, we got to build it back up," Thom says. "Take to the oars again and keep going as long as we can."

Jude looks up at his father. "You don't really believe that, though."

"No, maybe I don't," Thom says. "But it's a pretty thought to have. It's a good thing to believe, that we can keep going. And I want to be someone who believes now." He lets the words linger on his lips and lets them drift back into the silence from where they came.

Jude looks at the boards he sits on and at the stack beside them and the boxes of nails. "What's all this for?" Jude asks.

Thom looks down at the boards and then comes back to the work before him.

"I'm building a sunroom," he says, and he takes up the hammer again, working on the gutters.

Jude smiles to himself and imagines the sunroom in his head for a moment. He walks out into the yard and looks at the wolf. They stare at each other.

"What about me, Dad? What's left for me?" Jude calls out.

"I think you know the answer to that, son."

"Take the job in the county—?"

Thom looks over at his son. "If you take that job I'll kill you."

"What?"

"If you take that job and stay here, I'll kill you," Thom says. He stares at his son. "You know what you have to do. And I'll tell you this, too. If you're too scared to do it, too caught up in your own ego and shit, then you're not the man I ever knew you to be. If you don't do it now, if you don't go after her, you'll regret it for the rest of your life. You will walk the rest of your days wondering, 'what if,' and that's a lonely existence, Jude. It's cold and lonely."

Jude looks out at the Lake again. "You really think I need to go after her?"

"And whether or not you two get together, whether or not any of it works out, you need to make it right with her, to the extent that that's up to you. She has your heart, Jude. And so the only way to keep living is if you make it right with her."

"Couldn't I just text her?"

Thom looks at his son, bending his face with disgust. "Ugh, how hopeless."

Jude smiles and stands. He pulls off his shirt in the warm morning light and runs barefooted down to the dock. Thom watches him as he turns the rowboat over and guides it into the water. Jude steps into the Lake and the water soaks his jeans to the knees and he rolls them up and jumps into the boat. I'll follow you, he thinks, listening to the paddles churn in the water. I'll row out to you, Emily.

Thom watches his son from the top rung of the ladder. Jude takes up the oars and pulls hard against the water, rowing out across the calm glassy Lake. He rows fast and hard, feeling the wind on his back, feeling the blood surge through his heart and out into every part of him.

The shore and the house push farther away as he holds the oars and drifts in the morning tide. He thinks about nothing. He listens to the sound his heart makes within his chest, listens to the human noise he makes, and it sounds like the Lake. The world is running water, with a silence at its heart. He rows, and rows, and lets the Lake's fingers glide across his cheeks. He closes his eyes, pulling the oars, and he dreams of Emily. He feels the calm wind blowing warm from the south, and he pulls the oars hard, rowing across the clear blue waters of the Lake, no return in sight, as he has done a thousand times before.

Back on the shore, Thom balances on the ladder, hammering down the last nails of the gutter. Sixty-five degrees at nine a.m. He climbs down and looks out at his son rowing across the cove in the clear morning light. He looks at the Lake through the point in the air where his wife's tree once stood. Now it floats perfectly on the water and holds his son in its branches.

"Not a day goes by I don't think about you," he says aloud. "And I won't stop either. But I feel a little less cursed today, a little closer to paradise. And that's something, Helen. That's something beautiful."

He watches his son and smokes a cigarette, walking down toward the old dock, like a bear out of hibernation.

"And what are you going to do, after Jude leaves?" Joe whispers. "What will you do now that there's nothing left?"

"I'm going to build a sunroom," Thom says. "A sunroom will be nice."

JUDE

1

He bought a bouquet of hyacinth on his way to see her. Somehow through the chain of people in a small town he'd learned Beth was in the hospital again, more serious this time. Dying from some unknown illness. Dying from it for years. Jude wondered if everyone wasn't dying from that very same illness. One of heartbreak, of loneliness, of despair. Depression, because we are depressed. Outrage, because we are outraged. Sick and tired, because we are sick and tired. As he came into the hospital and waited for the elevator, he recalled something he'd read a while back, about how there are these hooks in our hearts attached to other people. They all pull, and you feel it. You pull and can only hope they feel it. Dramatic, sentimental even, but he liked something about it. There was poetry in that thought. He thinks about the hooks in his own heart. Those hooks that tear through his heart muscle are attached to his father and to Emily. With every beat of his heart he feels every beat of theirs. Every inch he pushes them away tugs him a little farther down the path toward losing himself, too. That is, only by losing himself for them can he find himself where he truly is.

He steps onto the elevator and the doors close and he is alone. He orients himself with the dizzying pattern of the tile under his feet, then looks at his reflection in the gold mirror of the closed elevator doors. His gut sinks as he rises in the building, floor after floor of death and dying and everything he never wants to be so close to as he is now. He looks at himself.

"You're a piece of shit," he says, looking himself in the

eye. "Whiny, pathetic, mopey. You've been a piece of shit for a while now."

But it's all right, he thinks. I'm human. Humans are shitty and whiny and pathetic and mopey. But I'm human, and there are beautiful things about that too, and I am also those things. I am all of those beautiful things, too. Yes, I contain multitudes.

The elevator stops and the doors open. A few other people get on. His mind is quiet. He moves to the corner, holding the flowers before him, filling his lungs with their scent.

To place trust in visible things: that is despair, he thinks. Yes, to reach for that which is invisible in the depths of my own nothingness, where the beautiful things are. I am those things too, he thinks, looking at himself amid the other faces now reflected in the doors, and the people look like flowers to him. We are all those beautiful things, too, he whispers. Not only broken, not only cursed, but stronger where we were broken, steadfast where we were once afraid. Yes, yes, beautiful. We are those things, too.

A woman turns and looks at him but says nothing.

He gets off on Beth's floor and wanders the corridors until he finds her room. He takes a breath and knocks, pushing the door open slowly.

"Hello?" he says, walking into the room.

Just around the corner, he sees Beth lying in the hospital bed. She rouses from a twilight sleep and forces her heavy eyes open. Before any words, she smiles at Jude.

"I heard you were in here," he says, standing beside the bed. "Just laying around being lazy, eh?"

"Oh, bullshit," Beth says, trying to sit up.

Jude moves closer, setting the flowers beside her. "No need to sit up," he says. He slides a chair closer and sits down.

"It's good to see you, sweet Jude."

"It's good to see you, too. They say anything to you?"

"Just that I'm dying," she says.

"I don't believe that. You'll outlive us all."

"Would you do me a favor, Jude?"

"I can try."

"My purse is across the room there. And all I want in this world is a cigarette, would you please?"

"I don't think you can smoke in here, Beth."

"I'm sick. I won't be here for long. You wouldn't deprive a dying woman of one last cigarette?"

Jude looks at her as she takes his hand and holds it tight. He can't help but to squeeze her hand and feel the hooks tugging at his heart.

He stands and looks through her purse. He shakes a cigarette from the pack and sits back in the chair. He lights it, takes a cool drag of the menthol, and places it between her long fingers. She pulls off the oxygen tubes curled around her ears and sticking into her nose and sits up in the bed. In every possible way, she doesn't seem to be sick at all, not dying, not ailing. And yet, she seems perfectly gone already, he thinks.

She sits there and smokes, grinning slyly at Jude as he sits beside her.

"What—?" he says.

"Nothing," she says, letting out a mouthful of smoke. "You'll see. And I'm just glad you're here."

He takes her hand again, leans back in the chair.

"I wonder how long until they come and yell at me."

"Any minute, probably," he says. "If you don't set off the sprinklers before that."

Beth laughs as she takes a drag, looking at Jude with a strange smile, one he hasn't seen in years.

"What is it? You're worrying me," he says.

"You'll see. It's just like it was meant to be. As if it were already happening, in some other version of this life."

"Like what was happening?" he says.

The door of the room creaks open, and Jude looks over.

"They didn't have Diet Coke, so I got you a Diet Slice instead," she says, walking into the room. She stops as she sees him. He stands, his jaw slack and eyes wide.

"Emily—?"

"Jude? What are you doing here?"

"I came to see your mom. I heard she was sick again. What . . . what are you doing home?"

"Jesus, Mom, you can't smoke in here." Emily takes the cigarette from her mother's lips and tosses it into the toilet in the bathroom. She comes back out, waving her hands to clear the smoke still hanging in the air. "Did you light that for her?"

"Well, I was just . . ."

"I asked him to," Beth says.

Emily stands at the foot of the bed, half-scowling at her mother.

"You shouldn't be sitting up, you should be sleeping."

"I'm not tired."

Emily opens the can of soda and sticks a straw in it, holding it to her mother's lips.

"So, how's Colorado?"

"It's nice. Different. Took me a while to get used to the elevation. My head felt like it was going to burst that first week."

"Are classes going well?"

"There aren't classes in June. Semester doesn't start until September."

"Oh, right." Jude sits again as Emily pulls a chair up on

the far side of the bed, Beth lying there between them, smiling as she sips from her drink.

"I drove by your house the other day when I got in," Emily says. "But no one was there."

"Yeah, we sold it. We got a little apartment in town, Dad and I. Right on the water."

"Did you hear Cherry's pregnant?"

"Yeah, I did. I saw Derek the other day. They're getting married, too. Next Saturday."

"That's wild, isn't it?"

"It's something."

Beth hands her drink back to Emily. She sets it on the side table and Beth slides down in the bed, readjusting the pillows behind her.

"Did you find a place yet?" Jude says.

"Yeah, I did. The school arranged it for me. Right next to campus."

"That's great."

"Yeah."

"Ughh," Beth suddenly growls.

"What's wrong, Mom?"

"You two," Beth says. "What is this bullshit conversation? Just talk normally. Not all these little nonsense things. It's killing me."

Emily sits back in her chair, awkward and embarrassed. "Hush, Mom, take a nap."

"Are you still working at the restaurant?"

"Yeah, still there. It's good though."

"No longer feeling mopey and pathetic about being a dishwasher then, eh?"

"No, it's a good job. I just didn't see it for a while. I was a little caught up, you know."

Emily looks at Jude. Just looks at him, sitting there,

leaning on his knees.

"What's the matter with you?" she says.

"What?"

"You look like something's the matter."

"Oh, no, nothing . . . I guess, I just wasn't expecting to see you here."

"No, you look like you want to say something."

Jude shakes his head, opens his mouth, closes it again, like a fish.

She sighs. "Fine. Whatever."

Emily pulls out her phone and starts scrolling through the screen.

"Well, I guess . . ." Jude clears his throat and stands. He looks and sees Beth's eyes have closed and her breathing slowed; she lies languid in the midday light. "She's asleep," he says, a bit needlessly. "I should probably go."

"Thanks for coming by," Emily says, not looking up.

Jude walks to the door and then stops, turning back to look at her.

"Emily?"

She looks up from her phone.

"Would you want to go for a walk with me?"

She puts her phone down and sits up in the chair.

"Why?"

"Just to walk," he says.

She looks over at her sleeping mother and stands.

"Okay," she says, and they walk out to the hall, closing the door gently behind them.

In the elevator, they stand amid a few other people. Jude sees himself in the reflection of the doors again, Emily there beside him. He moves his hand, not looking down, and slides his fingers into hers. He holds her hand in his, and she holds his, tight. In the reflection of the door, he sees her smile, just a little, just enough. He thinks he smells the hyacinth still lingering in the air, but he isn't sure. It doesn't matter. He holds her hand in his, and everything is silent, everything washes away. Just then, nothing else matters, and yet nothing has changed.

With each beat of his heart, he feels a tugging, and for a moment he thinks he can feel her own heart beating in perfect rhythm with his.

"What?" she says. "What's the matter?"

"Nothing," he says. "I should never have stopped holding your hand. I'm a fool."

"Yes, you are," she says, moving a little closer beside him.

They walk toward the courtyard of the hospital, hand in hand. The sunlight touches the new blossoms on the cherry trees. A few nurses sit at benches talking over coffee and cigarettes, far away from any entrance. It is warm and bright. Jude glances up at the trees, at the blue belly of sky and sun above them.

"When are you leaving for school?"

"It depends on mom," she says. "I was hoping to get out there in a week or two."

Jude nods, looking ahead at the bright shiny morning. "Would you mind if I maybe went with you?"

"To Denver?"

"Yeah. What if I moved there with you?"

Jude feels her hand grip tighter around his.

"You'd really want to?" she asks.

"Yes." He looks over at her. "I'd go with you to Antarctica if I had to."

"Yeah, I'd like that," she says. "What would you do there?"

"Not sure. I'd find something, though. There are always jobs no one else wants to do."

She raises her hand and kisses his fingers and they walk in silence through the courtyard. A breeze from the Lake drifts over them and carries the white blossoms off their young branches. They walk quietly and Jude thinks of nothing, feeling her hand in his.

THOM

1

There was this song his father used to sing, randomly, especially if he had had a few drinks. *"Would you like to swing
on a star, carry moonbeams home in a jar, and be better off than
you are, or would you rather be a fish?"* Often, Thom would
hear his father singing this, sometimes at full volume. Other
times, it was as if his father were singing it as he replayed
a memory of his own father singing it, solemnly, murmuring. As if talking to someone who wasn't there. But Thom
always answered the question. Yes, yes, he would like to do
those things. To carry moonbeams in a jar. Yes, he would
rather be a fish. And it was the fish that always stuck with
him. Like the Ron Padgett poem his wife used to recite to
him, whenever she found him mumbling those few lines.
He didn't like poetry, but he loved that one single poem by
Ron Padgett. Because, it was true to him. Yes, he would
rather be better off. Yes, to be a fish. To not exist, like how
fish don't exist. Thom Algonquin has never been sure if animals are equal to human beings. He didn't know if they had
souls. But he figured, at least, that fish certainly didn't. Such
a heavy thing, a soul. And fish show no signs of such heavi-
ness. Or, if they do, they carry it with a grace unknown by
mankind. Grace. Perhaps that is what we are after, Thom
thinks. Joe says nothing.

He sits in the sunroom he has built on to the back of the
house. It is a perfect room. The glass stretches flush, floor
to ceiling. The concrete lies level below him. The sunlight
throbs in waves in the early summer morning. It is a perfect room.

"And what is life but sitting in rooms?" Joe says.

Thom sings to himself, sitting calm and still in the sun-room, the sun on his face. Yes, he thinks, yes, I would rather be a fish.

To swim on endlessly, the ending its own beginning. Weightless, adrift, but not without purpose. Drifting as the purpose. Weightless, because it is to be so. To sink to the cold depths of the Lake, and rise again to the surface, toward the light he can never touch, to feel that air he can never breathe. Thom Algonquin, an old man now, useless by all accounts, stares out at the Lake from the sunroom that is no longer his. He looks at the waves, cold blue and alive, and he answers his father's song. Yes, I would like to be better off than I am.

"And aren't you?" Joe says. "Aren't you now?"

I guess I always thought I would be a great man, a hero even, he thinks.

"But there is no such thing, is there?" Joe says. "There is only the man you are."

And perhaps that is enough, Thom thinks.

The Lake is endless, both to eye and mind, and that is all that is needed to make it so. Endless in mystery, endless in beauty. But such endlessness is only a glimpse of some-thing more, something truly endless. Such a thought used to frighten him. Thom knows the Lake ends. He knows that just over there, there is something else, and something beyond, because the Lake is not the end. What surrounds him will die one day, he himself is but dust. But what he sees now is creation and those simple, little parts. A heron swoops and glides over the waters. A breeze shivers up the pines and wakes their branches. Someone mows a lawn a few houses away. An outboard motor churns on the water. The sun angles through the new clean glass and settles on his skin. Just before him, the thin line of the horizon pulls itself across the Lake. He has seen this before, heard all of it a thousand times over. But just now, as Thom looks at the Lake, the Lake is there. So long has he looked and stood apart from all of what he sees. Now, he sits, silent, listening. He empties himself with light, with the landscape, until he becomes a part of this morning view.

He has long felt both feet fettered to this raw earth, felt his soul crushed under body and flesh. Like that bear, he thinks. Like that bear, like all of this life. He sees now, though. He knows it doesn't have to be that way. The view is not new, the water centuries old. He has sat in this place all his life, and nothing has changed. Only he was asleep in those times. Now, he is awake. He breathes as a mighty wind comes in off the Lake and glides across the sunroom windows.

Thom rises from his chair, grabs his keys and coffee, and goes out to his truck. More work awaits.

First and foremost, I must thank my beautiful wife, Amanda. She is my first and greatest reader and has been the undying light in my darkest hours. She speaks her mind and is unflinching in her critiques, yet tender in her praise and unfaltering love. O, how you make my heart move. I love you, sugar.

To my son, Leo, to whom this book is dedicated. This entire book was written with you asleep in my arms. Whenever I faltered, or lost faith, I looked to you, little man. You inspire me to see new wonder each and every day. I am so excited to see the man you become. I love you, my little lion boy.

I want to thank my father who introduced me to the love of stories and the beauty of language as a kid. He is the bravest and most brilliant man I know. To my mother, who taught me to read and guided me to be a better man and a better writer every day of my life. I love you both.

To Joshua Hren and Wiseblood Books who took a gamble on me and this book. I am forever grateful for your faith in my work. I hope to make you proud.

To Katy Carl, a brilliant editor and writer who helped bring this story to life. I am so thankful for all of your hard work and for caring about these characters as much as I do. Thank you!

To my agent, Peter Carlsen. You are the very best of the best, it's as if we share heart and soul my friend.

To Kevin Morgan Watson of Press 53. You have been a dear friend and mentor since I first brought my book of terrible teenage poems for you to read so long ago. For the guidance, for the countless conversations, for believing in me, and for all you have taught me, I thank you, sir.

To my brother, Colton, and our countless conversations about this story as I was writing it. Your insights and patience during my ramblings helped more than you could ever know. I love you, Ike.

To my best friend, the poet Cordell Ponak, who sat and listened to me run on about books and writing for too many years now. For challenging me and always being there, for all the smokes and beers, and for being the greatest assistant produce manager this side of the Mississippi. I love you, buddy.

Special thank you to Dan Masset who read the very first draft of this book and believed in the story. Thank you to my sister Haley Roberson and her husband Rusty Roberson, to Amber Brown and all of my friends for your love and support. To my professors Sheryl Monks, Metta-Sama Melvin, Christopher Alexander, Blankford Parker, Michael Rager. To my Zen-friend, Ben Novak. To Brian Clarey at *Triad City Beat* for challenging me to always perfect the craft of writing.

A very special thank you to my grandfather and grandmother, Peter and Sue Nielsen, who always read my manuscripts first. I love you both. To my late grandmother, Chloe Ledbetter Brown, accomplished poet, for taking me to poetry readings as a child, and sparking within me a deep love of literature. I love you and miss you.

To everyone I have failed to mention here, to all of my friends and family, I thank you all. A book is never written alone, and you have all shaped my life in the most beautiful of ways. Thank you.

Benedictus Dominus, Benetictus sanctum nomen eius.

Note on the writing: This book was written by hand on legal pages with a Cross pen, and typed on a 1936 German Hermes Featherweight portable typewriter.

For research and inspiration, I am indebted to the poetry of Ron Padgett, Charles Wright, Li Po, Wang Wei, and the mythology of the Algonquin people of the Great Lakes. I am also forever grateful to the great Catholic Southern writers who came before me, most especially Walker Percy, Flannery O'Connor, Breece D'J Pancake, and John Kennedy O'Toole. I read *Building Small Boats* by Greg Rossel over twenty times and even designed and drew blue prints of the boat built in this book. One day, I'll build it.

Thomas Wolfe Fiction Prize finalist, Spencer K. M. Brown is a novelist and poet from North Carolina. Twice nominated for the Pushcart Prize and winner of the Penelope Niven Award and the Flying South Fiction Prize, his writing has appeared in numerous publications. He is the author of the novel *Move Over Mountain*. He lives in North Carolina with his wife and son.

Made in the USA
Monee, IL
06 March 2023

28963521R00184